Wendy and Me

Wendy and Me

John Gordon

ISBN: Softcover 978-1-4691-4603-4
Ebook 978-1-4691-4604-1

This is a work of fiction. Names, characters, places and incidents either are the product of the author's imagination or are used fictitiously, and any resemblance to any actual persons, living or dead, events, or locales is entirely coincidental.

This book was printed in the United States of America.

To order additional copies of this book, contact:
Xlibris Corporation
1-888-795-4274
www.Xlibris.com
Orders@Xlibris.com
110144

CHAPTER 1

Hia and I were smoking a cigarette in the Grove when God found us. She didn't exactly sneak up on us. She doesn't have to do that, she just kind of appears. Hia is a little more tuned into that kind of thing than I am. I should have known God was around when Hia shoved the cigarette into my hand. Even after all this time with Her though, we still sometimes thought we could get away with stuff. Not that we're trying. We were both good angels and we'd been with God forever, and She really does forgive everybody all the time and, of course She knew Hia had handed the butt to me. It's all good. You can't fool God and we just didn't always remember that.

When we were all still very young, God had created a special, magical place in the Grove for us to play in. We would play tag and hide and seek, and sometimes God would play with us. Those were the best games. We would hide and think that God couldn't find us and She would search and search and call out our names and say "Where are you funny little angels?" and we would think that She didn't know where we were, but of course, She did. Years later, when Adam and Eve were hiding from Her in the Garden, they too thought that they could deceive Her. God cried out to them, and they hid, and we all cringed and snickered because we were embarrassed for them. She was just giving them an opportunity to show themselves, because She obviously knew where they were, but that was then and this is now and what has passed was meant to pass and all is good in God's world.

"Where did you get the cigarettes, Hia?" God asked.

"We got them from one of the sailors," Hia replied.

"We?" I said.

"Well, me. I mean, I got it from one of those sailors," said Hia.

Of course God knew all this. It was just an exercise really; a test in honesty, so to speak. Hia was failing.

A tanker had gone down in a storm in the Caspian Sea two nights before. The crew was Albanian and the officers were British. The ship was registered in Liberia and had been ill equipped and barely seaworthy. She was carrying over 900 tons of Russian crude oil when the storm blew up suddenly out of the west, and the men on board panicked when they discovered only one serviceable lifeboat. The chief engineer was the most experienced hand on board and he directed the loading of the lifeboat. Then he went into the pitch black, cold water strapped to three others all wearing storm vests. The four of them lasted twenty-one hours into the next day before the sharks found them.

The chief engineer had given Hia the cigarettes.

"I'm sorry they're wet," he said.

"Oh, they'll dry up here," said Hia.

"Are you an angel?" asked the Albanian seaman.

"Why, yes," Hia batted her eyelashes at the poor man.

"I didn't know angels smoked," said the seaman.

"There are probably a lot of things you don't know about angels," Hia flirted.

Kieran and his brother were processing the new arrivals and watched the exchange between Hia and the sailor. They told me all about it before Hia had arrived in the Grove. We suspected Hia's behavior may get her in a spot of trouble, but I did not expect to see God so quickly.

"Angels do not smoke cigarettes, girls. I'd like to have a word with you, Hannah," said God.

"Me? I mean yes, Ma'am," I said. What had I done? I hadn't poached the cigarette or flirted with the sailor. I was a good angel. Well, I thought, I did take a puff of the wretched thing. It was terrible. It was certainly not worth getting into trouble with God.

"Shall we take a walk?" She asked.

"Oh, yes, that would be nice," I said. God was always so polite, and I loved being alone with Her. She always made me feel so special. I'm sure everybody felt the same way, but I didn't care. When I was with Her everything just seemed right. I instantly put Hia out of my mind. The Grove was no place for gossip or petty thoughts. What was to transpire between God and Hia was none of my business, and I somehow felt sure that God was not angry with me. She gave me confidence and clarity. She made me feel good about myself, and I had no anxiety about what She wanted to discuss with me.

"How long have you been back, Hannah?" God asked as we floated away from the others.

"Not long," I said because I wasn't really sure, but I knew She was sure. She knew exactly how long I'd been back and the circumstances of my return. I had died young this time, so I hadn't spent too much time in the world. It was so crowded these days, and it seemed to me that there was much more chaos and heartbreak. I had been on the continent of Africa which was spectacular, but tragic. The animals, the mountains, the jungle and savannahs, the sky, and the rivers were fantastic, but the people were so sad and desperate, and I had lived a very short, hungry, and barren life, and I was sure I hadn't accomplished much. God told me I had though. She said that I had brought enormous joy to my young orphaned mother; that I was all she had, all she had ever had or ever would have, and we died together swiftly which was a blessing. She was here now too, but I rarely saw her and she wouldn't know me if she saw me, but she's content and at peace now, and I'm happy for her.

All of the angels try to bring peace and contentment to the people of God. That's our job. Some of us are better at it than others, and I'm afraid sometimes that I don't do it as well as I should, but God knows I try and She is always very gracious with me and makes me feel good. Some angels are really good at spreading love and tolerance and patience and bringing joy to unhappy lives. Jesus doesn't go out much anymore, but he's the best. Everybody loves Jesus. Gabriel is a little jealous of Him and Jeremiah is always making fun of Gabriel, but all of the older prophets and saints and apostles seem to have a special knack when it comes to teaching compassion and love, and most of us angels just wing it. No pun intended. We're supposed to know what we're doing down there in the world, but sometimes I wonder.

We never know we're angels when we're with the living. We only remember our past lives when we're back in the Grove, and we're really only aware of being angels when we're actually being angels. It just stands to reason that some are better than others.

Theresa's back now. She had another very special and helpful and holy time in the world, but some of us think she's got her halo screwed down a little too tight. God doesn't like publicity.

"You've been back for long enough to recharge your batteries I think, Hannah, and now I'd like to give you a new assignment. You've never disappointed me, darling. I wish you knew that more surely. I know you sometimes doubt yourself, but you're a feisty little angel, and humility in one of my chosen children is certainly not a bad thing. You are very special to me, Hannah. You do your job well, and there is a girl that needs your help," said God.

"Oh, Mother, that sounds wonderful. Shall I be her husband or maybe a friend?" I asked.

"No," replied God, "you will be her daughter."

"Again?" I said. "I'm sorry. I didn't mean to make it sound like that. It's just that I thought the last one didn't go too well. Being a daughter I mean."

"But it did go well," said God. "You were wonderful. I told you that. You brought an unexpected joy into young Sarita's life."

"Of course, Mother, whatever you say." I tried to sound sincere, but I don't think I pulled it off.

"It's all right, little angel. Come to the Mountain when you and Hia are done with whatever you're doing."

"I will, Mother. Shall I see Moses?" I asked.

"Talk to Jacob, dear. Moses is getting so forgetful these days," the Lord chuckled.

CHAPTER 2

Wendy leaned so far into the toilet bowl her forehead touched the water. She recoiled and gagged and threw up some more. There was a little liquid bile, but her retching was mostly dry heaves now, and soon it was over. She slumped back onto the tile floor, and curled up in a ball, and sobbed.

It was the tequila, of course. She had only intended to have a beer or two with the staff last night, but then everybody had started drinking Sunrises which led to shots and now here she was on the floor of the bathroom again just like she had been a month before. She hadn't had anything to drink since the last incident and she was at least grateful that she remembered getting home this time. Heidi always drove to and from work. Wendy didn't have a car and the restaurant was about ten miles south on Route 7 in Shelburne. She remembered singing at the top of her lungs on the way home that night as her friend had navigated through a blinding snowstorm. Heidi drove a cute little green BMW with Maryland plates and blue pin striping on both sides. She was a student at the University, and Wendy figured that her parents probably had good money and that she probably didn't really need to wait tables at the Sirloin Saloon, but Wendy did. She needed this job, and she couldn't afford to lose it.

The last time she'd had this much to drink she'd been all over Matthew, the cute little Asian guy that covered the salad bar. She wasn't too sure what had happened that night. She didn't even know how she had gotten home and she had been too embarrassed to ask, but she did wake up in her own apartment. The only problem was that she'd found her panties in her coat pocket with her tip money and a napkin with Matthew's telephone number scrawled on it. She didn't know for sure that it was Matthew's number, but when she called a guy answered saying, "Sigma Nu." Wendy knew Matthew was in a fraternity at UVM. She was sure he'd say something or leer at her or that she would hear about what might have happened, but she never got a hint. He acted totally normally to her which was confusing. Usually guys followed up, or acted sweet, or at least ignored you. She was used to guys acting like they'd stolen something and they were afraid to return to the scene of the crime. She figured that most guys would probably be pretty surprised that sometimes a girl couldn't really tell whether she'd had sex the night before or not.

She absolutely had to quit drinking like this. She'd never had black outs before and she'd never felt this sick before either. Back in Providence, she could drink most boys under the table. That's how she'd met Cameron. He was the drummer in a lousy band going nowhere fast. It was the muscles of course; that and his beautiful color. She had never been with a black guy before and she'd been curious.

Cameron certainly wasn't really black. He wasn't even very dark. He was a beautiful color, and she suspected that one of his parents must have been white because he was a fine shade of mocha chocolate, and he talked like every other guy she had ever known in Providence and he didn't try to act hip or cool or from the ghetto or anything. She loved the music, she loved making the scene, she loved to dance, and she loved to drink, and she'd thought that night months ago that she was falling in love with the drummer in the band.

Thinking about it on the floor of her bathroom this morning, she realized that, beside the muscles and the beautiful skin and the soft eyes and the wicked drum licks, she didn't know very much about Cameron at all. She had left town with him after leaving a note on the kitchen counter for her drunken father and that had been that. Cameron talked about his sister in France once or twice, and he'd mentioned some of the other bands he had played with and some of the places he had visited, but when it got right down to it, Wendy realized that she had been living here in Winooski, Vermont, for the last few months with a perfect stranger. Cameron and the boys had a gig at a club four nights a week and they played some frat parties. Cam was out all night and slept all day, and Wendy was just passing time. And she was bored. She was cold too. She was tired of Vermont. She wasn't too crazy about this job, and now she wasn't even having fun anymore.

She threw up some more and considered that maybe something was really wrong with her. Maybe she had cancer and she was going to die like her mother. She didn't want to die in this creepy apartment in this creepy gray town. She had to get up and do something. Panic swelled through her and her ears filled with a rushing sound like an angry ocean. She had to get outside and breathe. She needed air, she needed space, and she needed to move. But she dry heaved again and collapsed on the cold tile.

The last thing she remembered thinking about was work and how glad she was that the place was closed on Monday's. She woke up shivering an hour later and crawled into bed and stayed there until the blue light of Tuesday peeked around the edges of her window blind. Cameron must not have come home at all last night. In fact, she realized suddenly that she hadn't seen him all weekend. Maybe those losers had a gig out of town somewhere. She got up to go to the bathroom thinking angry thoughts about why he hadn't told her that they were playing somewhere outside of Burlington, but when she walked in the bathroom to pee the nausea hit her, and she dropped to the floor and arched into the toilet bowl again. Nothing came up, there was nothing left in her. She hadn't eaten in two days and all the fluid was gagged out of her and now she knew that she was dying. She had cancer for sure. She was going to die just like her mother. It was probably pancreatic cancer. Stomach or maybe liver cancer she figured. She should probably get to the hospital, but she was sure it didn't matter. She was going to die anyway.

* * *

"You're pregnant," said the handsome young intern.

Wendy had managed to pull on some clothes and brush her teeth and walk to the Emergency Room of the Fletcher Allen Hospital. She was sure that it was a waste of time and that death was imminent, but she thought they might give her some pain pills or tranquilizers to make it go easier. Now she was staring into the ice blue eyes of this gorgeous doctor that had admitted her, taken her temperature and pulse, strapped the blood pressure device to her arm and drawn blood. She was in a hospital gown on a hospital bed in a little hospital room alone with a tall, handsome doctor with really white teeth and a twinkle in his eye. What had he just said?

"What did you just say?" she asked.

"I said, 'You're pregnant,'" he said again. "About six weeks, I figure. You've been experiencing morning sickness. It's quite normal really. At least that's what my mother used to tell me," he laughed. He had a wonderful laugh.

"Pregnant? That's impossible," said Wendy. She had been on birth control pills since she was fourteen and had never had any problems like this. When they got to Burlington last fall she'd gone to Planned Parenthood and gotten a refill, and she was sure she hadn't forgotten to take any.

"Okay, it's impossible, but I'm going to give you a script for some pre-natal vitamins and you can probably get it filled at the free clinic in town. Take the vitamins, lay off the booze and drugs and cigarettes, and try to eat well. You have a little blessing inside of you so take care of it."

"What? You are crazy man. I want to see an older doctor."

"Why don't you just go buy one of those little five dollar pregnancy test kits?" he said and then he walked away.

She was by herself in this cheery little hospital cubicle, and she had never felt more alone or less cheery in her life. Wendy's road had not been an easy one, but she was okay with that. She knew that she had grown up on the wrong side of the tracks in a dead end town, and she had dealt with that. She'd never asked for much. She worked and she had paid her own way since her father had quit his job and she had dropped out of school. She got out of Rhode Island and away from her crazy father because she didn't want to have to take care of him too. He was getting progressively worse. The booze hit him quicker, and he was a slob and he smelled all the time now and she needed out and she really didn't care what happened to him. She had not tried to get in touch with him since the night she'd left with Cameron, and he sure as hell didn't seem to be looking for her.

She was tough, and she was independent and she didn't need anybody in her life, but now she was scared. She felt alone, but for the first time in her life she realized that she wasn't really alone anymore. There was a baby inside her, and she was freaked out. Was she going to have a little black baby or was it going to be a little Filipino baby? She wasn't even sure what the hell Matthew was. Maybe he was Japanese. Maybe he had money. He went to college and she was sure that all Japanese people had money. His parents probably wouldn't be too happy about him knocking up a low life waitress, but she wasn't sure it was even his. This kid could be black, and she was positive that Cameron wouldn't be too interested in helping her raise the little thing.

Maybe she should just get rid of it. It was still early. She could get off this gurney, get dressed, and march right back down to Planned Parenthood. They would know how to deal with it. She couldn't have a baby. She was nineteen. What did she have to offer a kid? She could barely feed herself. What kind of life could she give a baby? She was doomed to raise a child in Winooski, Vermont, on food stamps and welfare, and this kid would have a worse life than she had ever had. She should have an abortion. Heck, it was common back home. Practically every girl she knew had done the abortion thing back home. This was no place to raise a biracial kid and if she was stuck with a little mutt she would never find a guy interested in marrying her. Not that that might happen anyway. She was always real careful about living in reality and not getting her hopes up. But she dreamed. Of course she sometimes thought about Prince Charming sweeping her off her feet and taking her to a little white cottage in the country with a picket fence and a dog. A girl had to dream.

"Are you still here?"said Prince Charming.

Oh my God, he is beautiful. Why couldn't I have had a one night stand with a guy like this? Better yet, why couldn't I have an affair with this guy? Why do I always go for the losers? I'm pretty, she thought, *I should be able to get a guy like this. I'm funny. I'm witty and cute and clean and smart*. Her mind was racing again. *What did he just say?*

"What did you just say?" she asked and she was surprised to hear her voice crack. She was squeaking.

"I said that I was . . . I just thought you might be gone already." He looked at the chart in his hand. "Wendy," he said.

"Yeah, I'm gone, big shot. Like I'm in Miami Beach already," she quipped. Why was she so sarcastic she wondered? She didn't mean to sound like a smart-ass, but she certainly did and she immediately felt bad about it.

"Okay, sorry," he said. "I'm glad you're still here, really. Do you have any questions for me? Can I help you at all? Is anybody coming to pick you up? Where do you live anyway?" He looked down at his clipboard again. "Oh, Winooski, did you walk over?"

Why am I babbling, he wondered? "It's just that you seem a little shell shocked and I'm kinda new at this too, and I hope I didn't hurt your feelings or insult you. You seem very nice, and I just wanted to, you know, help, I guess. If I can, I mean, but if you want to be alone . . . Hey, let me get you my card. I'll be right back. Stay put. I mean, please."

What was going on with this guy? Wendy wondered.

A big nurse walked in with her own clipboard. A real big, black as coal, wide eyed nurse in a starched white uniform with a silly little nurse's cap clinging desperately to the top of her mane of dreadlocks.

"Congratulations, darlin'," she said in a sing-song Caribbean accent. "You goin' home now and takin' care a dat leetle bundle of joy, so I'm here to get you and da baby all checked out a dis hospital and be on your way."

"Huh?"

"I got da 'scrition for you pills, and I need some signatures from you now, baby dear."

"Who are you?"

"I'm Josephine," she said in a lovely West Indian patois, "and I'm getting you two outta here, so paytention and sign what I tell you to sign, little parrot. You know you look just like a leetle parrot wit dos eyes a bulgin' big and wide?"

"Where are you from?" asked a suddenly interested Wendy.

"I'm from Saint John, but you don't know it and it don make no mind anywho peanut," said Josephine.

"But what are you doing here?" asked Wendy. Her voice was squeaking again.

"I'm a nurse, silly duck. What you tink I'm doin' here?"

"I mean, where do you live?" Wendy wanted to know.

Josephine said, "Winooski, same as you and I been cold in dis town for seven years now Miss Busy wit da questions."

"Are there other black people, I mean island people here in Vermont?" asked Wendy innocently.

"Course dere are," said Josephine. "Dere's my baby boy and my two girls and my crazy husband who stay out all night playin' foosball and dominoes."

"This baby might be black," said Wendy.

"Well den, we gonna love him jis a same little duck. Now git out the bed and get dressed. You leavin'," said Josephine.

"Okay, okay, sounds good to me," Wendy exclaimed. "What's the story with this doctor, Josephine?"

"What doctor, honey?" asked Josephine.

"The tall, dark, handsome, nervous one," answered Wendy.

"Ain't no doctor ducky, dat's Terrence," said the nurse.

"Terrence? I knew it. I knew he wasn't a real doctor. I want to see a real doctor. I want to see an older doctor," demanded Wendy.

"First of all, peoples wit no medical 'surance don't go demanding nutin, and second he ain't a doc yet but he gonna be. Terry's internin' honey. He's 'bout close to bein' the real ting widout chargin' you money, so hush up and put on your clothes," barked Josephine.

"Internin?" said Wendy. "You mean he's an intern?"

"Don' make fun of me, little girl. I'll drag your skinny butt out dat door, baby or no baby."

"I'm sorry. Of course, okay, I get it. He's an intern," said Wendy.

"Do I look slow to you? Baby, I deal wit sassy all day long," said Josephine.

"Please, I didn't mean anything. Don't get me wrong. He just seems so young I guess, and cute. Yeah, cute too," said Wendy.

"Oh he's cute dat Terry. You ain't da firs' to notice, peanut, but he gonna be a good doctor too. One a the best I tink. I jis hope he stays here, but he prolly won't. Too damn col' for him too, I believe," said Josephine. "Now les sign dese papers, suga'."

Terrence walked back into the examination room just as Wendy was buttoning up her jeans. He silently handed her a little business card and gave her a shy smile that made her knees wobble enough to make her lean back on the bed that she had just spent the last two hours in. She smiled back and felt her whole face flush.

"Are you all right?" the young intern asked.

"Fine, I mean no, I mean yeah, I'm alright Doctor . . ." she looked down at the card, "Frazier, is that your name?"

"No," said Terrence, "but I'm out of cards so I borrowed one from Doctor Frazier." He regretted it as soon as he said it. "I'm sorry, just kidding. Yes, Frazier is my name, but I'm not technically an MD yet. I will be in a couple more weeks though, but I do know how to read a blood report, and you are definitely 'with child' as they say, so if you need anything . . . anything at all, please call me. I put my home number on the back just in case it's late or you don't feel comfortable with the Emergency Room staff or, you know, you want to talk or get a hot chocolate . . . I'm sorry, I'm sure your husband wouldn't approve of that, but I couldn't help noticing that you didn't put, you know, I mean next of kin, well, I mean that's my job and I was just wondering. Oh brother, I'm sorry. I'm babbling again."

Wendy laughed and tears came to her eyes.

"Oh God, look what I've done. Oh please, oh Jesus, I'm sorry, Wendy. I didn't mean to pry. Please, Wendy, quit crying. I'm sorry really. Oh please forgive me it's none of my business. I'll shut up, Wendy. Don't answer me. It's okay. I just start . . ."

"Okay, okay. You can shut up. I'm just laughing. You're pretty funny, you know, and you could make a valium nervous, if nobody ever told you that," said Wendy as she wiped her face with the front of her shirt. "Some bedside manner," she muttered.

They stood looking at each other across the examination table. The window was behind Wendy. A soft rain was coming down, but the sun was shining through it and there was a halo around her head and a glow to her face. Terrence thought she looked very beautiful. Behind Terrence was the door leading to the chaos and noise and hustle of the hospital, but it seemed very quiet in the little room with the patient and the doctor staring into each other's eyes.

Josephine was leaning against the nurse's station across the hall with her beefy arms crossed loosely over her massive chest. "Uh oh," she mumbled to herself, "I seen this train wreck before."

CHAPTER 3

Spring was finally making its way to northern Vermont. Wendy felt the promise in the air and saw it on the faces of the students as she sat on a granite bench outside of Pomeroy Hall on the campus of the University of Vermont. The sky was clear, and two cardinals chased each other through the bare branches of maple trees just beginning to break into bud. She felt wonderful. The last two days had been an emotional rollercoaster, and this morning she had called the number scribbled on the back of the card that Terrence had given her the day before because she had popped awake terrified. But she was okay now. Her baby had spoken to her after Terrence had calmed her down, and the baby had told her that they would be all right. Her baby told her to be brave and to trust Terrence and to trust God. So she did, just like that. There had never been any trusting of God before in her life or even much consideration of God, but today she knew. She just knew.

When she had walked out of the hospital yesterday, her head was spinning. She'd started down Colchester Avenue back toward home, but there had been a bright light reflecting off of Lake Champlain in the distance, and when she'd gotten to Riverside Avenue it had pulled her.

She'd squinted against the glare coming down the hill, but once she got to the river she felt as though the lake was calling her and the light was softer and it was beautiful with the Adirondack Mountains in the distance. She'd followed Riverside for a couple of blocks and then cut over to Pearl Street to avoid the railroad bridge and the view of Canal Street and her depressing little apartment across the river in Winooski. She'd walked through the crowds on Church Street and stopped outside of a store called Good Stuff that she had never noticed before. There was a tiny pink bassinette in the window with a frilly white blanket draped casually over it as though the mother had tossed it there when she picked up her baby. Wendy had gone inside and lost an hour looking at baby furniture and talking to a sweet little man about dressing tables and changing stands and rocking horses. He'd asked her how far along she was with a glimmer in his eye and she knew that it showed not on her body but in her face. Her body hadn't changed. She was still slim and looked fit and sexy, but there was something new and different about her face. She glowed inside and out and she could feel it. She said "Six weeks" and burst into tears. He hugged her like her grandfather had done when she was a little girl. She kissed his soft cheek and smelled the Old Spice after-shave and wanted to hold onto him forever, but she pulled herself away and promised that she'd be back and he said that he'd be waiting for her.

Wendy had then walked back over to Winooski Avenue and stopped in front of a nursery school called Children's Space and watched the mad beasts tearing around the playground. She'd laughed and then she cried and then she'd laughed some more. She realized that she was making up names and inventing happy stories about their families and their lives. Her mistake had been going home.

She remembered noticing the car from a block away and thought that it might be Heidi's, but it wasn't.

* * *

Her thoughts of the previous day were interrupted by two cardinals that suddenly landed on the bench beside her and started a frantic racket like an angry old couple. They were face to face and seemed to be arguing. Wendy wondered if birds argued. She was a little surprised at this behavior. She hadn't really paid all that much attention to birds before and she was intrigued that these two would alight beside her and carry on as if she wasn't even there.

"Are you two married or something?" she asked above the din. They immediately stopped their chatter and looked at her, and this made Wendy very uncomfortable, like they would suddenly both jump on her face and start pecking at her eyes and tearing her hair.

"Sorry, I didn't mean to pry," she said.

The birds glanced at each other and then the brightly colored one, the male Wendy supposed, puffed out his little man chest and hopped right onto her knee. His mate turned away from them both and skipped up onto the armrest of the bench and turned her back as though she was ignoring them.

"Who's your friend?" asked Terrence.

She hadn't seen him approach, but she wasn't at all startled.

"Is this weird or what?" said Wendy. "Have you ever seen birds do this? It's like this guy has something to tell me and it's pissing his girlfriend off."

"I'm not surprised, happens all the time."

"With birds?"

"I really don't know," said Terrence. "Vets have two more years of school than us regular doctors."

"Were you in class, doctor?" asked Wendy.

"No, actually I was just seeing my advisor. Sorry I'm late. It went longer than expected," Terrence explained.

"Are you in trouble or something?"

"No," laughed Terrence. "We all meet pretty regularly with our advisors, and I've gotten to know Doctor Howe pretty well so we always just end up shooting the breeze. We're real comfortable with each other. I mean, I'm real comfortable with him, and I think he's casual with me."

"Casual?" Wendy asked.

"Yeah, totally, we've become friends, I guess. I know he cares about me and my career and he tells me all about his wife and kids and stuff."

"That's nice, Terry. Is it okay to call you Terry or should I stick to doctor?"

"Terry please, Wendy. Is it okay to call you Wendy?" Terrence asked.

"No, I prefer 'Waitress'," she laughed.

"Anyway, I'm glad to see you're in a better mood than you were when you called this morning. You're going through some scary stuff, especially if it's unexpected and all new to you," said Terrence.

"It's definitely all new, but I'm cool. This morning was a bit of a meltdown but after you and the baby talked to me I felt much better. Are all these people going to be doctors?" she asked looking at the rush of students emerging from the building.

"Well, that's the idea. This is Pomeroy, UVM's med school. Why do you ask? Never mind. I'm more interested in that comment about your baby talking to you."

"I dunno, they all just look so young, like a bunch of Doogie Howser's," said Wendy.

"Doogie Who's?"

"Never mind yourself, and yes, my baby has been talking to me. We're getting to know each other pretty well."

"Quite a change from the denial you were living in yesterday," said Terrence.

"A lot has changed in a very short time, Terry."

"Care to tell me about it?" asked Terrence.

"For some reason I do," said Wendy. "Do you have some time?"

"I've got all day for you, my pretty young mommy."

Wow, did he really say that?

"Wow, did you really say that?" asked Wendy.

Terrence blushed. "Yeah, I guess I did, but suddenly I regret it. Forgive me, I don't mean to be personal."

This guy is not for real, thought Wendy. "Okay, let's go to Starbucks or somewhere."

They fell into a comfortable walk down the hill toward town. They walked at the same speed, and Terrence almost took her hand but then thought better of it.

"So what were you and those cardinals talking about?" asked Terrence as they moved in synchronous stride, both unconsciously avoiding the cracks in the sidewalk.

"Well, before those two battling Bickersons showed up I was thinking about my day yesterday, and I was just getting to the ugly part so it's kind of cool that they decided to land on my bench and start squawking at each other. She was actually doing all the squawking, and she was the one that copped the attitude when I tried to interrupt. Typical, huh?"

"I won't touch that," said Terrence diplomatically.

They hit Church Street and took a left heading south through the ever present throng of Burlington's most popular thoroughfare. They walked past Good Stuff, and Wendy looked in the window hoping to see her friend from yesterday. He wasn't in sight, but she did notice what a great looking couple she and Terry made. *If only* . . . she thought. They got to Starbucks and walked in and were assaulted by Jimmy Buffett singing some island ditty way too loudly. The crowd was hip business casual and SUV soccer moms amping up on grandes and lattes and chais and the barristas all looked like they had stepped out of the same magazine ad and Terrence said, "I know another place," and they were back out on Church Street in a heartbeat.

"That was a pretty serious sensory overload," said Wendy once they had settled into a quiet booth in a little joint on Pine Street called Muddy Waters.

"No kidding," said Terrence. "Too much espresso in the air I think."

They sipped their coffees and sat quietly for a moment, taking in the room. They felt comfortable together, and the stillness of the moment was meditative and reassuring. They sat under a photograph of Theolonius Monk and listened to the soft rumble of John Coltrane. The atmosphere soothed them both. Burlington was following the path taken by Berkeley, Cambridge, and Boulder. The town was completing its transition from liberal, politically active authenticity to disingenuous, yuppiefied materialism, but like those other towns there were still holdouts of the socially conscious, creative, and caring hippies of yesterday. In villages and little towns, on farms and communes, and along the back bays of America, resilient pockets of aging hippies still held out hope for a kinder and gentler nation of brotherhood as envisioned in the promise of the sixties. It was a naïve notion to most, but one that the proprietors of this little coffee shop seemingly clung to. There were tapestries on the wall and macramé in the doorways and the smell of patchouli oil in the air.

"This is nice," said Wendy. "Do you come here a lot?"

"I don't really drink much coffee," Terrence replied, "but this place reminds me of my Uncle Jack."

"Was he a hippie?"

"Definitely," said Terrence. "Still lives in San Francisco. Oh yeah, big time hippie uncle. He was my mother's baby brother and he babysat me and my sister when we were kids. We were weaned on the Grateful Dead and Jim Morrison and Jimi Hendrix. I listened to music none of my friends had ever even heard of."

"Like who?" asked Wendy.

"Like Big Brother and the Holding Company and Hot Tuna and the Flying Burrito Brothers and Mike Bloomfield and Al Kooper's Super Sessions."

"Oh. Okay, you got me."

"Anyway, what happened after you talked to me this morning?" asked Terrence.

"No, well, I mean it started before that. Yesterday, yeah, well I walked out of Fletcher, and I was totally on automatic pilot so naturally I started back to my place which is a dump, so like I don't want to go there anyway, but I got distracted. I guess it was the lake. The sun was bouncing off the water, and I just started walking toward it and I ended up in a baby furniture store where I met this sweet little elf, and then I stood in a trance watching little kids in a playground and I felt good. I felt real good. I was in a good place, you know, and I haven't been in a real good place in a long time. I was kind of digesting this whole baby thing, processing it and walking back to my piece of crap apartment, and I saw this strange car outside. I mean it wasn't a strange car. It was an Audi. Like they only make about ten zillion of the things, but it was the same color as the beemer my friend has, so I thought it was hers. I mean Audi, BMW whatever. I'm not too good about these modern little preppy sports cars and it wasn't really the same color as Heidi's but it was close enough, you know? I work with Heidi. We're both waitresses at the Sirloin Saloon down toward Shelburne so I thought it was her, but it wasn't. I walk in the door and there was my loser boyfriend with some little Miss Money-pants doing bong hits in my living room. Sitting on my sofa in front of my TV, totally stoned out watching South Park, and I totally surprised them and they looked like I had caught them having sex or something which I didn't but it was clear they had."

Wendy stopped to catch her breath and the whole scene played across her face again. She looked like she was going to cry, so Terrence reached across the table and gently took her hand. She pulled it away instantly and then gave it back to him. Her hand was ice cold and his was warm and firm and they held hands for a long time until the hurt left her eyes.

"Do you want to go on?" he asked.

"Yes. I mean, no. I mean, yes," she stammered. "I mean okay, sure, but give me a minute."

"Of course," he said reassuringly.

She didn't take a minute. "So his name's Cameron, and he's a jerk and I don't even know her name and I really don't care, except I'm gonna find out because I'll bet Heidi knows her and I can slash her tires or something. Cameron's black," she said, and then she wondered why she'd mentioned that. She wished she had kept that little tidbit to herself. Terrence might not want to sleep with a girl that had been sleeping with a black dude. *Whoa girl, you're getting a little ahead of yourself,* she thought. "Not that that means anything. It doesn't really, does it? I mean it shouldn't," she said, but she needed to know.

"No. It doesn't mean anything," said Terrence. She was going a bit fast for him and it was getting slippery. He pushed the rest of his coffee away. He wouldn't prod her. She had to work through this at her own pace, but he could see that she was hurt, and it hurt him too. He knew how this felt and it sucked. He hadn't dared get into a relationship since his old girlfriend, Trish "the Dish" Goldberg, had cheated on him freshman year in college. It had been a blessing really. He'd buried himself in his studies and, now that he was finishing medical school, it was clear to him what a benefit the focus had been. But it still hurt. He wanted to hug this girl and make her feel better, but he was still Terrence Frazier, shy geek, and he didn't want to scare this little dove away.

"Anyway, they had spent the whole weekend at mommy and daddy's fancy ski pad in Stowe doing God knows what, but I do and you do too, and I'm like so done with that jerk, but I don't know, it hurts, you know? No, you probably don't. I don't imagine that you've ever been cheated on in your life. I mean we were boyfriend and girlfriend living together, and the place was a real hole, but I tried to keep it clean and make it nice, and he had no right bringing that rich slut into our place and sitting there like everything's cool and smoking my weed. I mean our weed, I mean it was his weed anyway so I don't care, and I'm done smoking pot so it shouldn't matter and I shouldn't give a flying shit, but I do I guess and I'm pissed. And I do, I guess, I mean care, but arrivederci baby. It's over and I'm glad, but I just feel used and I told him to get out and he said okay and now I'm like 'okay?' you know, but that's it. Sorry. I'm sorry, Terry." And then Wendy really started to cry. Terrence got up and walked around the table and pulled her up into his arms and hugged her as hard as he thought he could without breaking her ribs. She sobbed into his sweater for a couple of minutes and then blew her nose into his chest and they both laughed. The other people in the café that were watching all started to laugh too, and suddenly there was a wonderful feeling of relief and the chubby old lady behind the counter waddled around the milk and sugar table in her old Birkenstocks wiping her hands on her apron and she grabbed the two of them in a big bear hug and all the other customers suddenly started clapping.

“That was pretty cool,” Wendy said when they had walked about a block from the coffee shop. They were headed down to the lake. A gaggle of Canada geese was starting their little pre-flight honking ritual, and as Terrence and Wendy walked out onto the ferry dock hundreds of geese rose from the glassy water as one, making a thunderous racket and roiling the water into a churning silvery froth. A guy on a bicycle started yelling something and a car load of kids in an old jeep honked the horn again and again competing with the geese.

“Life is pretty cool,” agreed Terrence.

CHAPTER 4

Cameron moved out, and a week later Terrence moved in. Wendy and Terrence took most of the furniture to the Goodwill store and painted the whole apartment in bright, springy shades of pastel pinks, greens, and blues. They brought Terrence's old bed and his desk over from the dorm and spent the next couple of weeks driving around Vermont and upstate New York going to funky little antique shops. The dingy apartment that Wendy had hated was slowly transformed from a dark, dirty caterpillar to a beautiful, bright butterfly. Terrence traveled light. The bed and desk were from his parent's house in Pennsylvania. He had one garbage bag of clothes and six heavy boxes of books. Wendy started accumulating plants and soon there were ferns and spider plants and ivy plants all over the little apartment. They found two big old milk cans in a junk pile at the end of a farm lane down by Hinesburg and painted them sky blue with puffy white clouds and planted striped sea grass in them and placed them on either side of the porch door.

Terrence was working his shift at the hospital. The days were getting longer and Wendy wandered around her little nest clutching a cup of tea with both hands as the evening sun peeked under the bamboo window blinds. She was two months pregnant now. May had brought the sun back to Vermont and life and hope back into Wendy's world. She was in love. She was head over heels, think about him every waking minute, full blown, knockdown, drag out in love with Terrence Frazier, M.D., and she realized with a cold shiver that she was afraid. Good things didn't happen to her. Good things just didn't last, not in her world. *Oh my God,* she thought. *Don't let the other shoe drop.*

"Sweetie, I'm home."

Sweetie, I'm home? Wendy was sitting in the back bedroom at Terrence's desk looking at his computer. He had started to give her a couple of lessons and had even registered an e-mail address for her, but she didn't really have anybody to e-mail and the thing made her nervous anyway. "I'm back here in the bedroom," she called. *Where the heck else would I be?* There were only two rooms in the apartment anyway.

Go give him a hug.

Who said that? thought Wendy. Did she really just hear someone tell her to go hug him? She eyed the computer suspiciously. *This thing is haunted,* she thought. Maybe Terry'd had it wired up to watch her. It was probably spying on her all day and now he was making it talk, or maybe he . . . what was the word? Maybe he'd programmed it somehow. She was spooked. Somebody or something had just told her to go hug him. She looked around the room and squinted out the window and then back at the computer. She wasn't even sure the darn thing was on.

Terrence walked into the room wearing a big smile, but before he could even say anything Wendy jumped up with an angry look on her face and said, "Is this computer on?"

"No, I don't think so. I mean it doesn't look like it's on from here anyway. What's wrong?" asked Terrence.

"What's wrong? What's wrong? I don't know, this whole deal seems a little bizarre to me. I mean I didn't exactly grow up like this, this, this 'Honey I'm home' business. Maybe in your little world back in Paoli, Pa, that stuff is normal but, I don't know, I mean we're not exactly Ozzie and Harriet. Am I supposed to come running to the door and hug you after a long hard day at work or something?"

"No Wendy," said Terrence. "You don't have to hug me."

"Then who's telling me I do?" demanded Wendy. She jumped up and stomped into the kitchenette and stood there with her hands on her hips.

"Okay, let's just have a seat and calm down a minute Wendy. Do you feel okay?" asked Terrence. "Would you like a cup of coffee or tea?"

That was it. She'd been drinking too much tea. She was hallucinating. *Oh crap. Was that thud the sound of the other shoe dropping?*

"No, I do not want another cup of tea, and I do not want to calm down. Something just told me to come hug you. Plain as day, didn't you hear it?" she pleaded.

It was me Mommy. Don't freak out, babies talk to their mommies all the time and nobody else has to know about it. Okay?

Oh my God! She was losing it. She was losing her mind for sure now. She had said that her baby had spoken to her when she first met Terry, but now she was sure that it really had.

"There, there, it did it again. Did you hear that?" begged Wendy. "Oh, Terry, please tell me you just heard that little voice. It was the baby. I think it's a girl. I'm going to have a little baby girl, Terry. She spoke to me."

"Wendy. Slow down. We won't do a sonogram until the end of the first trimester. There's no point really. It's still way too early to determine the baby's sex, at least by modern day conventional means. I mean I guess . . ."

"Will you shut up?" screamed Wendy. "I just told you my baby spoke to me."

He's not ready for this Mommy.

"You shut up, too!" Wendy yelled at her belly. "Oh, baby, I'm sorry, I didn't mean to yell at you."

Terrence was leaning way back on the kitchen stool with his coat still draped over his arm and his mouth wide open. His bag had dropped to the floor, and he stared at Wendy with big eyes popping out of his head.

"Okay, okay," he said. "Now listen, Wendy, you've had a rough day, and I think what you need is . . ."

"Up your butt and around the corner, big shot. I know what I heard and I'm not crazy so close your mouth and leave me alone. I need to be alone. I need to talk this out with my baby. Put your eyes back in your head and go in the other room and leave us alone, damn it," she said, and then looking down at her stomach again, "Excuse me, honey."

"Up my butt and around the corner?" he repeated to himself. *What the heck is happening?* thought Terrence as he quickly retreated around the divider into the other room. This was the room that served as a living room, dining room, den, mudroom, and everything else. *Where did that crack come from?* he wondered. He put his coat back on and sat down in front of the television but didn't bother to turn it on. Two minutes before everything had been perfectly normal. He had been looking forward to a nice, quiet evening with this girl that he was just getting to know. How do people fall in love without knowing each other? What did he really know about Wendy? He knew where she had grown up. She had told him a little bit about the tragedy of her mother's early death and her father's problem with alcohol, but what else hadn't she told him? Was there any history of mental illness in her family? Was she prone to drama and unpredictability? Did she have any other living relatives?

They were really just living day by day at this point. They hadn't discussed any kind of a future. She had asked him if he'd wanted to move in, and he had said yes. That was it, period, no plans, they were living in the moment and taking things in stride, and it seemed to be working. He had some career considerations to address, but now that he thought about it, he didn't even know what kind of a lease Wendy had on this place. He had met her friend Heidi, but didn't know anything else about her job or friends. He didn't even really know what she did when he was at the hospital, and he didn't feel the need to know. He didn't feel at all threatened or jealous or anxious about this relationship. He trusted her. He trusted them. His instinct told him that this was going to work out and that was good enough for him. He didn't know exactly how everything would play out, and he wasn't worried about it. He had told Dr. Howe about his change in living arrangements and he had gotten the distinct impression that he approved. He was more than Terrence's academic advisor. He was his mentor and his confidant and he was a bit of a father figure for him. He had said simply, "Follow your heart, son." That was good enough for Terrence.

The Frazier's were old money, main line Philadelphia socialites. Terrence's mother was from a long line of snooty blue bloods that traced their lineage and their attitudes back to the Mayflower. She was an Abercrombie and she never let anybody forget it. Terrence had purposely not given it much thought, but he knew that a marriage to Wendy could be an ugly affair. His dad was cool. Both his father and his granddad were modest doctors, and they didn't take themselves too seriously. They belonged to the right clubs and summered in the right places, but Harold Frazier would only care that his son found love in a relationship. The girl's pedigree wouldn't mean a darn thing to him and if Terrence and Wendy wanted to get hitched on a Mexican beach or at a California winery instead of St. Mary's Episcopal with the dutiful reception at Chester Valley Country Club that would be just fine with him. His mother, of course, was a whole different kettle of fish. She had insisted that his little sister, Sarah, go to Bryn Mawr because that had been her alma mater. Terrence had broken tradition by going to Gettysburg College because he was interested in history and warfare and that had not gone down too well. His dad had supported him though, and once Terrence had realized that his father wanted him to be his own man, he had started taking the science and math courses he would need for pre-med. Medicine had always been his first love. He admired his father and grandfather very much. He was impressed at the way people treated them and deferred to them because they were successful yet humble physicians. Terrence wanted that too.

He got up and crept back toward the bedroom. The door was ajar, and he heard Wendy mumbling to somebody. Was she talking to the baby again? Maybe she was on the phone? He looked in through the cracked door and was startled to see his girlfriend on her knees beside the bed. She must be looking for her shoes under the bed. He could see that she was barefoot, and he noticed that her cute little toes were wiggling. She had pink toenail polish on, and he hadn't noticed that before.

"Are you okay, Wendy?" he asked. "Did you lose something?"

"I'm praying," she said.

"Oh."

"I mean, I'm trying to. I've never prayed before, not really, not like get down on your knees and bow your head and pray to God praying."

"Me neither," said Terrence. "I didn't really . . . I didn't know, you . . . I mean, I went to church. My mother made us. It didn't do much for me. Are you religious?" he asked.

Wendy held out her hand to him. She was reaching for him with her palm up and her face still bowed into the bedcover. "Please come here beside me, Terry," she said.

So he did. He walked across the room, taking his coat off again and dropping it on the floor. He knelt down beside her and folded his hands like Jesus did in the picture over his mother's vanity. He bowed his head onto the soft bedspread and closed his eyes. In a moment he realized that he wasn't breathing and he inhaled deeply and held his breath for a couple of beats and then exhaled slowly. He did this again a couple of times until he started to feel more relaxed, and then he realized that Wendy was breathing with him and the two of them breathed deeply and slowly together for awhile. Terrence started to feel more peaceful, and they both slowed their breathing even more and seemed to sink into a rhythm as their bodies relaxed and their shoulders melted together.

"This is nice," Terrence whispered.

"Real nice," Wendy whispered back.

"Are you praying?" he asked.

"I'm not sure," she said. "I'm not saying anything. I guess I'm just thinking."

"I don't even think I'm thinking," said Terrence. "I'm just kinda zoning. It feels real mellow."

"Maybe we're meditating," suggested Wendy.

"Yeah, meditating," agreed Terrence. "Should we try to pray?"

"Okay. Here goes," Wendy said. "Dear God, Hi, it's Terry and me. How are you?"

Terrence snickered.

"What?" Wendy demanded. "I just asked Her how She was."

"Her?" questioned Terrence.

"Yeah, Her. What's wrong with Her?"

"God's a woman?"

"Yup."

"Okay," said Terrence. "Go on."

"I'm done."

"You're done?"

"Yeah Mister Smarty-pants, you broke the spell. I was really diggin' that, and you blew it," Wendy said as she pushed herself up from the floor.

"Well, I was diggin' it too," said Terrence. "I'm sorry, Wendy. Can we do it again?"

"Maybe." But she was already marching out of the bedroom.

Terrence heard her snap the TV on and open the refrigerator. He stayed on his knees for another couple of minutes before following her into the next room. "Hey, you want me to run down and get a pizza or something?" he asked her.

He's trying Mommy. Just take baby steps.

"No, it's okay, Terry. I'm fine. That was nice. We can just take baby steps. I was making lasagna from a recipe I saw in the *Free Press*. Maybe we can try that again sometime. Praying, I mean."

"I'd like that," said Terrence. "Anytime you want to pray again is cool with me. I don't feel funny or weird about it at all. I feel very comfortable with you, Wendy. I'm sorry if I spoiled the moment."

"Don't be sorry. We're all just getting to know each other."

The grace of God will be with us, and miracles will happen in our lives as long as we stay together and stay with Mother.

"I hope so," Wendy mumbled to herself.

Terrence looked at her curiously and then decided to pretend not to hear.

CHAPTER 5

It's still too cold for flip-flops and you forgot to take your vitamins.

Okay, you're right about the flip-flops, but I was coming right back to take my vitamins, thought Wendy as she turned around on Canal Street and headed back to the apartment. The little voice didn't bother her anymore, but she didn't tell anybody about it either. She was wonderfully happy, and if she was a little nuts that was fine with her. She suspected that really happy people were all probably slightly nuts anyway, and she wouldn't mind being totally around the bend if it meant a life of rapturous joy.

"Hey, I thought you were going to the store, punkin," said Terrence as he stepped out of the shower.

"It's still too cold for flip-flops," said Wendy. "Let me put on my sneaks and take my vitamins and I'll run out and get you your corn flakes in a flash."

She loved doing things for Terry. Running out to the store because they were out of cereal was a blessing to her. It was an opportunity to do something for the man she was growing to love more and more each day. He was such a little boy in so many ways. She had never known any guys that had such funny rituals. He ate a bowl of cereal for breakfast each morning. *How queer is that?* she thought. He cut bananas lengthwise and then sliced them into the bowl. He shook out the damp dishtowel and hung it neatly from the utensil drawer to dry. He rolled up the toothpaste tube and put the toilet paper roll on with the leading edge forward so it delivered from the top. She wondered if these little quirks would quit being cute. Maybe this was the kind of thing that would make her ballistic in a couple of years.

They liked the same stuff, though. Peanut butter had to be smooth Jif. They used Heinz ketchup and real butter and low fat milk and sea salt. He liked a lot of pepper, and they were both crazy about Ben and Jerry's frozen yogurt. Terrence had to have a salad practically every day and even when they got pizza he made a salad and he made a production of it; cutting up peppers and tomatoes and celery and whatever else they had in the fridge. They didn't watch much television, but they both liked the History channel and they both read novels in bed and they both hated his car. That was fun because they laughed about it, and they were always on the lookout for a new one so they were constantly checking out other people's cars and discussing the pros and cons of various models, new or used, different colors, makes, models, the whole bit.

Terrence wasn't a clothes horse at all, but he was very picky about what he wore. He had to have clean underwear and socks. That was a good thing, but she laughed to herself when she found him ironing his shirts and slacks. They lived on a pretty tight budget, but it wasn't a problem at all. She was making good enough money at the Saloon and he was getting a steady paycheck as an intern, but they watched their pennies and never even considered taking clothes to the cleaners to be cleaned and pressed. Although he had showed up at the apartment with his clothes jammed in a plastic garbage bag, they were certainly good clothes. All of his shirts had an alligator or a little horse on them. He usually wore button-fly Levis, but always went to the hospital in a pair of clean, pressed and pleated L.L. Bean khakis. He only had one winter jacket, but it was a good one from Land's End, and he had two pair of shoes; Merrill boots and soft Merrill loafers. He had a UVM sweatshirt and a couple of Brooks Brothers V neck sweaters and one nice sport coat with a J. Press tag in it, but most of all Wendy liked his undies. He wore long, tight boxers, and he could have been the model on the box. He had great abs, a great butt, and nice muscles. It cracked her up that he was so shy for a guy with such a great body. Most guys with his physique would parade it around for the whole world to see. They made love in the dark, and he was gentle and considerate and maybe a little too conservative, but Wendy loved that about him. He was a softie, a sweet, sensitive boy in a man's body and she knew what a hunk all the women at the hospital and around the campus thought he was. But he was her hunk, and she did not intend to lose him. So she took care of their little nest and took care of herself and did her best to watch her growing figure, but she knew that he found her body fascinating and they were enjoying the change together.

Wendy didn't have any designer labels. She was strictly a Penny'-s and Mandee'-s type of gal, but she was changing that. She wasn't exactly embarrassed about her wardrobe, she mostly liked jeans and loose tops, but she was starting to get a little funky. She went to the Salvation Army Thrift Shop on Colchester and picked up some peasant blouses and long flowing skirts with loud prints. She had to wear a uniform at work so that wasn't an issue, but she bought a good pair of espadrilles and found a great old blue jean jacket with a rising sun embroidered on the back at a cute place called Tootsie's on College Street. She was a bit surprised at her new attitude toward Terry's friends, the University students and preppies in general. She didn't seem to be as harsh or defiant as she used to be. She was a lot more accepting of people in general and she suspected that she just wasn't so afraid of everybody and everything anymore.

Back in Providence her friends had all wanted to go to bars down on Water St. and Main St. and try to hook up with guys from Brown or RISD, but she was not into what she perceived as the rich, spoiled type. Boy, would those old friends be surprised to see her now, making house with a handsome young doctor from the good part of Philly. Plus he was straight, totally straight as an arrow, responsible and old fashioned. Terrence had started paying the bills too. She didn't know exactly how that had happened, but she just gave him her weekly check and he took care of the rent and the utilities and the phone and cable and everything else. She used her tip money for groceries, but they didn't even eat much. She had given up coffee and was into herbal tea now, and her pediatrician had given her an old dog eared copy of *What to Expect_When Your Expecting* which she read every morning along with a couple of daily meditation books.

"Are you going to see Dr. Mitchell today?" Terrence was standing at the kitchen sink washing out his cereal bowl. They didn't have a dishwasher which was fine, they didn't need one, but the apartment had come with a slick, miniature, over/under washer dryer unit and a window air conditioner in the bedroom. Wendy was starting to wake up in the middle of the night overheated so she was glad that they had the a/c unit. She was sure that it was probably just her imagination, but she was happy to have the cool breeze blowing on her anyway.

"Yup," said Wendy. "I can't wait. I love Grace; she's so cool about pregnancy. You can tell she thinks it's a gift, like a miracle for women that we should all be grateful for, and I agree. It's like we have this secret power that you guys will never really understand."

Terrence nodded and smiled at her. "What time?"

"Ten-thirty," said Wendy as she moved into the bedroom. "No rush, I have plenty of time."

Terrence followed her into the other room after brushing his teeth and found her on her knees praying. "May I join you?" he asked as he slid to the floor.

Wendy nodded her head, but didn't open her eyes. "Thank you for this beautiful morning, God. Thank you for a good night's sleep, a warm bed and cozy home, and thank you for all of our blessings," she prayed.

"Thank you for this wonderful person beside me, God. Please watch over us both as we go about our day. Help me to be kind and considerate and tolerant today. Help me to stay focused and to be helpful to people in need. Help me to return to Wendy in one piece and please hold her hand as she meets with her doctor," prayed Terrence.

"Thank you for all that you have given us, God." She leaned over and kissed Terrence on the cheek. "All three of us," she finished.

"Amen," said Terrence.

May we be at peace and may our hearts remain open.

"Thank you," said Wendy.

"You're welcome," responded Terrence.

"Not you, silly," she giggled.

"Huh?"

"Let's get a puppy," Wendy squealed as she jumped to her feet.

"What?"

"Or maybe a kitten," she said.

"Wait a minute."

"Oh, I'm just kidding—for now, but someday I'd like a dog and a cat," said Wendy. "Grace is taking me to her yoga class this afternoon. I'm going to start doing yoga."

"That's great," said Terrence. "What's next, transcendental meditation?"

"Maybe," said Wendy with her hands on her hips. "Grace wears Earth shoes too."

"What are Earth shoes?"

"And she is going to give me this totally cool peace sign necklace she made out of silver and turquoise."

"You are getting to be quite the love child," said Terrence.

"No, Terry," she said. "I'm carrying the love child."

CHAPTER 6

"What's it called again?" asked Wendy.

"Ho'oponopono," said Dr. Mitchell. "It's basically a Hawaiian philosophical practice of repentance, forgiveness and transmutation. It's a path to happiness Wendy; a tool to move through some of the resentment and anger that we all store and that gets in the way of living a peaceful, divine life free of blame and self pity. You have a special soul Wendy. I could see that the very first time I met you. You also have some shame and bitterness that you may want to address so that they are not carried on to this little one. We can talk about it more after yoga this afternoon, if you would like."

"I would."

"Great, so back to business; I can schedule a sonogram in a couple of weeks, but as I said before it's certainly not a requirement. The baby is healthy. She is right on schedule, growing little hands and feet that look like clenched baby otter paddles right now. She has doubled in size from two weeks ago, and she has a little tail that will go away and eyelids and earlobes that will be with her for about the next ninety years. Blood work will determine any problems like Down syndrome so a sonogram is strictly optional. We can't tell the baby's sex yet anyway."

"I just feel like a sonogram is spying. I don't want to invade my baby's space. She's in her little nest and she's happy; I can tell. Let's leave her alone."

"That's what I mean about you, girl," said Dr. Mitchell. "You have an intuitive sensitivity. This little baby is very lucky to have you for her mother. So, I'm figuring April first as the day of conception. April Fool's Day, Wendy."

"You got that right."

I like her.

They were walking through the reception area and Wendy said, "I do too."

"Pardon me?" said the receptionist.

"Oh, nothing," said Wendy.

Four hours later they were on a mat on the wooden floor of an old colonial house up on Spear Street. The entire first floor had been gutted and transformed into an open studio with mirrors on the soft pastel walls.

"I could stay right here forever," thought the little love child as she rolled around in the soft silence of her mother's womb.

Wendy was doing her yoga exercises and was lost in the stillness of the moment. She wished that she could stay in this peaceful state of mind forever.

"Yeah," Hannah thought. "I could get real used to this." She swished gently back and forth in her wet nest listening contentedly to the steady beat of her mother's heart. Her mommy was in a meditative place Hannah knew, and she was happy which meant that they were both happy. Hannah loved the synchronicity of being inside the body of another. Their hearts beat together, their pulses pulsed together. When Terrence came into Wendy's world, Wendy's heart beat faster, and Hannah felt the excitement too. She loved the slow rumble of his voice, and she loved how he made her mommy feel. Wendy hummed and sang quietly all the time now and it made the unborn child inside of her feel peaceful and loved.

Sometimes she missed talking with God and with Hia, but she always felt that she was with them, and she knew intuitively from inside Wendy's belly that all was well with the world. She felt as though she was helping this mommy too. Wendy was calmer and more focused on living well and doing good things for herself, for her baby and for others. The incident with the tacos was a lesson well learned, and Hannah knew that it would be awhile before Terrence and Wendy ate spicy food again, but her mommy was growing so much. Not just physically of course; Wendy's mental and spiritual development were soaring. She was living with love and divine intention. She was communicating with Mother and listening to Her and reaching out to others and experiencing the wonderful coincidences of life without shame, anger, or self pity. Having a baby inside of her was making Wendy a better person, and Hannah was very, very happy about that.

She knew that she was in a temporary state of intuition and experience and that as soon as she passed through the birth canal and started breathing with her own little lungs that she would no longer be aware of being an angel; she would no longer have a direct link with God and with her other angel friends. She would no longer remember this time or the experiences of the past when she had lived on earth before, and of course, in the Grove. Right know she knew that the Grove was a place, that Heaven was a human state of mind, and that she would always return and always be safe and be with Mother, but once she became a human and began being and doing as a human, she would not have the perspective of experience or the eye of the ancients or the knowledge that she had now. She knew that she would see Hia in the world, and that they would somehow know each other, but she had no idea what form or place that might take. Hia was such an exciting and dynamic soul that Hannah figured she would run across her singing in a rock band or ski racing or deep sea diving. Maybe she would be a political activist or a famous revolutionary. Twenty or thirty years from now, Hannah might read about a brave explorer or an astronaut or somebody saving starving children in India or defending hunted gorillas in Africa, and she would know that it was her old friend. She would just know. Coincidence was a big part of living with God, and she knew that this mommy would soon rejoice in chance meetings and events and experiences. For now, though, she could use her past knowledge and experience to help Wendy, and that was surely enough. That was what God expected of her.

* * *

"Let's go see your father."

Wendy was making a tuna noodle casserole and she turned to Terrence who was sitting on the couch leafing through a color catalog of national parks.

"Let's go see my father," she said wiping her wet hands on her blue jeans.

"Really?" asked Terrence.

"Sure," said Wendy. "I just had this really strong feeling. I want to see my dad. I'm worried about him, and I'm tired of being angry, and I want him to know he's going to have a granddaughter."

"Or maybe a grandson," Terrence said.

Okay, thought Wendy. *It's a girl, but I don't have to go there with him. He's the doctor. Science must prevail.*

"Maybe we could drive down to Providence in like two weeks," Terrence continued. "I'm trying to set up an interview in Boston anyway."

Sirens and bells and whistles and bright lights started going off in Wendy's brain. "An interview for what?" she asked, though she wasn't sure she wanted to hear the answer.

"My residency," said Terrence.

"What's that?"

"Well, my internship here at the hospital will be over in August, and the next move is two years of residency. They're pushing me to stay here, but I don't know. I kind of feel like I felt freshman year at Gettysburg; not sure what major to declare, you know?"

"What are you talking about, Terry?" Wendy was suddenly scared.

"I'm not sure what I want to do, Wendy. I could specialize in a particular field of medicine; I could concentrate on research or I could continue on toward becoming a G.P."

"I thought you already were a doctor," said Wendy. She felt a surge of nausea and realized that her palms were sweating. The tuna smell was making her sick.

"I am a doctor. I mean, I completed medical school. I got my degree last summer, and I've been doing my first year of internship ever since. I have a bunch of options at this point, Wendy. Before I met you I was sure I wanted to be a country doctor like my dad and my granddad; not that they actually practiced medicine out in the country anywhere. But, anyway, that means becoming a general practitioner, and I need a couple more years of residency in a hospital to do that. I'm thinking about being a pediatrician too, and I'm interested in oncology as well. I just don't know yet, but I need some more time in a hospital somewhere, and I feel like I've been in Burlington long enough."

"So you're moving?" asked Wendy.

"I'm thinking about it," said Terrence.

Don't worry, he's taking us.

"Are you taking us? I mean, I'm sorry, I don't mean to push, or, uh, put you on the spot, but I guess I'm curious. No damn it, I'm not curious. I want to know. What are your intentions Terry?" Wendy was clearly flustered at this unexpected turn.

"My intentions?" asked Terrence. He laughed. "My intentions, Wendy, are to ask you to come with me when I relocate to a different hospital to finish my residency. As a matter of fact, I thought I'd whittle my options down to a couple of choices and ask you where you would like to move. I want to stay with you, Wendy. I want you to be with me."

"Do you?" she asked with a sigh of relief.

"Yeah, kiddo, I do, and there are a couple of choices we can make together," he said. "There's Boston and a great place in New Haven I've been looking at and Children's in Philadelphia too, but I'm not sure that I . . . , I mean we, want to be that close to my mother."

"What's wrong with your mother?" asked Wendy innocently. She was back at the sink cutting cucumbers for a salad.

"That's a loaded question and a long story," said Terrence. "You'll find out soon enough."

"Really, what do you mean?"

"Let's plan a trip," Terrence said. "We can go down to Providence and see your dad and then onto Philly to see my folks, and I can interview at a couple of hospitals along the way. We'll go in a week or two if you can get some time off. It'll be great weather and we can hit the shore and make a little working vacation out of it; just the two of us."

Three.

"Three," said Wendy.

"What? Oh, yeah, three," agreed Terrence.

"That sounds like fun, Terry. I'm sure I can get some time off or get Heidi to cover for me. She already told me she's staying in Burlington for the summer. She has the hots for an older guy in town. He's divorced and he has a cool sailboat on the lake, so she'll be leaving the sorority house at the end of the semester and moving in with him on his boat."

"Sounds cramped," said Terrence.

"You haven't seen this boat," said Wendy. "Let's eat."

We are truly blessed.

"Terry, I really feel blessed to be with you and to have this baby in me," said Wendy as she put the plates on the little coffee table in front of the television. "I'm excited about this trip. I'm excited about us and about our future and I have to tell you I'm scared."

"Why are you scared?" asked Terrence.

"Because good things just don't happen to me," answered Wendy. "And I'm afraid it's all going to fall apart. Like you're suddenly going to realize that I'm six years younger than you and I'm carrying another man's baby and one night you're just not going to come home and I'll never see you again."

She started to whimper and she ran back into the kitchen and tried to stop but she couldn't and it got worse. She was crying and then she was sobbing and then she was on the linoleum floor curled into a ball and the sobs were racking her body, and then Terrence was on the floor beside her and he was holding her. He had her whole body in his lap, and he was rocking her and trying to soothe her but she couldn't hear him because she couldn't stop crying.

"Wendy, Wendy, Wendy, hush, shh. It's okay, sweetie. I'm not going anywhere. I want to be with you, Wendy. I've never felt like this before with any other girl. I want us to be together, Wendy, to stay together, just the three of us. Age doesn't matter. The baby's father doesn't matter. I want this baby to be ours. I want to be this baby's father, Wendy. I want us to be a family. I want to take care of you. I love you, Wendy."

That did it. Wendy looked up into Terrence's face. Her eyes were red and wet and her nose was running. She didn't look so great just then.

"You do?"

Terrence laughed. He couldn't help it, but he regretted it immediately.

"What the hell's so funny?" Wendy demanded.

"Nothing," said Terrence. "Yes, I do love you, Wendy." He laughed again. The situation was pretty funny, he thought. She looked like a little kid that had lost her doll and fallen off her bike and skinned her knee.

"I'm sorry, you're just so cute," said Terrence.

He loves you, Mommy.

"Do you really love me?" Wendy asked again.

"I really love you," said Terrence. "Dear Lord, thank you for bringing this adorable, goofy girl into my boring life."

"Thank you, God, for letting me hear those words and for believing them for the first time in my life. Thank you for all that you have given me, especially the hardship that I have survived so that I could appreciate this moment so much."

"Thank you for our happy home," said Terrence. "For each other, for this nice meal that we are about to enjoy and for this hard kitchen floor that we have chosen as the most appropriate place to express our love and to give our thanks to You."

"Stop fooling around," said Wendy, and she hit him playfully on the arm.

"Who's fooling around?"

And thank you, Mother, for letting me share in this love.

"For sure," said Wendy.

"What?"

"Never mind," she said. "Amen."

"Amen."

Amen.

CHAPTER 7

The fox was wounded and hungry and cold. The blizzard was raging in the night and he found the nest under a rock and crawled in. The rabbit was frozen in fear but knew that the fox was hurt and when it fell into a deep feverish sleep she began to lick his damaged paw.

Wendy woke up with the dream still vivid in her mind. She felt as though her unborn baby had been reading a bedtime story to her. She saw the blizzard and the burrow and the fox and the rabbit. The rabbit was ready to deliver the bunnies in her womb and here she was sharing her nest with an injured predator and nursing it back to health. The fox was handsome and strong, but badly hurt, and he let this rabbit tend to him.

"I had the coolest dream last night, and I can't get it out of my head," said Wendy as she poured grapefruit juice into two glasses.

"What was it about?" asked Terrence tentatively.

"Not you," Wendy laughed. "It was about a fox and a rabbit."

"That could be about us," said Terrence.

"I guess," Wendy mused. "But I don't know the ending yet."

"Do you want to go back to sleep?" laughed Terrence.

"No," Wendy laughed too. "I feel like going for a drive though. Are you off today?"

"You bet. How about a little cruise down to Charlotte Bay? I'd like to check out Heidi's boyfriend's sailboat," Terrence ventured.

"Me too," said Wendy. "But we should probably wait for an invitation. I'm tired of Route 7 anyway. Let's go to the mountains."

"Stowe?"

"No way," Wendy said quickly. "How about the Mad River Valley? I love it down there." She certainly didn't want to run the risk of bumping into Cameron and his girlfriend in the swank little town of Stowe.

"Okay, that sounds good. You can tell me about your dream on the way down," said Terrence.

"It won't take that long," said Wendy.

* * *

Terrence was just starting to wonder if his clunker was going to make it over Appalachian Gap when they reached the top. The view behind them out over Lake Champlain was beautiful and the view before them of the Presidential Range in New Hampshire was breathtaking. They paused to look north toward Camel's Hump and Mount Mansfield and then Terrence dropped it into neutral and let the old car roll gently into the valley of Mad River.

They were surprised that there was still snow on the mountain and even more surprised when a group of young skiers emerged from the woods alongside of them and whooped and hollered through the trees following the road down the mountain pass. The skiers cut back into the dense forest along some unseen trail and were gone as quickly as they had materialized.

"Wow," said Wendy. "That looked like fun."

"No kidding," replied Terrence.

"Do you ski, Terry?" she asked.

"Not really, I mean, I have, but not lately." he said. "My parents gave us a taste of everything. We took skiing lessons and golf lessons and tennis lessons, swimming lessons, riding lessons and squash lessons. We went to dance school and camp and took art and piano lessons. I'm a pretty good water skier, but it's a lot easier than snow skiing. I never surfed, though, or snowboarded."

"I can ice skate," said Wendy proudly. "And sail. I went to YWCA camp three summers in a row and learned to swim and sail in Narragansett Bay. That was before mother . . . ." Her voice trailed off and she changed the subject. "I hate to say it, but it almost sounds like your mom and dad didn't want you around much."

"You may be right," laughed Terrence. "They certainly spent a lot of money to have other people spend a lot of time with us."

And knit.

"Yeah," whispered Wendy, "and knit."

"Sorry?"

She didn't answer. They were winding down the mountain switchbacks and had emerged from the last turn in the road to the base of the ski area. Wendy looked at the idle chairlift climbing up the mountain tower after tower. It was a single chair. There was only one seat and it looked very lonely, and the loneliness swept over her like a wave.

She spoke softly staring up the mountain at the towers blending into the deep blue sky. "My mother taught me how to knit before she died. I was barely twelve years old, and I would sit on her bed with her all day. Daddy didn't make me go to school. We just knit until . . . we just knit. Knitted, I guess. I don't know. Which is it? I haven't knitted since."

He saw her chin quiver and knew that she was thinking about her mother. He could see the hurt on her face, and it touched him deeply. He wanted to pull over and hold her, but he let it go.

They entered the village of Waitsfield and cruised aimlessly and wordlessly around looking at the shops and the people for awhile. They found themselves back on Route 100 and were heading south when they saw a sign for Warren. They took a left and drove around that little village and ended up on a road headed straight up a mountain and just kept going, twisting and turning and pointing out farms and houses and animals to each other. It was a comfortable time. The day was beautiful and warm, but there was still snow on the tops of the mountains. The people all seemed so healthy and energetic. There were bicyclists and horseback riders and folks with skis and kayaks on their car roofs and dog walkers and joggers and gliders circled the valley and soared over the ridge tops. They followed a road that pointed over Lincoln Gap, but it was closed up near the top so they turned around and headed back the way they had come. They didn't want to go all the way down to Rochester and over to Middlebury so they stopped in the cute little Warren Store and got sandwiches and asked directions.

"Man, my uncle would love this place," said Terrence.

"It's like a throwback to the sixties," said Wendy.

"No kidding, hippies with cell phones and computers."

Winding their way back up Appalachian Gap they ran into the same gang of skiers hanging out in the dirt parking lot across from the ski area which appeared to be closed for the season. They were young and exuberant and flushed with skiing, wine, and marijuana. They all had big smiles on their sunburned faces and wore uniforms of oversized sweaters and old baggy ski pants patched with duct tape. Their clothes looked old but their equipment—skis, boots and packs—looked professional and serviceable and well used. They had long hair and white teeth and the relaxed confidence of athletes. The two girls looked about sixteen, but they exuded a self-assuredness that they could run or ski all day. Wendy felt envious of their youth and their joy, and when they waved Terrence pulled over and asked, "Do you guys hike up to ski down? It looks like the lifts are closed."

One of the young men stepped forward and said, "We did today." And they all laughed.

"Scoot's truck blew a gasket this morning half way up, but usually we all pile in one vehicle and somebody gets designated driver duty. Wasn't happenin' today though, dude. Want some wine or a hit of this spliff? It's killer homegrown, bro."

Terrence laughed and said, "No thanks, I'm actually with the Burlington Police Department," and all the kids took a step back and froze.

"I'm sorry," he said quickly. "Just kidding."

"That was mean, Terry," admonished Wendy.

"Whoa," said the oldest looking skier. "Hurt the buzz, bro, but you're cool. I knew you were shinin' us on."

"You did not," said one of the pretty young girls.

"No, I didn't," he admitted. "You got me, bro."

"I'm sorry, really. You all look like you're having such a great time. I hope I didn't ruin it," said Terrence.

"Hey that's cool, Terry, my man, but Scoot's gonna have to change his shorts now," one of the other guys exclaimed.

They all laughed together and pounded on Terrence's car, and the guy named Scoot said, "Fly now, brother and sister; be gone and may the light of the snow gods lead you safely home."

"Home from the land of the sun catchers," said Scoot's buddy.

"The land of the tree dancers," said the quiet boy standing behind the pick-up truck.

"Sky dancers," said the other young girl.

"We are stardust," said the first girl again. "We are tree dancing, sun catching, sky dancers and we're happy you stopped and shared our space."

"Good-bye," said Wendy as Terrence restarted the car.

"Adios, amiga," said another and Wendy and Terrence started back over the Gap.

"That was fun," Wendy said when they had once again safely crested the mountain top.

"Right on, amiga," joked Terrence.

They're connected.

"Yeah, connected to the earth I'd say."

"Excuse me?" asked Terrence.

"Oh, nothing," said Wendy.

CHAPTER 8

"These are terrific, Wendy," said Terrence, leafing through some papers with pencil drawings on them. He had sat down on the couch after work to untie his boots and found a stack of a dozen pictures of foxes, rabbits, and hawks on the end table. There were a couple of landscapes too, and Terrence was impressed. "I didn't know you could draw."

"What?"

"I said, 'I didn't know you could draw,'" Terrence said again louder.

"I didn't either," hollered Wendy from the bedroom. She was lying on the floor doing some yoga exercises in a pool of late afternoon sunlight streaming through the window. "I told you about that dream I had the other night, remember? This morning I just got an inspiration. I doodled a fox on the back of an envelope, and it came out pretty good so I grabbed some paper and just started drawing. Those are the good ones. The disasters got thrown away. I found some pictures of animals in your stack of Smithsonian magazines and just tried to draw what I saw."

"They're great," Terrence yelled into the bedroom.

"Thank you, Terry," Wendy tried to yell back but she was lying on her back with her legs over her head, and her belly was muffling her voice. "I thought I'd put them in my little story."

"What little story?" Terrence asked. He had moved closer into the kitchen and was standing in front of the refrigerator with the door open. "Do we have any more apple cider?"

"It's not really cider season," yelled Wendy into her stomach. "It costs about twice as much now as it does in October. I thought I might try to tell the story of the rabbit and the fox and illustrate it; like for little kids, you know?

"I think it's been done, Wendy."

"Not the way I'm doing it, wise guy," said Wendy, emerging from the bedroom with a towel around her neck. She was wearing a black sports bra and black tights. Her face was flushed and her silky brown hair was pulled up tight on the top of her head.

"Wow, you look great," said Terrence closing the refrigerator door.

Say thank you.

"Thank you, Terry. How's the hospital hunt going?"

"Really good," Terrence replied. "I think I've got it narrowed down to six or seven. I sent out letters of introduction last week and asked for interviews. Dr. Howe said he's going to call each director to be kind of pro-active about it."

"Wow, this is really sounding serious," Wendy said, joining him in the little kitchen and wrapping her arm around his waist. "It scares me, you know."

"I know it does, and I'm sorry, but you have nothing to be worried about, my dear. We'll cruise down to Boston so I can talk to the people at Massachusetts General and New England Sinai, and just for kicks, I sent a letter to the New England Medical Center at Tufts too." Terrence was trying to be businesslike, hoping that would sound more reassuring. "I'm not sold on Tufts and that would probably mean two days in Boston, but we could drop in on your dad in between or I could leave you there for a day or even two or more if you'd like. I definitely want to interview at the Yale/New Haven Pediatrics Hospital, though, so we'll work those interviews around our visit to Providence."

"Bristol," said Wendy.

"I'm sorry?" said Terrence.

"I said Bristol, Terry. We're actually in Bristol, not Providence. I grew up in Bristol, Rhode Island between Narragansett Bay and Mount Hope Bay; it ain't Paoli, brother." Wendy walked into the bedroom so Terrence couldn't see the look on her face. "I'm not sure how much time I want to spend with daddy anyway; that kinda depends on him I guess."

"Are you okay, Wendy?" Terrence followed her into the other room. "I've never heard you call him daddy. That's sweet."

"Well I grew up calling him Daddy, and it was sweet. I loved him very much and then Mom . . . Mommy died and he . . . he just . . . oh, Terry, I'm not sure about this." Her eyes were welling up, and she was about to let loose so she buried her face in his chest and did. She cried. She cried a lot, and she realized that this was getting to be a pretty common routine. She had cried more in the last seven weeks then she had in the previous seven years.

"Let it out, Wendy. It's okay. I don't think you've let your guard down for a very long time. I don't know the circumstances of your mother's death or your father's trouble with booze, but I'm willing to bet that since I don't, you probably haven't really dealt with all of this." Terrence knew he was in uncharted waters, and he wanted to go very slowly and be very careful. "We all have to grieve our losses, sweetie. Everybody needs to process pain and emotion, and I'm getting to know you pretty well and I know that you have a boatload of both. I'm here for you, please, Wendy, believe that."

Trust him Mommy. He loves you.

"Oh Terry, okay, I trust you!" That was hard to say. "So what's next, after New Haven?"

"Alright," said Terry. "Stamford General, Morristown Hospital in New Jersey; they have a wonderful cancer center, and then Children's in Philadelphia. Along the way I'll take you to the Jersey shore and a couple of my old Pennsylvania haunts. The daffodils and crocuses and tulips will be out. Heck we can even go to D.C. for the cherry blossoms if it's not too late."

"Your wish is my command, fair prince. Why don't you make dinner?"

Three days later Terrence had firmed up his appointments sufficiently enough to start planning their adventure. The hospital administrators that he'd hoped to speak with were all surprisingly flexible and anxious to sit with him at his convenience. Terrence suspected that was because of Dr. Howe's phone calls and for that he was very grateful.

* * *

"Hullo."

"Daddy?"

"Wendy? Wendy! Wendy! Oh my God. Oh sweet Jesus, is it really you? My baby! Oh Wendy, Wendy darling, where are you? Are you okay? Are you alright, my baby? Where are you calling from, sweetie? Oh God, oh praise God, I didn't know if I would ever hear your sweet voice again. Oh, my little girl. Wendy, Wendy, Wendy, I have missed you so much. Thank God you called. Where are you, sweetheart?"

Wendy's father was a little excited. She took a wild guess that he was happy to hear from her.

"I have been so worried about you, little girl. You just dropped off the face of the earth. I've been looking for you for a year . . . no, ten months. You've been gone for ten months, baby. It's okay, that's okay. Where are you? Can I see you? Are you coming home?"

"Daddy, please. Take a deep breath. I want to see you too. That's why I'm calling, silly."

"Oh thank you, God. My prayers have been answered. I've really missed you, little girl. Where are you? I can come to you, Wendy." He was starting to calm down a little. "You're calling me daddy again? You sound good, little girl. Where have you been?"

"I've been in Vermont, and I was hoping I could stop in and see you tomorrow or Tuesday, whenever is convenient you know?"

"Convenient?" her father practically shouted. "You can come and see me anytime; right now is good. You're my only child, Wendy Applegate. I want to see you this minute, and I don't want you to ever leave again. Vermont? Are you in some kind of trouble? Don't worry, we can work it out. Everything will be fine again. I mean, I don't mean 'again', I just mean now. Everything will be fine . . . good, everything will be good. Oh, honey, I can't wait to see you."

"Daddy, calm down. I'm okay. Everything is fine. We're coming to Boston tomorrow and I can come down to the Bay then or the next day. Whatever is best for you," said Wendy.

"We?" asked her father. "Who's we? Are you still with that black guy? I tracked down that band you left with. Your friend Jill told me about this guy, but that band has a white drummer now. I wasn't spying on you, or anything Wendy, but I was worried. I was scared sick and when I couldn't find this black drummer . . . the other kids in the band didn't know where you two had gone and I just thought . . ."

"Daddy, will you please get a grip? No, I am not with Cameron anymore. That didn't work out. I've never heard you say anything prejudiced about black people," said Wendy.

"I'm not prejudiced about anybody, Wendy. I'm your father, and I've been doing a lousy job of it for too long now, and I feel terrible and I was just trying to find you because I love you and I want to say 'I'm sorry' and try to make it up to you somehow and, and, and . . ."

"Daddy," Wendy raised her voice. "You're babbling now. We'll talk when I get there. Terry is going to Massachusetts General in the morning and after . . ."

"Is somebody sick?" interjected her father. "Are you sick, Wendy? Who's Terry?"

"Nobody's sick," Wendy assured him. "Terry is my boyfriend and he has an interview at the hospital. We're going to a couple of hospitals in Connecticut, Jersey, and Philadelphia, and we're working on a rough agenda."

"An agenda for hospitals?" asked Wendy's dad. "Interviews? Who is this guy? Is he a doctor? Is this a white guy, Wendy?"

"Daddy!" Now she was yelling. "Yes he's white, and yes, he's a doctor. He's a white doctor, and if you don't quit talking like that we're not coming to see you after all. Have you been drinking already this morning?"

That shut him up. There was a long silence and then Joe Applegate said, "No, Wendy, I have not been drinking. I can't wait to see you. Come anytime you want and bring your boyfriend. The house looks great and I'll be waiting for you. Let me give you my cell number in case I run out for groceries or something."

"You have a cell phone, Daddy?"

"We have a lot to talk about, little girl. I'm so anxious to see you. I love you, Wendy. I love you more than I have ever loved anything in this world."

Be nice, he's your only father.

"I love you too, Daddy. We'll call when we get close. Bye-bye."

"Good bye, sweetheart."

Terrence was sitting on the bed with his legs stretched out and a book in his lap. "Everything okay?" he asked.

"I think so . . . maybe. Maybe we shouldn't stay with him. He sounds kind of manic. Suddenly I'm not so sure this is such a great idea. Maybe we should get a room in a hotel close by. Can we afford that?"

"Of course we can afford it. Let me go on line and see what I can find around Bristol," said Terrence.

"Not much I'm afraid," said Wendy. "There's the Harbor Inn, but that's a little pricey I think. The Bristol Motor Lodge would probably be a better choice as long as it's not prom night."

"And what do you know about prom night at the Bristol Motor Lodge, ma'am?"

"Nothing I'm telling you about, mister."

CHAPTER 9

Let's not get hungry.

Wendy started making sandwiches and packing a lunch in the canvas bag she used for groceries. She was more tuned in to environmental issues these days and had recently begun bringing her own bag to the market. She made Terry two peanut butter and ham sandwiches on wheat. How could he eat these things, she wondered? Peanut butter and ham was a childhood favorite of his, but it grossed her out. She cut up a couple of apples and slipped them into a baggie and then started making some tuna fish for a sandwich of her own. Celery, pepper, chives, mayo, peppers, carrots, and tuna with tomato slices on more wheat toast. Yum, now that was a sandwich.

"Hey, what are doing, sweetie? We can get something to eat along the way."

Wendy had been up for hours already. She was excited about this trip and nervous about seeing her father. She had gone for a long run and meditated and cleaned the apartment again and left a message on Josephine's machine about watering the plants. She had become very close to Josephine and was always happy to watch her little boy when they needed a sitter.

"Good morning, sleepyhead," she said to Terrence as he walked into the kitchen and wrapped his arms around her waist. She pushed him away with her bottom as she washed her hands in the sink and said, "I just thought that we didn't want to be cruising down Interstate 89 looking for a place to stop to get something to eat. A little birdie whispered in my ear, 'Hey, let's not get hungry.'"

"I love that little bird. Wow, my favorite sands, definitely better than McDonalds," said Terrence walking out the door carrying two suitcases with a backpack slung over his shoulder.

They didn't drive much; Terrence walked to work and Wendy rode with Heidi to the restaurant. Everything they needed was close by and within walking distance so the ugly little Chevette usually sat by itself in a corner of the apartment complex lot. Last night though, Terrence had taken it out for a car wash and a fill up. He checked the oil, the tire pressure, the lights, and the battery. When he returned he was lucky enough to find a spot right in front of their apartment.

Wendy followed him out the door a moment later with the canvas lunch bag, a small carrying case, and a couple of books and magazines tucked under her arm. "Should I lock it?" she yelled.

"No, no, wait, I have to get my briefcase," Terrence yelled back. He took the steps two at a time, passing Wendy on the landing and ran into the little apartment and grabbed his case off the bed. He made a quick survey checking the oven and unplugging the TV and then pulled the door tightly behind him.

"All set," he said and threw his case in the backseat and climbed in.

They backed out of the lot and puttered across campus heading for the interstate cloverleaf. They were both quiet; lost in their own thoughts. The radio hadn't worked in years, and the silence was comfortable. The old car purred contentedly until they hit the highway and then the increased RPM's made a steady whine like a baseball card in the spokes of a bicycle tire.

"Are we going to make it, Mr. Scott?"

"That's all the power she's got, Captain," said Terrence in his best Scottish brogue. The car was older than both of them but not quite as old as Star Trek.

Mother, we offer ourselves to you, to protect us and watch over us on our journey.

They headed southeast and didn't speak until they passed the town of Williston. Summer was still officially a couple of days away, but northern Vermont had not yet received the memo, and the trees blanketing the mountains had the pale green translucent color of spring. Forsythia had been planted in the wide median separating the northbound and southbound traffic and the smell of dirt and decay and new life was in the air. Wendy reached across the gear shift and put her hand on Terrence's thigh and let it rest gently there.

"God, we offer ourselves to You this day to protect us and watch over us on this journey. Please keep us safe and help us to accept the unexpected. There may be plenty of that."

Terrence looked over at her and chuckled. He put his hand over hers and continued the prayer. "Thank You for our blessings, Lord, and thank You for each other and help us to be patient, tolerant, kind and considerate." He stopped and let the thoughts sink in and then he said, "I think we're starting to get pretty good at this. I'm still not sure what we're doing, but it makes me feel good."

"Me too," said Wendy. "I used to pray when I was a little girl, but that was different. I have a whole new feeling about it these days."

"Were you religious growing up? I mean your parents, did you guys go to church?" asked Terrence. They were winding down toward Richmond and Mount Mansfield was hovering over the northern sky to their left dominating the entire landscape of sky and clouds and sun and trees. The yellow forsythia dazzled as they flashed by it at the Chevette's top speed. The road was beautifully landscaped; huge rock outcroppings suddenly appeared hiding the oncoming cars across the wide median strip and mossy bogs filled with cattails and swooping birds made them feel like they were alone at times on a quiet empty highway.

"Presbyterian, we were Presbyterian. Mom and Dad took me to church practically every Sunday. I liked it, but after my mother died that just stopped. No more church, no more God, I think Daddy was pissed. What about you?" She wanted to steer the conversation away from her family.

"Oh yeah, we were big time Episcopalians, still are I guess. Mom was on every committee and dad ushered and was a greeter, the whole shebang. St. Mary's Episcopal every Sunday and the Country Club for brunch afterward. Sarah and I did Sunday school until we got confirmed, and then we suffered through Dr. Pine's endless sermons. I liked communion just because it was a change of pace. Coffee hour afterward was torture, but the club was even worse. I spent the entire time standing at the table beside my chair like a good little soldier watching my breakfast get cold and shaking old people's hands.

'How do you do Mrs. Moneybags?' 'My how you've grown, young man,' he mimicked. "I hated it. I used to call St. Mary's the home of the frozen chosen."

Wendy laughed. "Sounds like fun."

They were quiet again for a couple of miles. The road skirted past Waterbury and in and out of Montpelier and then up a steep hill above Barre. The views were breathtaking. "When we came through here last year the leaves were just starting to turn. It was spectacular. I thought I was moving to some kind of magical place with elves and fairies and leprechauns and imps and stuff. I mean I've seen trees change, but I had never seen anything like this. I was really full of hope. I don't know what happened. Sometime around Thanksgiving it started losing its luster. The days got darker and shorter and the weather got colder and I started to feel very alone, and trapped. Maybe it was the holidays, I missed the holidays with my mommy and daddy and grandparents. I used to love it. I was the center of attention, and then up here I was all by myself. I tried to make Christmas nice, but we both had to work and . . . I dunno, I feel like I was robbed. Like I had a life and it was stolen from me."

Blame never helps.

"I'm sorry, Wendy."

"It's not your fault," she said softly. "December and January and February were just so hard. I realize now how depressed I let myself get. I thought March would bring back warmth and sun, but it didn't and then about halfway through April I felt it start to lift. Then I found out I was pregnant and I met you, both on the same day, by the way, and it all changed overnight. I still feel sad sometimes, Terry, but now something's different. Now I have hope."

"Now we have each other."

Now there is promise.

"I truly believe that everything will work out now, that everything will be okay. I'm optimistic. Am I being gullible or can I believe in promise again? Oh yeah . . . Daddy. Maybe I am being a little naïve."

"Why is that, Wendy? Whatever happens will happen. You can't control it. You can't live his life and one thing I've learned is you certainly can't change other people. All you can do is accept the situation and move on. Concentrate on you. There is promise in your life and there is life inside of you and that is truly a blessing."

"He was such a wonderful father when I was a little girl. After Mommy died everything just went to hell. Grandma and Granddad had moved to Orlando, and we were living in the big house and Daddy was running the business, and we were such a happy little family.

"We stopped at the liquor store on the way home from the funeral. I'll never forget it. He came out with a case of Heineken and put it in the trunk and didn't take it out when we got to the house. The place was filled with people and there was a ton of food and tons of booze and then they all finally left, and Daddy and I slept together in my bed. We took Grandma and Granddad to the airport the next day and, for about a month, we had ladies dropping off casseroles, but we never ate them. I went right back to school and Daddy went right back to work and we tried to keep everything the same, but of course everything was different. I had missed way too much school and one day I got called to the principal's office and Daddy was there. They told him that I had fallen too far behind and that I would have to repeat sixth grade. I thought he was going to argue with them, but he just kept staring at the ground. We picked up another pizza on the way home and he got that case of beer out of the trunk and sat up all night and drank the whole thing. I didn't go to school the next day. Actually I didn't go to school much at all the rest of the year. Daddy was always asleep. I don't know why I'm telling you all this."

What we don't let go of keeps a grip on us.

"No, go on, please," said Terrence. "This is good for you, Wendy. You need to do this."

"Well, the summer was lousy. No camp, no sailing, no nothing. Daddy had graduated to vodka and he passed out on the couch every night. I tried to be the woman of the house and take care of things, but I . . . I . . . I was twelve years old for crying out loud. Mrs. Shannon started calling from work. She was Granddad's old secretary. God, I still remember that voice, 'Is your father going to be coming in today,

Wendy, dear?' I hated those phone calls, and of course he wasn't coming in. He was done working. He was done living. He wasn't mean or dirty or sloppy or hard to take care of. He was just gone. He wasn't there anymore. When the vacuum cleaner broke I started borrowing Mrs. Yurkowski's. She lived in the house beside us. She knew what was going on. She was so worried about us. When school started again, I tried to get off on the right track. I went to the mall with Jill and her mother and I bought some new clothes, and I made my little lunches and I would make sure Daddy was okay before I left for the bus, but it sucked. All my friends were in seventh grade and I was back in sixth. The work was easy, I'd done it before, but everything was different, and I didn't have Mommy to help me or to talk to. I was the oldest girl in my class and I had boobs and got my period, and I didn't have a mother. Oh damn, I'm sorry." She started to cry and Terry didn't say a word. He held her hand and let her cry.

"Granddad fought in Vietnam," she said. "I don't know where that came from."

"It's okay," said Terrence.

"He survived three Tet offensives. All his buddies died. He came home from the war and started working at Mr. Brosini's Gulf station, and then Mr. Brosini sold it to him, well to him and the bank I guess. Granddad turned it into a distributorship and gave it to Daddy when he retired and then Daddy sold it. I came home from school one day, and Granddad was in the kitchen screaming at Daddy. How could he sell his business? How could he turn into a pathetic drunk? How could he insult the memory of his daughter and neglect his granddaughter. He was mad. I left and went over to Jill's house and spent the night with her. I remember her mother giving me a pair of Jill's underpants, but I went home in the morning to make sure daddy was okay and I took a shower and changed anyway. Granddad was gone. I was late for school."

They had been driving directly south for an hour or so and they were coming up on White River Junction with the Connecticut River valley stretched out before them. They crossed the river into New Hampshire and left Vermont in the rearview mirror.

"What kind of distributorship?" asked Terrence to try to lighten up the mood.

"Oil."

"Oil? You mean like fuel oil?"

"I'm not sure," said Wendy.

"Fuel oil," continued Terrence, "like home heating fuel, like for furnaces."

"Oh no," said Wendy. "It was oil, like motor oil, like 10w30 kind of oil. He had contracts with the bus companies and the taxi companies up in Providence and some of the car dealers that changed people's oil, that kind of thing. Daddy started selling hydraulic oil and stuff to construction companies and all kinds of places I guess. It was a good business. They had these cute little tanker trucks they put the oil in and then Linus and Gurnak would deliver it all over Rhode Island and southern Mass. and eastern Connecticut. I loved those guys. They were so sweet to me. They were Ecuadoran or something and they called me the 'Leetle Princess.' I wonder what happened to them."

"Sounds like a pretty good business," said Terrence.

"Yeah, I think it was. Granddad was sure mad about losing it."

The traffic was getting heavy outside of Concord when they got off Interstate 89 and onto the Interstate 293 toll road down toward Manchester. The toll road ended as they followed the signs for 93 and Massachusetts and in no time they were leaving New Hampshire and crossing into the Bay State.

"We forgot to eat our sandwiches," said Wendy.

"Hey, not good, give me one of those babies, please."

They were back in civilization now. The road was crowded, and the forests and mountains had been replaced with strip malls and gas stations and businesses and homes. Wendy felt as though they were being swept along in a powerful current that would dump them right into the Atlantic Ocean. The old Chevette was dwarfed by huge tractor trailers and SUV-'s. There were speedy little sports cars zipping around them like water bugs, and it was all a bit of sensory overload for two people that had spent a quiet winter in northern Vermont.

Besides two complete sets of new tires installed over the years, the only change the old Chevrolet had seen since the early eighties was the installation of modern seatbelts. When Terrence had gotten the car the two front seats each had a lap belt which he had replaced with double cross shoulder restraining belts like those found in racing cars. Wendy had made fun of them the first time she sat in the old clunker, but she tightened the belt now. Their conversation had been pretty emotional coming down through Vermont and New Hampshire and the scenery and sharing had made them both feel very relaxed, but now they were cranked up on edge. This was scary driving. It was dangerous. These people were crazy. They approached Boston in an army of speeding vehicles, too nervous to appreciate the panorama of the city unfolding before them. The Zakim Bridge was magnificent and they crossed it too fast looking left and right at all the sights but afraid to take their eyes off the road for too long. A quick glance at the Boston Bridge and down at the water below and then they flew safely back over land.

"There's the Old North Church," Terrence nodded to his left keeping both hands tightly on the wheel. Wendy glanced over and thought she caught sight of a white church steeple but then she saw their exit in a flurry of signs.

"Terry, there's exit twenty-four," she practically yelled. He cut across two lanes of traffic and they swung down the ramp at full speed. They came to a stop at the light at the bottom of the ramp and took a deep breath. There was a blue sign across the boulevard with the international symbol for hospital and the initials MGH on the bottom. The arrow on it pointed to the right so Terrence flipped on his right blinker and Wendy rolled down her window and leaned out to ask the cars in the right lane to let them in. No such luck.

"Go back to Vermont idiot," a guy with a New England twang yelled at them. Wendy looked at his Volvo and almost gave him the finger but then thought about that forgiveness and acceptance stuff that she had been working on and smiled at him instead. He zipped around the corner and she saw his peace sign on the back window and a bumper sticker that said, "War is Not the Answer," and she smiled.

"Well I have to agree with that, 'War is Not the Answer.'"

"Agreed," said Terrence looking nervously in all four directions at once as cars continued to fly around them. "Except in the case of slavery, terrorism, fascism, Communism or Nazism, war is definitely not the answer."

Wendy laughed as the traffic paused long enough for Terrence to make his right turn. "Okay, now we're looking for the Cambridge Street location, right?"

"Right, it's a big place, there are a bunch of buildings, but that's where the guy I'm supposed to meet is."

"Are you nervous, Terry?"

"Yes, I am, but I shouldn't be. He sounded like a real nice chap on the phone. Boston doctors are chaps, you know."

"Okay, whoa, here it is, here it is. Now all we have to do is find a place to park," she said. "Like maybe Vermont."

"No kidding." They found a place, but it was six blocks away and it cost them eighteen dollars for the first hour.

"What do you want to do?" asked Terrence.

"Well, I'll walk with you and then I'm going to explore a little. I'm getting over my culture shock and I pretty much scoped things out on Mapquest and I thought I would walk through Beacon Hill over to Boston Common."

"Mapquest? Hey girl, you've been practicing behind my back," exclaimed Terrence. "I'm impressed."

"No flies on me, handsome. That's the John Hancock building," she said pointing up at the gleaming silver structure looming sixty stories above them. "How long do you think you'll be?"

"No idea, but let's try to meet back here in an hour if we can and maybe we can keep the parking to eighteen bucks."

"Sounds good cowboy" and they walked silently and quickly and with purpose like experienced city dwellers. Wendy kissed Terrence's cheek at the hospital entrance and gave his butt a squeeze and said, "Break a leg."

He was already leaning against the car when she returned and Wendy could tell by the smile on his face that his interview had gone well.

"That was quick," she said.

"His office was right on the ground floor and he said he was expecting me and I walked right in and his secretary put a coffee tray down on the table in his office and he poured me a cup of coffee without even asking and then he said, 'Terry, I've read your resume. I've read your bio. I've spoken with Dr. Howe, and all I want to know is when can you start?'"

"Terry!" Wendy squealed and jumped into his arms and began kissing him all over his neck and face.

"Wait a minute, I'm not done, and then he said the hospital could only authorize him to offer me seventy-thousand for my first year of residency, but he promised that would be up for review after the first quarter."

"Oh my God," she yelled again. "Is that normal?"

"Heck no, it's a lot more than I expected. They must really need help here, but I told him I had to run it by you and that I had a couple other interviews set up and he said, 'Remember we asked you first' and then told me to finish my coffee and go knock off those other interviews and get back to him as soon as possible. Wendy, I'm in shock."

"This is wild."

"He said that there was a reason that I came to the best place first and that I should follow my instincts because they're good ones. He wants me to come back tomorrow for a tour and to meet some of the staff, and he wants to take us out to dinner."

"Unbelievable, do you want to go to Sinai now?"

"No," said Terry. "I thought this would take a lot longer and I was planning on Sinai and Tufts tomorrow, but Dr. Pickens said that I'm just wasting my time because his would be the best offer I would get, and if it wasn't he would match any other hospital's offer anyway. Unbelievable is right. I say we head down to Bristol so I can meet your dad."

"What the heck are you so anxious about? I'm not sure we want to ruin this good day. I really don't know what's waiting for us down there. Terry, this could be bad."

"If it is, it is. We have a hotel reservation, remember? Say, it's not prom night tonight, is it?" laughed Terrence.

"Tell me his first name isn't Slim."

"Who isn't Slim? Dr. Pickens? It's James, but you can call him Slim Jim."

Good girl, Mommy. Remember, hope stands on tiptoes.

CHAPTER 10

Don't be afraid, Mommy. We will not regret the past or fear the future. It's okay to look back, just don't stare.

"Okay, that sounds like good advice."

"What sounds like good advice?" asked Terrence.

"Don't regret the past or be afraid of the future."

"Easier said than done," said Terrence. "Who gave you that advice?"

"My little birdie," answered Wendy.

"When do I get to meet this little birdie?" Terrence asked.

"Soon enough, big boy. You will meet the little winged one soon enough."

"Wendy, have I ever told you that sometimes you spook me out?"

They were back on the Interstate now looking for signs for 95 and points south. The rat race on wheels had begun again. It was still early in the day; Wendy had expected a later arrival. She had visualized walking into the house at dusk, spending ten embarrassing minutes with her father, and then beating a quick retreat to the Bristol Motor Lodge and a room service crab cake dinner.

They fought the mid day traffic for about fifteen miles until they merged onto Interstate 95 and then continued another thirty miles or so into Providence. They found the exit for North Swansea and followed Route 136 right down into Bristol. The whole trip took less than an hour and it was way too fast for Wendy. They cruised through the little town of Bristol until Wendy told Terrence to make a right hand turn onto Mt. Hope Road.

"Hey, this is pretty nice territory, Miss Wrong Side of the Tracks," quipped Terrence.

Wendy wasn't in the mood. She felt like she was going to throw up. "Left here," she said.

"Here? DeWolf Avenue?"

"Yeah, yeah, here," said Wendy.

"No kidding, Wendy, this is a nice neighborhood. I really had the wrong impression. The oil business isn't so bad after all, huh?"

"Okay, Terry, enough already. I think it's about to get ugly. Hopefully he hasn't started yet. It's here, on the right." She pointed. "That one, just pull over, Terry, please."

"Right here?" he asked.

"Yes, here, damn it. Anywhere, just stop the damn car and let's get this over with."

"Wendy, calm down."

It's okay, Mommy. You'll see. It's going to be okay.

Easy for you to say, thought Wendy. Terrence pulled to the curb and turned off the engine. They were going to need gas, he noticed.

Wendy was staring at the house. She hadn't moved a muscle. A black cat hopped off a wicker chair on the front porch of the house next door and started ambling down the steps eyeing the car.

"Nice cat," said Terrence.

"Sammy!" yelled Wendy and jumped out of the car. She ran across the lawn toward the cat, and the poor thing froze. Then the cat recognized Wendy and ran to her and jumped into her arms. Terrence could hear her purr from the street. She sounded like a motorboat.

"Oh, Sammy, Sammy, Sammy, I missed you so much." She buried her face in the cat's side, and when she pulled away tears were streaming down her face with black fur stuck on her cheeks.

Terrence shoved his hands in his pockets and slowly started up onto the neighbor's lawn.

"Terry, this is my best friend in the world. Her name is Samantha, and she has slept with me her whole life. Until I left her, I mean." The tears started again but they were interrupted by a loud wail.

"Wendy Applegate, my precious girl, as I live and breathe." It was Mrs. Yurkowski, the neighbor, and she was struggling down the steps with one hand on the railing and the other flailing in the air. "Come here, my darling, come here, come and give me a hug. Oh, I've been so worried. Oh good, Sam's found you. Well that's as should be. Come see me, you sweet girl."

The hugs and the tears were coming fast now, and Terrence stood back and took it all in. The cat and Wendy and the little round lady from next door were hugging up a storm and crying and laughing all at the same time. Mrs. Yurkowski was kind of hopping too. Her tiny feet were jumping up and down about a half inch off the ground. Terrence tried not to laugh. *This is great*, he thought, and then the little elf noticed him for the first time.

"Who is your handsome chauffer, Wendy Applegate?"

"Mrs. Yurkowski, I'd like you to meet Dr. Terry Frazier. Dr. Frazier this is Anita Yurkowski. You may call her Nit if you behave."

"It's a pleasure to meet you, Nit," said Terrence and he walked across the lawn and extended his hand.

"Oh dear, oh dear me," said Mrs. Yurkowski pulling away from Wendy and clutching her throat. "A doctor?" She turned to Wendy. "A doctor, Wendy?"

Wendy laughed. "Yes, ma'am, a doctor."

The change that had come over Wendy in the last three minutes was phenomenal. She hitched her kitty up higher on her chest, squared her shoulders, and turned purposely toward her childhood home. "Okay," she said to no one in particular. "Let's get her done."

"Wendy, darling, you're in for quite a surprise," said Nit with a big smile on her face.

Wendy looked at her quizzically and marched over to the house and up the front steps. She shifted Sammy onto her shoulder and reached for the doorknob, but the door swung open before she could grab it. Terrence and Nit stood back quietly as a thin, attractive, raven haired woman stepped forward.

"Hello, Wendy," she said with a big smile on her face. "I'm Rebecca. I've really been looking forward to meeting you. Please come in. Oh, excuse me; it's your house of course. I don't think your father was expecting you so early in the day. You're even prettier than your pictures. Your dad's done some rearranging, and he has photos of you all over this house. I would have recognized you in a Turkish bazaar; I've seen so many pictures of you. Hi, Nit, come on in, I made iced tea. Please pardon me, Wendy, I'm a little nervous, I guess."

"Let's go, handsome," said Nit grabbing Terrence's arm. "We don't want to miss this."

What the heck is going on here? Terrence wondered to himself.

Wendy was wondering the same thing when Sammy wiggled out of her arms and ran through the door and into the kitchen. The house was immaculate. It was spotless, and it smelled clean and fresh. The old sofa was gone, and the window curtains and shades were wide open letting sunlight pour into the living room. The old rug was gone too, and the hardwood floor had been refinished and the pine shined brightly. There was a fresh coat of paint on the walls, and the fireplace was clean as a whistle.

"Wow," said Wendy.

"Your father's done a lot of work," said Rebecca.

"I've been supervising, Wendy," said Nit. "The man has been a whirlwind. He has scrubbed and painted and redecorated this old house from top to bottom. Your grandmother would be proud. All except your room that is, Wendy; he hasn't changed a thing in your room, has he, Becca?"

"Well I didn't see it all before he started, but . . . I'm sorry Wendy this must all be a bit of a shock to you. I mean I know how change can unbalance a person. I'm sure it's hard. I wish your father was here. I feel like an intruder."

"Where is daddy?" asked Wendy.

"He's at his meeting," said Mrs. Yurkowski.

"Meeting?" questioned Wendy. Her father was a member of the Elks. Her grandfather had been a proud member of the VFW and the American Legion, and even though Joe Applegate wasn't ever in the service he spent time at both of those places too. "It's the middle of the day." She didn't want to think about what he would be doing at the Legion Hall at two in the afternoon.

Do not be disheartened, Mommy. Hope is the key that unlocks the door of discouragement.

"You didn't live through it, baby."

"He goes to A.A. now," said Nit, ignoring Wendy's comment. "Every day, sometimes twice. He's a new man, Wendy." Nit seemed very proud of her neighbor. Rebecca had quietly slipped into the kitchen and was putting together a tray of refreshments. Wendy wandered around the first floor of the house with her mouth open. She was clearly overwhelmed.

"Wendy, are you all right?" asked Terrence.

"Yeah, fine," she said. "Yeah, yeah I'm just fine. I need to sit down, I think."

"Let's sit on the porch; it's a nice day," said Terrence.

"Good idea doctor," said Nit. "I was sure glad to see that ratty old couch out on the curb last year. He's got some real nice porch furniture again. Oh, Wendy, I wish your mom and grandma could see this old place now."

Rebecca came out on the porch with a tray of iced tea glasses with sliced lemons on a plate and sugar in a bowl. She shot Nit a look that said—"Shut up"—and then asked, "Does anybody want some cookies or apples? I could cut up a couple apples."

Wendy looked dazed. "A.A., like Alcoholics Anonymous you mean, so he's not drinking?" She had a hopeful, expectant look on her face.

"Nope," said Nit. "He went on the wagon right after you ran off. I didn't think it was going to take, but God bless him . . ."

"Anita," Rebecca cut in forcefully. "I think Wendy should hear this from her father. He'll be home soon, Wendy."

Anita Yurkowski couldn't shut up. "It's Monday. Monday's he goes over to Fall River and sometimes up to Providence for the big speaker's meeting at night too."

"Nit, please," said Rebecca again.

"It's okay, I'm proud of him. I was telling the girls at my beauty parlor . . ."

"How long have you lived next door, Nit?" Terrence interrupted. Rebecca looked at him approvingly.

"Me? Well, Sidney and I have been here for almost fifty years. I remember when Annabelle was born. I'm still waiting for my invitation to Orlando. Wendy's grandma and I have been neighbors since we were girls."

"Fifty years?" said Terrence. "I'd love to see your house."

"Oh, it's a mess, but if you're a doctor I guess you've seen a lot of messy houses. Come on, Terry, bring your glass. Joe won't mind. We'll bring 'em back"

Terrence and Nit made their way down the steps and across the lawn. Terrence held her arm and she beamed up at him. "Well, you know, I had to take care of the cat after Wendy left, Mr. Doctor." And she continued to prattle on as Terrence helped her up her own steps and in through the front door.

Rebecca chuckled and said, "He's good. Where'd you find him?"

"Yeah, he's sweet. He found me, I guess."

"Better yet," said Rebecca.

"I am a little surprised at the situation here, I'm uh . . . I don't mean to be rude Rebecca . . ."

"Becca please, Wendy."

"Okay, sure, Becca. So what's your deal? Are you and my dad . . . ?"

"No, Wendy, we're not, I mean we're not . . . Well, I'm not really sure what I mean. Your father is a sweet man, and I've just been helping him get back on his feet. Please don't jump to any conclusions. I mostly listen to him talk, and he mostly talks about you and your mother. He is dealing with a lot of guilt and shame, and no one can walk that path for him. I had my trouble with drugs and booze, and I've been in recovery for a long time so I have a little perspective and sometimes I can help him to not blame himself so much. He has a lot to talk with you about, Wendy, and it's not my place to get involved. He loves you very much. His heart has been broken since the day you left, but coming from a severely alcoholic, dysfunctional family myself, I've pointed out to him that you did exactly what you had to do, and I don't blame you one bit. From what I know about you, Wendy, you are a warrior and a survivor and I'm real proud to have finally met you. I'm not here to get in between anybody. That man adores you, and he's been a nervous wreck since you called."

She's special, Mommy, and she's carrying an angel.

"Thank you for watching over my father, Becca. I think we're all going to get along just fine. How far along are you?"

"Far along? What do you mean far along? Do you mean . . . oh dear. Wendy, do you know I'm pregnant? I didn't even think I was starting to show yet."

"Only in your eyes, Becca. Is it Daddy's?"

"Oh my, I didn't think we were going to get here so fast. Your father doesn't even know. I just found out, really, not too long ago. Oh, Wendy, this must be difficult, I'm sorry, but honesty is my policy, so at the risk of derailing a relationship I was truly hoping to foster, I must say, yes, of course the baby is your father's. Can I ask you, though, to please keep this just between us girls? Heck, Nit doesn't even know which means it's still my secret . . . our secret now, I hope."

"It's cool. It totally clears things up. I'm okay with it, Becca. I'm happy for you really. Things have changed a lot in my life. I guess that's because of Terry, I'm not sure, but I just feel like I have a whole new attitude about forgiveness and tolerance and life." She smiled at Rebecca and held out her hand to her. "I've always wanted a baby sister."

"But how did you know? Most twenty-year-old girls aren't so intuitive. At least I wasn't. Wait a minute." Rebecca paused and put down her glass. She took Wendy's hand with both of hers, and squeezed tight, and said, "Oh my God, you're pregnant too."

"Yup, and I'm nineteen, thank you very much. I still feel like a girl, pregnant or not, and that twenty thing still sounds old to me. I never thought I'd be twenty."

Terrence and Nit emerged from the house next door. He looked over at the two of them on the porch and made a quick decision. "Say, Nit, I need gas. Can you show me where a station is in town?"

"You bet," said Nit. "I'll give you the grand tour. Did you know I was born in this town almost . . . well, a lot of years ago?" They tottered across the lawn; Terrence opened the door for Mrs. Yurkowski and she parked herself in that old hunk like a queen in her carriage. Terrence waved and winked up at the porch as he walked around the car. "We won't be too long," he yelled, and they pulled into the street and down to the corner.

"Wow, he's terrific," said Rebecca.

"He sure is, Becca. I'm scared to death; I'm so in love with him. So how did you know I was carrying?"

"It's so weird. I've never been pregnant before. I'm only ten years older than you, but I swear this baby talks to me. Please don't laugh, Wendy. I know I sound loony. She tells me the most amazing things, though."

"You know it's a girl," confirmed Wendy.

"Oh yeah, no doubt," said Becca. "This sounds crazy, but she gives me advice, good advice. She tells me how to handle your father, for instance, and that's delicate stuff. He didn't drink for too long compared with some of the other people we know in the program, but he drank hard, and he drank with remorse and shame and guilt, and he lost a lot of self esteem along the way, and the little peanut in my belly tells me just the right things to say to him at just the right times. It's eerie, Wendy."

"You're in A.A. too?" Wendy asked.

"Yup, sober nine years New Years Day."

"That must have been a tough New Years Eve."

"Damn straight. That was the worst night of my life," said Becca. "I can't get over your knowing that I was pregnant."

"I'll tell you, Becca, honesty surely is the best policy. I've learned that recently and sometimes it's a struggle for me. I used to always lie, even when I didn't have to. I don't know where that comes from. Certainly not from Daddy, but I just never heard a story that I didn't think I couldn't make a little better, you know? Like I was smarter than everybody else; man, look where that got me. Anyway, my little birdie told me you were carrying an angel. Is this normal? Do all pregnant women get these premonitions?"

"I don't think so, Wendy, but I'm sure glad you do too, because I was starting to think I was crazy," said Rebecca.

"Yeah, me too, at least at first I thought I was nuts, but then I just kind of went with it. I felt like I had a secret, you know? Terry is totally clueless, and it freaks him out when I talk to my baby. She says things out of the clear blue, and I just answer her before I think about where I am or who might hear me."

"I know what you mean. I figure people must think I'm talking to one of those cell phones stuck in my ear."

"Hey, that's great," said Wendy. "I never thought of that."

They were silent for a moment, just staring at each other on the front porch together still holding hands and neither one of them felt the least bit self conscious.

"This is amazing," started Wendy. "I really like you. I mean, I don't mean it to sound like that, but I've known you now for, what, twenty minutes maybe? And I feel like we've known each other forever. I feel really good with you, Becca."

"I feel really good with you too, and I'm not just saying that. I have no agenda here Wendy, no ulterior motives. I have to tell you that I'm crazy about your dad. He's one of those real special people that come along only rarely in a person's life, and I'm scared too. I think I love him, Wendy, and I don't want to lose him, but I don't want to get between you two in any way either. He's so proper, Wendy. He has never let me spend the night here, which is cool, but believe me Nit notices."

"He's a little conservative, I guess, but he's lucky to have you, Becca and I'm glad you two have found each other. I know he loves me and he'll always love my mother, but he was not meant to live alone. He needs someone like you. He needs you, and I'm glad he's got you. I feel really good about this whole thing. Oh, Becca, I'm so glad I came home.

I was expecting the worst, but I think things were meant to turn out just the way they are."

This is good.

"This is good," said Wendy and Rebecca at the same time, and then they laughed together like two old souls.

CHAPTER 11

Terrence and Nit pulled into the Gulf station in town, and Terrence was just starting to pump gas into the old bomb when Nit screeched.

"Joseph! Hello, hello, what are you doing here?"

A handsome man who looked to be in about his early forties was sitting on the bench in front of the station with his faced turned to the sun and his eyes closed. Terrence knew right away that it was Wendy's father. The resemblance was unmistakable, but the body language and easy demeanor really gave it away. Joe Applegate was slender and looked to be in very good shape; the kind of man who didn't look like he had to work too hard to stay in good condition. His dark hair was receding gracefully, and he looked very tranquil with his hands hanging comfortably between his legs. He wore a blue polo shirt and stylish blue jeans and looked pretty cool for a guy pushing middle age. He had the air of a poised athlete and he slowly opened his eyes and smiled at Nit.

"I guess I would recognize that voice anywhere, Anita. I'm not doing anything, but thanks for asking," said Wendy's father.

"Well stop meditating and come over here and meet Wendy's doctor," said Nit.

Joe's eyes grew wide, and the poised attitude disappeared instantly. He jumped to his feet and came right out of one of his flip flops as he staggered toward them. Retreating a step to reclaim the escaped sandal he tried to hide his embarrassment with, "Well, why didn't you tell me, you nutty old woman?" but it sounded too harsh and he immediately regretted saying it. "I'm sorry, Nit, that was mean. I didn't mean to . . ."

"Oh don't be nervous, you silly boy, just come shake Terry's hand."

" . . . insult you. Hi, Terry, excuse me, nice to meet you." He stuck out his hand. "I was just sitting here catching some rays. I've got the car on the lift inside, needs an oil change. Well it doesn't really need it, but . . . wow, I didn't expect you two 'til later. Nice to meet you." He was shaking Terrence's hand. "Sorry, I guess I just said that."

"It's nice to finally meet you too, Mr. Applegate. Wendy's told me a lot about you," said Terrence, keeping one eye on the gas nozzle.

"That's okay," said Joe. "There have been a lot of changes in the last couple of months, right Nit?"

"You betcha, but Terry's already heard about all that. He hijacked me so Wendy and your Becca could spend some time alone." She cast an eye toward Terrence. "I may be old doctor but I don't have the Alzheimer's yet." Nit giggled. "I'm anxious to get back home and see what's happening on the porch, though, so finish up, Terry. How long are you gonna be Joe?"

"Why don't you ride back with us, Mr. Applegate?" suggested Terrence.

"Joe, Terry, please call me Joe. We don't stand on formality around here, do we, Nit?"

"Only when the tourists are watching," laughed Nit. She was having the time of her life. "Get in the car, Joe. An old girl doesn't get too many chances to ride around with two handsome young men"

"Well," Joe hesitated and looked back at the garage. "Okay, let me run in and tell the boys to call me when they get done. This place isn't run the way it used to be anyhow." Joe jogged back across the small tarmac and in through the office door under the orange Gulf sign.

"Joe used to own this place," Nit whispered conspiratorially. "He's right; Jack Hodge doesn't know how to run a business."

Jack was an old high school buddy of Joe's and he had bought the place when Joe was at his lowest with the drinking and the loss of his wife. Nit thought that he had taken advantage of Joe and so did pretty much everybody else in town. Terrence placed the nozzle back in the holder on the pump and walked toward the building to pay. Joe was inside when he came in the door, and he heard Joe tell a little guy with a goatee that he'd think about it.

"Sorry to interrupt," said Terrence. "I've got twenty-four dollars on the far pump—regular." He handed a credit card to the man who looked at it without taking it.

"We don't take American Express," said the goatee.

"Put it on my tab, Jack," said Joe.

"Don't be silly," said Terrence pulling out a twenty and a five. "I've got it, Mr. Applegate, thanks anyway."

"See that, Mr. Applegate," the goatee said sarcastically. "Real money." He handed Terrence back a dollar out of his pocket. Terrence and Joe walked out to the car together wordlessly. Nit had wiggled into the back seat so Joe slipped into the front.

Joe and Terrence could not have squeezed a word in edgewise if they had wanted to. Anita talked the whole way back to the house, which, mercifully, wasn't too far. She kept up a constant banter about the weather, the town, the traffic, the deterioration of the neighborhood, youth today, global warming, and the evil people that didn't pick up after their dogs. Terrence and Joe exchanged glances and shared a common grin with Joe throwing in an occasional eye roll.

They pulled up to the house and Joe said, "Pull in the driveway, Terry. I'll pick up the car tomorrow; we're not going anywhere, I don't think."

The two girls were still in the same chairs on the front porch, looking intently at each other and didn't even notice the car had pulled into the drive until Nit let out a robust, "Let me out. I've got places to go and people to see. Hi, girls," she hollered and waved. "We're back. Oh my, what time is it? I have to go home and whip up some dinner for Sidney. Oh never mind, he can wait. We might get an invitation from our neighbors anyway. Right, Joe?"

Sam was sitting in Wendy's lap, and Rebecca had asked her how a pretty and dainty female had ended up with the name Sam, so Wendy told her about Bewitched. Wendy and Annabelle used to watch it together every afternoon when Wendy was a little girl. Wendy loved it. She'd believed her mommy could make magic happen if she helped her wiggle her nose for her which had often brought tears to Annabelle's eyes, but had always brought joy to her heart. This was one of the many very special times with her mother that always flooded Wendy's memory. She had pretended she was Tabitha and her mommy was Samantha and it had all seemed about right because as soon as the show was over every day, Joe arrived home from work. It stood to reason, therefore, in a little girl's mind, that her Daddy was Darrin. The little black kitten had arrived on Wendy's fourth birthday, and she was instantly Wendy's best friend and confidante. She was named Samantha, and she shared the little girl's every thought and secret. Wendy tried to wiggle her little black nose too, but the kitten wouldn't have anything to do with that game.

"She's seen it all, I guess," said Wendy. "Sammy is almost sixteen now, and she has been in this home and this family all of her life and most of mine. I still feel terrible about leaving her, but I knew that no matter how bad Daddy ever got, he would take care of my kitty. I had to leave, Becca," she whispered and her chin quivered and her eyes filled, and Rebecca reached over and took her hand again.

"Of course you did," she said. "And look how things have worked out. You did what you had to do and your higher power took care of the rest. Stay positive, Wendy, stay focused on doing the next right thing, keep following your heart, God is watching over us all."

"I believe that, you know." Wendy sounded a little surprised to hear herself say it, but she really did believe that things were going to be okay.

She expected setbacks. She was pragmatic and had experienced some tough lessons, but she truly believed that she would prevail, and she felt that her optimism and positive attitude were crucial to that belief.

Hardship is the pathway to peace, Mommy.

"Then I should be downright serene, I guess," Wendy mumbled to herself. Rebecca arched her eyebrows and gave her a look, but said nothing.

"Tell me how you got involved with A.A., Becca. You don't seem like the kind of person that would have a problem with booze."

"As long as I keep spiritually fit and do the work I know I need to do, I can keep alcohol from ever being a problem in my life again." She watched as Terrence, Joe, and Anita crawled out of the car and stood in the driveway chatting. Sensing that they still had a few moments alone together, she continued. "I was an art student at NYU a hundred years ago, and my girlfriends and I used to go bar hopping in the Village. I was the restless one. I never wanted to go back to the dorm. I would stay in the bars and close them, and I attracted a lot of unwanted attention. I loved the whole scene. I loved the music and the smoke and the action, and I loved to dance and I learned how to drink for free. My friends would just leave me. I guess they knew I had a problem before I did, but once I started partying, I never wanted to stop. I didn't go home to bed, I passed out, and sometimes I didn't make it home. My grades were suffering, I started to lose weight and get puffy and blotchy, and pretty soon all the bouncers and bartenders knew my name. I could sense trouble. My art was a struggle. I was losing myself.

"I knew I had to stop, but I couldn't. One night I woke up in Battery Park in the back of a cab with a Puerto Rican guy on top of me and that was it. That was my New Years Eve. I called the hotline number the next morning and went to a meeting on Second Avenue that night and I never looked back. I'm one of the lucky ones; a first time winner. Never drank again, that was it. The group called itself the Clean and Dry Group and some of us called ourselves the Scream and Cry Group. I worked through a lot of tears and some childhood trauma that I've been able to put behind me now, and I got my art degree and got the hell out of Manhattan, but I've never left A.A. That's about it, the down and dirty quick version of my life's story." She finished and looked nervously over at the group in the driveway.

"Wow," said Wendy. "How did you meet my father?"

"I thirteenth stepped him," laughed Rebecca.

"Huh?"

"I'm just kidding really. The foundation of A.A. is the principle of the twelve steps of recovery. Admitting you have a problem, asking for help, making restitution, and helping others, in a nutshell. Thirteen steppers are the inevitable sharks you find in the program that prey on newcomers. People are pretty vulnerable when they come into the rooms, and the world is filled with assholes. A.A. is no exception. Your dad actually asked me out for coffee after he was coming around for five or six months. I ran it by my sponsor and she told me to keep my distance, but I ignored her. I'd been watching your dad since the first day I saw him and I could see how much he wanted to get sober. He talked about you and your mother, and he was very sincere and I was touched. We had coffee, and he told me that his sponsor told him to keep his distance too." She laughed and they watched Nit walk back over to her house and Joe and Terrence head into the garage. "Hey, we ain't saints."

"No, we sure ain't. That's a pretty cool story. Do you think we should we do something about dinner?" Wendy asked Rebecca.

Joe and Terrence were still in the garage and the girls on the porch were staring at the door.

"I guess," said Rebecca. "What do you think is going on in there?"

"Beats me, what's in there?"

"I honestly do not know. I've never set foot in that garage," answered Rebecca just as the two men emerged chatting and laughing like old buddies.

"Granddad's car," realized Wendy. "That's the only thing in there, I think. Well maybe the boat."

"Hey," hollered Joe. "Do you two want to go out somewhere to get a bite to eat? Nothing fancy, maybe crab cakes at Tweet's or the shrimp basket, I love that."

"Tweet's?" asked Rebecca.

"Tweet's is a great little place," said Wendy. "I waited tables there one summer. It's right up the block. We could walk."

"Sounds fine to me," said Terrence. "I'm tired of driving. A little exercise sounds like a good thing. I wonder if I could use the phone inside to confirm my appointments tomorrow before it gets too late.

I forgot to charge my cell last night. Oh wait, what about a room? I should probably go over to The Bristol Motor Lodge and get a room. I can call from there." He glanced at Wendy, "as long as it's not prom night that is."

"Prom night?" asked Rebecca.

"It's a private joke," said Wendy. "No offense."

I'm hungry.

"Don't be silly," said Joe. "You're both staying here, and of course you can use the phone, Terry. The one in the kitchen is closest."

"Great, thanks, Joe, I'll get my briefcase."

"Don't worry, sweetie, we're going to get some food," Wendy said.

"Do you have one of those cell phones stuck in your ear?" teased Rebecca. "What about me, Joe? Do I get to sleep over too?"

Joe Applegate blushed and stammered and looked at his daughter and said, "Well, you live here. I mean, uh . . . well . . ."

"Don't get nervous Daddy."

* * *

Dinner was a blast. The four of them got along like long lost friends, and the conversation was lively and fun. The guys had coffee and the girls had tea, and then they started walking back to the house and fell into the same familiar formation they had adopted on their stroll up to the restaurant; Joe and Terrence in front and Wendy and Rebecca walking side by side behind them a couple of yards. On the way up, the guys had discussed cars, and the girls talked about yoga and whispered about morning sickness. Joe explained that he had never really been too interested in automobiles or engines even though that was the business that he had inherited from Annabelle's father. He instinctively knew how to run a business though. He was scrupulously honest, and he treated his employees, customers, and suppliers with respect and dignity. He had become a reluctant expert in the field of lubricants because he read all of the bulletins and brochures and paid attention to the salesmen and engineering guys that came around from the big oil companies. He didn't miss it, though, that much was clear. Joe explained to Terrence that the conversation that he had walked in on earlier in the day was another attempt on Jack Hodge's part to get Joe to return to the business to bail Jack out, and that that sure as heck was not going to happen.

Wendy told Rebecca about the new discovery in her life: yoga. She didn't know how she had lived so long without it and wished that she had gotten into it when she was younger and struggling with the physical changes of a young girl's body and the emotional turmoil of losing her mother. The meditative aspect of yoga had become an integral part of her life and she could tell by her mood when she had gone too many days without practicing. Rebecca loved yoga too. They seemed to have so much in common, and they agreed that tomorrow they would go to Rebecca's early morning class together.

They chatted quietly about pregnancy, of course. Wendy had been a little worried about the sights and smells of a restaurant; she had suffered for a month at the Sirloin Saloon trying not to get sick every time she delivered a steak to a table, but she had been fine tonight. Rebecca had the same experiences and had lived for two weeks on saltines and ginger ale before things finally settled down. They laughed conspiratorially and held onto one another and fell into a comfortable and peaceful silence.

The walk back home was quieter and more relaxed on stomachs filled with good food. The baby in Wendy's tummy seemed satiated and content. Nobody felt the need to make idle conversation under a starry sky with the salty smell of the ocean blowing gently off the bay.

* * *

"Let's go for a walk, Terry," Wendy said when they reached the house. "I'll show you the bridge."

"Okay, well I'm going to go home," said Rebecca. "Wendy, I'll pick you up about five thirty if that isn't too early. I like to get there as soon as Freida opens up and spend a little quiet time. I'll bring an extra mat."

"That sounds great, Becca. Thank you very much. I never thought about bringing my yoga mat along when I was packing stuff for this trip. Come to think of it, the only thing I thought about was what clothes I was going to wear when I met Terry's mom."

"Yeah, that's a scary thought," said Terrence. "See you tomorrow, Becca."

"I'll see you tomorrow, Terry. It's been a real pleasure meeting you," Rebecca replied.

"I think I've pretty much finished my book," Wendy told Terrence out of the clear blue after they had walked awhile in silence.

They were strolling along the sidewalk heading south down the peninsula that is Bristol. The road was smaller here than it was up near the highway, and the breeze had picked up and clouds were beginning to cast shadows as they floated across the moon. They entered a grassy park-like area that was the beginning of the Roger Williams University campus. They could see the lights of the Mt. Hope Bridge from far away as they wandered along the meandering paths of the school. Muted lamp posts lit the paths helping them to see and adding a romantic touch to the evening.

"That's wonderful, Wendy. You're really quite amazing you know; full of surprises. This whole day has been one big surprise after another for me. Your dad, your house, your town; it's all so different from what I expected. When did you find the time to write this book?"

"It's for children, Terry. It was easy. The story just unfolded in my mind and the drawings are really very simple. I don't expect to even get the thing published, but it was fun," said Wendy.

"Nonsense, you should send it to someone. I don't have a clue who, though. How do you find a publisher or an editor or a printer? It's totally out of my league, I'm afraid."

"I don't know either, and I'm not going to worry about it. It's a beautiful night Terry. I've been cold for months; this warm breeze feels so nice. Let's not worry about books or anything else. Today was wonderful; our drive down, your interview, meeting Becca, holding

Sammy, and Daddy. Oh, Daddy . . . oh, Terry I just can't believe it. Pinch me. Is it really true? He looks so good and he sounds so good, and I just love Rebecca. She's perfect for him. She's wonderful. I would never have dared to dream that things could have changed so much. And Daddy really likes you. Wow, Terry, my father likes a guy I'm in love with. Life is good."

Tell him about the octopus mommy.

"No, I think it's a little premature for that."

"What?" said Terrence, "What's a little premature? You're doing it again, Wendy."

"Sorry, sweetie. I was just thinking out loud."

So tell him. He loves this stuff, Mommy, and he's very supportive and that makes us all feel good.

"Okay, okay, I'm thinking about another kid's book too, but don't get excited, nobody's going to end up on Oprah writing books about foxes and bunnies and octopuses," Wendy said to Terrence. "Hey, look, now you can see the whole bridge."

"Octopuses?"

"Yeah, now do you want to hear a scary story? A real life scary story?" asked Wendy.

"Um, okay, I guess. Am I going to be able to sleep tonight? By the way, where am I going to sleep tonight?"

"I'm not sure," said Wendy. "That's kind of a delicate subject, isn't it? Let's just let it ride and we'll see what happens. So do you want to hear my bridge story of terror or not? It's also the story of 'up your butt and around the corner'."

"I think the tale of terror I could do without, but I've been wondering where the butt thing came from since the day you barked it at me," Terrence laughed. "And when did the scary story turn into the scary bridge story? That bridge?" He pointed at the graceful structure in front of them.

"Yeah, that bridge."

They sat down on a little stone bench overlooking the water and the bridge. Mt. Hope Bay was on their left and Narragansett Bay was on their right and it looked like they joined together underneath the bridge. Terrence could imagine that the water must be treacherous right off this point. The bridge towered above it all and the double string of lights outlining its form and length was festive and impressive at the same time. A tanker was off in the distance making its way north toward Providence and a fishing boat looked to be heading south into the open water of the Atlantic. A tug boat roared past them no more than a hundred feet from the spot where they were sitting.

"First, tell me about the Octopus," said Terrence.

Wendy laughed. "His name is Justin, and he's going to be the central character of my new book. He lives in a reef in the Virgin Islands, and he protects all the little baby fish by scaring away the tourists. Josephine told me all about Cinnamon Bay in St. John and the underwater snorkeling trail and how people are not supposed to disturb the environment or the fish or anything, and I just kind of took it from there. I mean you know there has to be the occasional little brat from Pittsburgh or Buffalo or somewhere that tries to net a pretty tropical fish or stuff a starfish in his trunks or something. Well, that's what Justin's there for. He's the cop on the beat. The mother fish don't let their babies swim inside the reef near the touristos without Justin being in the neighborhood to protect them.

"He has a cool little cave with a garden of brightly colored sea glass and fragments of Red Stripe beer bottles in his front yard. I will love drawing all of this: the colorful tiny fish; Justin's cave and garden; the fat, ugly, sunburned tourists. Justin's last name is Case. Get it? The mommy fish tell their babies that they have to have you-know-who around, Justin Case. He'll have a cute mailbox outside of his cave with his name on it and the little fishes will have their masks and snorkels and pails and shovels, just like human kids and they'll have to go to his cave and wake old grumpy up to come scare the swimmers away so that they can play in the warm, shallow water, and the Park Rangers will warn the people to stay away from the mean old octopus.

"Maybe the little cuties will have baseball caps and bats and soccer balls. The baby girl fish could be riding baby seahorses you know, something like that. I think it sounds like fun and it will be real colorful and tropical and I'll throw in brightly painted buses on shore and chubby native ladies that look like Josephine, that kind of thing. What do you think? And boats too, yeah, boat bottoms and churning propellers they have to look out for. That's it. That's the basis of book number two."

"Justin Case. I love it, Wendy. You're so full of such fresh ideas, so creative. Where does all this creativity come from?"

Me!

"Do we dare go onto the scary story or do you want to hear about your dad's proposed trade?" Terrence smiled.

"What trade?" demanded Wendy.

"He wants you to move back home and he told me he would trade Rebecca for you," joked Terrence.

Wendy hit him in the arm, and she knew it was a little too hard. "Oops, too hard, I'm sorry."

"Ouch, no kidding, that was hard. This is wild, but it's not as important as your real life scary story. You've got me intrigued now," said Terrence.

"You've got me intrigued."

"You first," Terrence insisted.

"Okay, a couple of summers ago we were all down at the park drinking beer and smoking hash. Collie's brother goes to Harvard, and he was there with this exotic gooey Lebanese hashish he bought in Cambridge and we were all getting real silly, and Collie and Drake decided that we should go for a boat ride. They have a friend down at St. George's off Sachuest Bay, and they were going to have him meet us on the beach or something. I can't remember the details."

"Wait a minute," said Terrence. Who are Collie and Drake, and where did they get such dorky names?"

"They're brothers; Colliard and Drake Pierponte. Their dad is a big shot banker in Providence and their mother is old money Boston and they have a house in Wellfleet and all the kids went to prep schools and then Ivy League. They have a sister at Wellesley; I forget her name . . .

Phillipa maybe. That's it, yeah, they call her Pill. Jill knows her. They aren't exactly friends, but I guess their parents are. Jill and I ran into her in town a couple years ago, and Jill told her how pretty her pearls were—just girl talk. Out of nowhere this snob informs us that Wellesley girls only take their pearls off for one thing, wink, wink. Like gag me, I wanted to barf on her."

"That just doesn't sound like the girl I know," said Terrence.

Love and tolerance, Mommy.

"I know, Terry. It's not me. I'm beyond being cynical and angry now. We're all just people."

"But the brothers are Colliard and Drake?"

"Yeah, Collie goes to Yale, and there's another one—he's older, went to MIT I think. Actually I think Drake went to your school," continued Wendy.

"Lawrenceville?"

"Right, Lawrenceville. He was supposed to go to Princeton, but he got kicked out of Lawrenceville and ended up at Kent in Connecticut I think. I lose track."

"Drake Pierponte? I don't remember . . . wait, there was a little nerd in the class behind me named Pierponte, they called him PeeWee."

"Yeah, his name is Peter Drake Pierponte. That's him. He had the hash. I think he flunked out of Harvard too," Wendy said. "Anyway, we all traipse down to the marina. It's like three in the morning. There were about ten of us, and we climb onto this fancy yacht, the Pierponte family barge, and slip lines and head off. Collie cuts right across the channel and we go out past Hog Island, and then I guess the boys kind of lose their bearings because it's a dark night and the island is dark and we can't see the bridge or the lights from the mainland on the other side of the island and I know there's some bad water out there. This one kid starts getting real panicky and keeps yelling 'Where are we? Where are we? Where's the bridge?' and that's when yours truly said 'It's up your butt and around the corner' because we were just coming around the island, and presto there it was. It really was around the corner. So everyone's laughing at this kid and Collie spots a buoy and everybody's relieved and this jerk turns around and clocks me and I go head over heels right in the drink."

"Oh my God," Terrence exclaimed.

Hurt people hurt people.

"Uh huh, it was scary, man. I think I told him he was gay or something. Anyway, I come up spitting and hollering, but nobody hears me and nobody else saw what had happened, but there's this jerk standing in the stern with his hands on his hips and a grin on his face and that boat is leaving me behind. I was shocked. I was sure they were going to come back for me, but they didn't. He never told anybody. He was going to let me drown and let me tell you, Terry that is dangerous water out there. The tide comes in and out about ten or twelve feet, and the currents are probably eight or ten knots and I'm being pulled out to sea like something's got me by the leg. I'm screaming and swimming as hard as I can and the water is cold and I was crying and so darn scared and the boat and the bridge are getting further away and there are barges and tankers out there. It was terrible."

"What happened? Oh Wendy, baby, how terrifying. What happened?"

"I just let go. I knew I was doomed and I just rolled over on my back and let go. I surrendered, Terry. I said 'Okay, God, I've been a bad girl. I hate myself. I hate my life and I want to be with my mother, so go ahead. Do what you gotta do.' I floated along with the current right down the middle of the channel, staring up at the sky and crying and telling my mom I would be with her, and pretty soon I totally relaxed and just let the water take me and I felt warm and peaceful and I didn't really care. Then Oscar landed a life ring perfectly over my head and pulled me into his boat."

"Oscar?"

"Oscar DeLaguerre, my savior, a little Portuguese fisherman just heading in from three days out. He spotted me bobbing along and thought I was dead. He was going to use the gaffe he said, but it was below and I was moving too fast so he threw the ring and scored. He brought me back to Bristol, it was daylight by now. I'd been in the water for a couple of hours, and I made him promise not to tell anyone. Now there are only three people in the world that know the whole story. Oscar said he would kill Randy Hoffman for me if I wanted him to, but I said no. And that is the end of the 'Up your butt and around the corner' story."

It is the weak that are cruel, only the gentle and strong are kind.

"Thank you, baby, I'm starting to realize that."

Terrence stared at Wendy for a moment, trying to comprehend the obvious confusion and trauma at work in her mind.

"Wow, jeez, Wendy, that is terrible. He should have been brought up on charges; attempted manslaughter or something."

"Maybe, I don't know, Terry. I think about it. I almost told Oscar to go ahead and kill him. He wanted to, but we weren't supposed to be on that boat or out that late or drinking beer and getting stoned. Plus I'd told my dad I was spending the night at Jill's. I did a lot of that back then. Karma got him, though."

"What happened?" asked Terrence.

"Two winters ago he was found in a dumpster outside a go-go joint in East Providence."

"Dead?" Terrence said expectantly.

"No, almost, I guess. He was half frozen. He had a broken jaw and a concussion and a couple of broken ribs, and he was missing a lot of teeth. I was glad when I heard, but happy too that I hadn't told anyone about that night but Oscar," said Wendy.

"Do you think Oscar . . ."

"No doubt, Oscar did it. He was good friends with Gurnak and Linus. Those people live by a code and they all know my family and what we were going through. Those guys loved my mother and they watched out for me," Wendy choked up a little and said, "Okay, what's this trade?"

"Hah, you sure have a habit of changing the subject when things get edgy," said Terrence.

Let's thank Mother for our blessings and for your good fortune, Mommy.

"Terry, please pray with me," Wendy said as she slid off the bench onto her knees and tilted her head back to the stars above.

"Mother, thank You for saving my life so that I might have this wonderful man beside me tonight, and that my father would be saved from his alcoholism, and that he would be successful on his journey of sobriety and his renewed sense of confidence and self esteem. Thank You, Lord, for this precious gift living inside me. I am overwhelmed with gratitude and I thank You, and I love You, and I'm so happy that I have the faith to pray and to love and to believe."

Terrence had slipped to his knees as well, and he listened to Wendy and he kept his thoughts to himself. He too felt blessed, and it was new to him and he wasn't sure how to express it, but it felt okay to be quiet.

* * *

"Technically it's Bahama yellow, not brown, and it's a '67," Wendy said authoritatively. "I think they changed the taillights in 1968 or something. Porsche never made radical changes to the 911 or 912, but a year or two after Granddaddy bought his they did something to make them different. The crappy mid-engine things that came out later were a real departure from the classic line. He hated those new ones." Wendy knew more about the car in the garage than anybody else in the family including her mother's father.

They were walking back to the house now, hand in hand. It was a beautiful night, and it had been a wonderful day for both of them. After spending some serious meditative time on their knees in the damp grass, Terrence had pulled Wendy to her feet and held her for a long embrace. They fit so well together and neither one of them felt like moving, but finally they parted and began slowly retracing their steps away from the waterfront and back up through the deserted college campus. It was a Monday night in the middle of June and they were absolutely alone.

"Anyway, what do you think?" asked Terrence. He had quickly related his conversation with her father in the garage that afternoon. Joe wanted to trade the Chevette for the Porsche. He said that Wendy had always loved it and that he had been saving it for her. He kept it in tip top condition and he wanted to fix up the little Chevy and donate it to a charity he had in mind. He was looking for a new project and when he rode home from the station with Anita and Terrence it struck him that this would be the perfect arrangement. Terrence told Joe that he was kind of fond of his old ride, but he wasn't stupid. The Porsche was truly a classic.

"It really is a classic, of course," confirmed Wendy. "It's a race car and Porsche really struggled making a corporate decision to retrofit those two models to be street legal in this country, but they never compromised. It's precision German engineering. Granddaddy used to take me on Sunday drives down to Newport and out on the Cape and even to Mystic once in awhile. We would be gone together for the whole day, and I loved it. I loved him. The 912 never came as a convertible, and the color was pretty putrid I guess. Granddaddy called it baby diarrhea brown, but Porsche called it Bahama yellow and it certainly got a lot of attention, even in Newport, where there are some truly amazing vehicles tooling around on Sunday afternoons. The transmission was designed for the track, and believe me it's tight. That little air-cooled engine may be only four cylinders, but the car is light as a feather and it has incredible torque and stamina on the open road. The steering is what it's all about though, that baby holds a curve with the RPM's maxed out which is why it was so successful on the Le Mans and Grand Prix tracks of Europe. Granddaddy bought it when he came home from the war and there weren't a lot of mechanics around that understood it. The Volkswagen guys were about the most familiar with that set-up. I read everything I could find on Porsche's back when I was little and all my friends were into big, ugly American muscle cars. I'll bet it's got less than fifty thousand miles on it."

"Fifty six according to the odometer," said Terrence. "So what do you think?"

"I think Daddy's crazy."

It's not about the car, Mommy. Your daddy wants to do something nice for you.

"But I know it's not about the car. Daddy just wants to do something nice for me. I always thought it was going to end up being mine someday, but of course it's his call and he wants to show me that he loves me. Thank goodness money never got tight or he might have considered selling it, and it's worth twenty Chevy Chevettes. It's not a commuting car, though Terry. It's much too good to be used like a regular car.

Granddaddy kept it in that garage under a chamois cover for close to forty years. It has no clearance; these lousy roads would pothole the poor thing to death, but then again it wasn't built to sit in a garage or a museum. It was meant to be driven. Okay, let's do it, but let's take care of it, Terry. If we end up somewhere here in the Northeast let's get a van or a truck and just use the Porsche for Sunday drives like granddaddy and I did."

"Okay," Terrence laughed. "I'm glad you worked your way through that decision. It's very entertaining to watch you work over a problem. I'll let your dad know it's a deal."

"Not tonight apparently." They had reached the house, and all the lights but the front porch light and the hall light were off. Joe had gone to bed by the look of things. Terrence expected a note or directions to the guest room, but they were on their own.

"I'd like to take a shower if I could. Should I put my bag in the guest room?"

"You can put your bag anywhere you want, cowboy, and you can certainly take a shower. You can sleep in the guest room if you want too, but rest assured, wherever you sleep, I'm sleeping with you."

"Are you sure?"

"I'm very sure, and I'd prefer that you sleep in my room in my bed where I'm willing to bet my old kitty is sleeping right now." Wendy flipped off the porch light and grabbed her bag in one hand and Terrence's hand in the other and headed up the stairs. "That's my bathroom," she said pointing to a door at the end of the hall. "Take your time: I'll be in here," she said motioning with her head to the open door at the top of the stairs.

As soon as Terrence got the water in the shower just right Wendy joined him.

CHAPTER 12

"Wake up, sleepyheads," coaxed Rebecca in a stage whisper. "I started the Mr. Coffee machine. Joe's up and out already. He likes going to the seven o'clock meeting, and he said he wanted to stop and pick up donuts."

Wendy and Terrence were twisted together like a giant pretzel, and Sammy was asleep in the middle of them. Rebecca pulled her head back out of the room and closed the door gently as Wendy rolled over and pulled a pillow from underneath Terrence's head and draped it over her own. Terrence laughed and pulled it back and tossed the covers off the two of them, sending a grumpy old cat meowing off the bed. Sammy scratched at the door to go out, and Terrence got up and accommodated her. He got dressed quietly, watching Wendy trying to pull the sheet back over herself.

"I've got my first appointment at Sinai at nine and then Tufts at noon. Then I'm going to take Dr. Pickens up on his offer of a tour at General. I'll call him when I get back into Boston. You should probably get up, little darlin', considering your new best friend is downstairs making coffee."

Wendy moaned, rolled up and put her feet on the ground, bent over and moaned again. "It takes me a little longer every morning," she mumbled half to herself. "Well, okay, yoga at five thirty. What time is it Terry?"

"Um," he looked at his watch. "It's five forty. Oops."

"Oops? Uh oh, I wonder what time the class actually starts."

"Are you two up?" a holler came from the bottom of the steps. "I'm running a little late, but that's all right, the class doesn't actually start until seven."

"There's your answer." Terrence crossed the room and opened the door. "Thanks, Becca," he said to the bottom of the steps. "We're up."

"Not me," said Wendy as she collapsed back onto the soft mattress and pulled the covers up to her chin. "Where's my kitty?"

"Get up," laughed Terrence and he headed down the hall to the bathroom.

Ten minutes later they were all in the kitchen. Terrence was blowing on a hot cup of coffee, Wendy was sipping a glass of cranberry juice, and Rebecca was slicing strawberries.

"Are you always this up and at 'em, Becca?" asked Wendy.

"No," said Rebecca forcefully. "I'm trying to impress you two. How am I doing?"

"You're doing good," said Terrence. "I'm impressed."

"Doing well, Terry," Wendy corrected.

"All right, you two, have a great day. I'm outta here. How do I look?"

"You look well, Terry," mocked Rebecca. "Knock 'em dead."

"Wendy, tell your dad about our conversation last night, please. I'm really excited. Wait a minute," he paused. "I think I dreamed about that car last night. Everybody was speaking French and wearing little one piece racing outfits. It's an omen. This is going to be a good day."

He kissed Wendy on the lips, and then he kissed Rebecca too and both girls said, "Aww."

They cleaned up the dishes together, and Wendy found Sammy's food where it was always kept and fed her too. Everything in the kitchen was the same, to Wendy's relief. They left the coffee machine on, grabbed their yoga mats, and headed out to Rebecca's little VW Golf for the short ride to the studio.

Wendy was introduced to all of Rebecca's friends and after the yoga class she got a long tour of her tiny apartment. They stopped for croissants and tea in town on the way back to the house. Rebecca shared an art studio with a handful of other artists and she pointed it out as they drove along the Bay on Hope Street.

Joe was home when they got there. They made breakfast and talked. After a little while, the sunny morning clouded over and the rain began to fall. They made lunch and talked some more and listened to the steady drumming on the roof. Wendy had a feeling of cleansing, and release and she could not remember the last time she had felt this good.

"Unbelievable," Terrence responded that afternoon when Joe asked him how his day had gone. "Everybody was just great, and I really felt wanted at both Sinai and Tufts, like this country is running out of interns or something. The tour and the people at General were just amazing. Dr. Pickens was right about his offer being the best, and the facilities are top notch. What really blew me away was the 'call' system. Each resident has mandatory time when he or she is 'on call', but a lot of these guys have families or other obligations and they trade or swap or even just give their 'call' hours away. The guy that was showing me around takes all the 'call' time he can get and at $230/shift he makes almost an extra grand a week. General has primary response duty for the local prison, so some of the calls are pretty brutal, but it's got to be good trauma training."

"Massachusetts General also has an excellent detox center," said Joe. "My home group takes a meeting into there every Wednesday night. There are plenty of uninterested drunks that just show up for the cigarettes, but some guys have seen the light and gotten sober there too. It's a safe place to begin recovery."

"I don't know much about the disease of alcoholism, Joe," started Terrence. "I was surprised how little time we spent on compulsions and addiction in med school. I guess they basically leave that for psychiatry school, but I'm curious about your experience."

"Rebecca might be a better source for you, Terry," said Joe. "She's been at this a lot longer than me."

Terrence looked surprised and Rebecca laughed.

"Gee, Wendy, you're pretty good at this anonymity business," she said.

Wendy just looked at everybody with a twinkle in her eye. Terrence looked confused.

"You're in A.A. too?" he said.

"She's kind of my mentor, my sponsor, and my guiding light. She is definitely a good example of what the program can do for a person," said Joe. "I was in bad shape. I didn't realize Wendy was even gone for a couple of days, and then I absolutely freaked out. It rained hard for a day or two after you left, honey." Joe looked at his daughter. "I'm sorry, maybe this isn't an appropriate conversation."

"Oh no, Daddy, please, I'm interested too. How did you get sober?"

"Well, I called everybody I could think of looking for you. Don't feel badly, Wendy. You absolutely did what you had to do. I understand that now. Becca's been a big part of helping me to come to terms with that. The way you and I lived in the years following your mother's death amounted to nothing less than child abuse. I totally neglected you to salve my own selfish self pity, and I realize that today and wish I could change it, but I can't. And now you've given me the opportunity to try to make amends and in some small way, to try to make it up to you. That's probably impossible, little girl, but I have to try. You spent six or seven of the most important, most formidable years of your life trying to look after me, trying to take care of a pathetic, desperate, drunken and broken fool, and I know I'll never be able to give you those years back, Wendy, but . . . I don't know. I have to try to make it right and the only way I know how to do that now is to grow the heck up and take care of myself and to be responsible and available for you."

Wendy began to cry.

"I'm sorry, now is not the time."

What does not come from the heart does not reach the heart.

"No, Daddy," choked Wendy. "Go on, please go on," she cried.

Joe started to well up too, but he struggled on. "Anyway, I flipped and everybody in town knew you had skipped out, and, believe me, baby, nobody was blaming you. I tried to put the garbage out on the curb when it finally stopped raining, but I was a day late and I didn't even know it. Then I slipped on the wet driveway and fell on my back, and I was so drunk I couldn't get up. I was just lying there crying and feeling sorry for myself when Tommy pulled up."

"Mr. Gunn?" said Wendy.

"Yeah, Tommy was in the company pick-up. He had just swept the lot and cruised down our street coincidentally to make sure I was okay, when he found me lying in the driveway. He and his brother still own their father's marina, and you know we've been friends since kindergarten. We played baseball and basketball in high school and fished all the time and chased girls together. He was your mother's first boyfriend until I stole her away from him. Tommy got sober in '87 when we were about twenty-one or two. He never even got out of the truck. He just leaned out the window and said, 'Are you done yet?'"

Joe stopped and looked up at the living room ceiling and thought for a moment. He bit his lip. "Yeah, I was done. He said he'd be back in the morning and that I had better be sober, and then he drove away and left me sprawled out on the ground. I didn't know what to expect, but I didn't drink the rest of that night and I didn't have anything in the morning and he walked in the front door and said, 'Come on, I've been saving your seat for you.' I went to my first Alcoholics Anonymous meeting that day, November first, and I haven't had a drink since. They gave me a Big Book that morning, and I took it home and read it cover to cover. Tommy Gunn pulled in the driveway on November second and we did it again."

"What's the Big Book?" asked Terrence.

"It's *Alcoholics Anonymous*. That's the title of the Big Book. Bill Wilson and the early pioneers of A.A. wrote it," said Joe.

"How big is it?"

"It's not any bigger than most books, that's just what they call it. I don't know why. Do you, Becca?"

Rebecca chuckled and said, "No, I don't and I'm not sure I've ever heard anyone ask that question. There's a lot more literature now, but that's the original Bible of sobriety so to speak. Those first guys back in the '30's, Bill W. and Dr. Bob, are like gods to some people."

They are prophets chosen by God, maybe even saints.

"Works for me."

"What, Wendy?"

"Nothing, Daddy, go on."

"Well, there's not much more to tell. It's still a mystery to me. I have no idea why the compulsion to drink was suddenly lifted from me. Oh, I struggled. I had my moments when a tall glass of vodka seemed like the answer to a lot of my problems, but I had Tommy and some other guys sticking close to me and keeping me busy, and then of course along came this dark haired beauty." He nodded to Rebecca. "I've been saved, and I've been blessed and good things just keep coming my way and I don't know why but I've quit asking. I've learned that I'm not stronger than alcohol and I'm not stronger than God. I asked God to fight this battle for me and He's done it. I'm a tough guy and I'm brave and I have a boat load of self will and personal determination, but none of that could help me stop drinking. Peace and serenity don't come out of self sufficiency, and even when I was drinking I understood that they don't come out of a bottle either."

"So you found God, Daddy? I mean, I think I have too. It's like this big 'Aha' that was missing in our lives for all those years."

"Yes, Wendy. I have found God, but He was never lost. At first I struggled with the whole Higher Power thing, but I knew that the meetings were keeping me sober. I started praying to your mother. I still do, everyday. And then it dawned on me; I was praying to Annabelle Applegate, A.A., and Alcoholics Anonymous, A.A., was keeping me sober. I know it sounds dumb, but it worked for me. I prayed to your mom to watch over both of us, Wendy, and she did. She still does. I know Annabelle is looking down on all four of us right now, and I know she's happy."

Mother is watching over your mommy, and your mommy is watching over us and they are both very happy.

"And I am too," said Wendy.

Peter told the exiles at Cappadocia that Mother would give them the gift of a new birth and that it would be a living hope.

"God has given us the gift of hope, Daddy."

"You grew up when I wasn't paying attention, Wendy," said Joseph Applegate. "I love you very much, Princess."

"I love you too, my dear daddy, and I feel very comfortable leaving you now. We're going to be okay, aren't we?"

"We are indeed, what's for dinner?"

"Pizza," said Rebecca. "And you're going to go get it."

"Let's go, Terry, duty calls. Let me give you a few driving tips in that old 912."

They traded owner's cards in the morning, and Terrence and Wendy threw their bags in the Porsche and climbed in after them. Joe slipped an envelope into Wendy's purse and kissed her good-bye for the umpteenth time. The next stop was Stamford, Connecticut, and nobody was in a hurry. They'd had a wonderful reunion, and Wendy felt more at peace with the world than she ever had felt before. Her father cried on Rebecca's shoulder when the snappy little sports car turned the corner at the end of the block.

CHAPTER 13

"A.A. totally intrigues me," said Terrence as they breezed along Interstate 95 in the early morning sunshine. The ocean was off to the left of them, and they whizzed by sailboats and speedboats and working vessels as they made their way westward with the windows down in their sporty new car. The salty smell of the water filled their nostrils.

"Me too," said Wendy. "I'd like to learn more about it. These guys that started it must have been some kind of special."

Wilson and Smith are two of Mother's ancient souls. There are a number of original angels in heaven that return to this world over and over again to provide solace and direction and hope. Over the last one hundred generations there have been teachers like Jesus, Buddha, Socrates, Mohammed, Krishna, Hiawatha, the prophets and sages, Epictetus, Seneca, Gandhi, Galileo, Rembrandt, Newton, Mozart, Da Vinci, Jalal Rumi, Madame Curie, Salk, Cicero, Aristotle, Emerson, Witherspoon, Lao Tsu, Edwards, Burke, Lincoln, Joyce, Michelangelo and millions more. Most of us return as humble travelers and lead unspectacular lives concentrating on spreading love, charity and forgiveness. We were all with God at the beginning of the great light, except of course, the Visitors. Most of us don't know where they came from, and I'm not sure that we're supposed to know, but they'll return. I know that. I don't know how, but I feel it deeply.

"Whoa, baby, too much info!"

"What's that?" Terrence asked above the noise of the road.

"I just got a lesson on spiritual history from my baby and it was a little heavy. This kid can get pretty intense, I'm starting to find out," said Wendy.

Terrence looked concerned. "Do you think you might want to talk about this with a psychologist or somebody familiar with this type of phenomena, Wendy? I'm sure it's not that out of the ordinary to hear voices, and you seem pretty chill about it, but still . . . I mean there are people that, you know . . ." He paused and looked at her thoughtfully. "Okay, you want me to shut up, right?"

Wendy looked over at Terrence, smiled, and felt a warm glow in her heart. She felt as though they were in a bubble of light. She looked beyond his profile across West Mystic to the water of Fisher's Island Sound and saw visions of yesterday and tomorrow. Closing her eyes she saw a huge winged creature dip gracefully out of a deep red sky and scoop something from the waves. She saw long canoes with painted men dropping paddles into the placid water. She saw small wooden sailing ships with tattered sails hanging on broken masts and she saw breeching blue whales blowing fine streams of water into rainbows. Silver saucers skirted across the horizon, and roiling gray clouds spit daggers of fire at long flat ships surrounded by elegant dolphins with colorful striped fins. Her mind was a kaleidoscopic video.

"That's okay, Terry. I don't want you to shut up. I like it when you're concerned about me. I hear my baby talking and I see things I could never before have imagined seeing and I'm not frightened. It doesn't scare me at all. We are the gentle ones Terry and as long as we stay within the cycle of cooperation with our Creator we will be safe."

That was beautiful, Mommy.

"Thank you, baby."

Terrence just shook his head and kept his eyes on the road. The Porsche chewed up the miles through the beautiful morning with the warm sun rising higher behind them. West Haven, Milford, Bridgeport, and finally into Norwalk they drove. He started looking for Exit 6 and the Stamford Hospital sign and began to feel a little hungry. "I guess we should have stopped at that Dunkin' Donuts back there. I'm getting hungry."

"We are too," said Wendy. "Oh, here's the exit. We take this to Stillwater, then to Broad Street, and then we'll see Shelburne Road."

"Right, it's beside the U of Connecticut campus I think, or maybe in it. I'm not sure."

They spotted the sign for the hospital and also a sign for Tully Health Center and found a spot in the parking lot. Terrence was anxious to start his interview, so Wendy said that she'd wander over to the campus and see if she could find a salad and a cup of tea or juice.

An hour later, they were back at the car and anxious to keep moving. Wendy and the baby were fed and happy, and Terrence was once again pleased with his reception.

"Thank God 'Trish the Dish' dumped me freshman year," he said. "My academic record is really paving the way and opening doors I never could have expected."

"Who is 'Trish the Dish' and why would any sane female ever dump you?"

"Ah," said Terrence. "That was nice, but the truth is I probably wasn't a very attentive boyfriend." He pulled the sporty little car out of the parking lot and back into the traffic of Stamford. "Which way is the highway? Hey, there's a sign for the Merritt Parkway, let's take that. The Merritt is like the last old road in America I think. It was built a long time ago for people with a different attitude about travel. It's scenic and curvy and it has gas stations and rest areas in the median, and it's grassy and landscaped and too darn small for the way people drive today, but it'll take us where we want to go. Actually, I think the Taconic is like that too; probably built by the same guy."

"Who is 'Trish the Dish'?"

"Okay," Terrence exhaled. "You're not going to let this go are you?"

"No," said Wendy emphatically.

"Trish Goldberg was my high school sweetheart and she blew me off and broke my heart when we went our separate ways to college, which turned out to be a blessing in disguise because I buried myself in the books and didn't look up for three years. The next thing I knew,

I had a four-point-oh grade point average and I got into every medical school I applied to, and that is who 'Trish the Dish' is."

"Her loss," said Wendy.

They crossed the George Washington Bridge in crawling bumper-to-bumper traffic, which was fine with Wendy because she was enjoying the sights of New York City to the south. A truck inched up on their left, blocking out the view down the Hudson but she just shifted her attention to the other side with the towering Palisades and the scene of the mighty river upstream. "This is fabulous," she said.

"There's a lot of early American history right here," Terrence said. "I always like to think about what this all looked like before Europeans came to these shores. Imagine being a little Native American kid right here four hundred years ago? It must have been fantastic. We're going to cut through a pretty dense part of New Jersey on the other side of the GW but Morristown is only about thirty minutes away, and it's the heart of the Revolution in my opinion. Washington stayed there a lot and in Pennsylvania too. Between Jockey Hollow and Valley Forge, the Continental Army got the breaks it needed to regroup and refit and take it to the Brits. I love this stuff."

Wendy could see it. The bridge and the cars and trucks and apartment buildings and barges and tug boats disappeared, and she saw Indian children frolicking on the banks of the mighty river and felt a sense of overwhelming tranquility. She felt the earth circle its star a million times in an instant and witnessed a fleeting parade of native culture in her mind. The people were calm and at peace with one another and the environment. She felt very connected to the Earth Mother.

Morristown was nothing like she had ever imagined New Jersey to be. She liked it instantly and after Terrence finished his interview with the hospital administrator she was happy that the director of the Carol Simon Cancer Center wanted to chat with him so that she could walk through the quaint little town. The village square was a throwback to older times. A saleslady in a cute cheese shop called it 'the green', and Wendy sat on a park bench watching the birds and the people with dogs and admiring the neat little stores until Terrence pulled up in the Porsche. "Hey, lady, are you lost?"

"Terry, this place is great. Get a job here. Look at these beautiful trees."

Trees spend all day looking up at God.

"I have a job if I want one," he said as he swung open the door. "Come on, I'll show you more of New Jersey that might surprise you."

She hopped in the car and they headed west on Route 24. Terrence explained that he knew Jersey from prep school and coming up to this area to compete in sports against other schools. Princeton was very special he explained, but it had that liberal college town thing going, and that attitude bugged him. This part of the state, out here in New Vernon and Mendham and Chester and Bernardsville and Bedminster and Far Hills was where the old money was, and these people were very low key about it. Wendy fell in love with Peapack and Gladstone and felt very comfortable as they drove further west in the rolling farms of Hunterdon County.

"Terry, if Morristown General makes a good offer, go for it. I'll move here in a heartbeat."

"They did," Terrence said simply.

Crossing the Delaware River from Lambertville to New Hope, Pennsylvania, was a step back in time for Wendy. "This is so New Englandy," she said. "I love this. What a quaint little bridge. I expect to see horses and buggies and kids in knickers rolling hoops."

"It really is cool here," Terrence agreed. "We used to come over here from school to hear bands on Saturday nights."

"Bands?" said Wendy. "What kind of music do they play in this little 'burgh?"

"New Hope would surprise you. There is a real artsy crowd here. A lot of New York people have weekend places here, and the music scene is really hip. I guess a lot of acts do a gig here between their New York and Philadelphia dates. I've seen Ry Cooder and John Sebastian and James Taylor and the Young Rascals and Blood, Sweat and Tears and a bunch of other acts here. I saw Don Henley, he was a gas. Plus there are a lot of rippin' local bands that have been together for a long time that play all the roadhouses and bars and clubs throughout Jersey. Some of these guys would amaze you. I remember the Blue Sparks from Hell and the Hot Damn Brothers and a bunch more. I know a great place for dinner, and we can stay at any of a bunch of bed and breakfasts tonight. What do you think?"

"I'll follow you anywhere, big boy."

They cruised around the little river town for an hour getting a feel for the place. Terrence pointed out the old railroad station and the granary and the remnants of the canal, and they drove past shops and galleries and about a half mile up the western hillside out of town they found a bed and breakfast called The Fox and Hound. They checked into the sprawling nineteenth century inn and got arranged in a charming room before walking back down into the village for dinner. Terrence pointed out a well known restaurant called Mother's, and Wendy thought that the name was very appropriate. Mother's was serving and the place was jumping. A local crowd was at the bar and a lively three piece band was rocking the joint. Mother's seemed like the most popular spot in New Hope but when they emerged onto the street after a delicious dinner the sidewalks were more crowded than they had been late that afternoon.

"What's going on here, Terry?" Wendy wanted to know. "What are all these people doing in the street at nine at night?"

"I think it's just a typical summer Wednesday night," said Terrence as they joined the throng on Main Street. "We used to have a blast here when we were in high school. You had to get a pass to leave campus on the weekend so there was a whole trade in counterfeit passes and fake ID's. Pennsylvania has stricter liquor laws than Jersey so we would buy beer on the Jersey side of the river and come over here to party. Actually, all we did was what we're doing now. We just cruised around. We loved to make the scene and walk around and look at girls. There used to be a cool hippie head shop in that little store at the foot of the bridge. Guys bought rolling papers there and chillums and pipes and stuff."

"Chillums?"

"Yeah, I think that's what we called them. They were little hand held fireplaces for smoking weed," explained Terrence. "Man, this whole scene brings me back. Goat almost got us killed right here years ago. He was toasted and he started taunting this biker. We ran away and the guy found us later walking across the bridge back to Lambertville in the middle of the night. We had all had too much to drink, not just Goat. There were about twenty of them on Harleys, and they pulled knives and started chasing us and we eventually ran into the police station on the Jersey side. We got back to campus just as the breakfast bell was ringing.

"What a night that was. Come on, I'm pooped. Let's head back to the B&B. Tomorrow might be a workout."

"Your interview?" asked Wendy.

"No, my parents," said Terrence.

"Becca would love this place," said Wendy when they had escaped the lights of New Hope and found themselves walking under a twinkling canopy of stars in the dark night.

* * *

"Your breakfast is served, master." Wendy had slipped out of bed and walked around the grounds barefoot in the early morning dew talking to her baby and praying to God and feeling loved and grateful. She could not have been in a better mood as she crept into the room with a tray of coffee, juice, and scones. She had been imagining again, thinking about what this place had been like a couple of centuries earlier with the wildlife and native children playing placidly under the late stars of the predawn sky. They were children of the stars, luminous beings of pure light, and she had dreamed about them the night before as though they were smoky whispers in her mind, just out of reach, but calling to her and gesturing for her to follow them.

"I have a hangover," Terrence moaned.

"I would believe that since you're such a lightweight, but unfortunately you didn't have anything to drink last night."

"Yes, I did," insisted Terrence as he rolled up from under the soft quilt. "I waited until you fell asleep, and then I snuck down to the karaoke bar and got blitzed and sang 'Stairway to Heaven'. I was very good. Young damsels tried following me home and pestered me for my autograph. I had to use a pseudonym."

"Wild dreams?"

"Wow, you're not kidding. Thanks for the coffee. We have the Philadelphia Children's Hospital at ten and my mother is expecting us for lunch at noon I guess. Actually the proper name is Children's Hospital of Philadelphia which is why savvy people say 'CHOP'.

"I dreamed about my mother, which is never a good thing, but I know you were worried about seeing your dad, and that worked out better than either of us could have imagined so I'm staying positive and hoping for the best."

Good idea.

"Good idea, Terry. Affirm in the positive," said Wendy. "I had some pretty crazy dreams too, but they didn't really go away when I woke up, which is cool. It's all good. I'm really enjoying this little trip together. Thank you, Terry."

"You're welcome . . . I think."

*   *   *

"Hello, Terrence Frazier here."

They were driving down along the river admiring the green shoreline of New Jersey on what had turned into another brilliant, sunny summer morning. Terrence had been telling Wendy about Washington's momentous crossing of the Delaware on that cold Christmas night over two hundred and thirty years ago when his cell phone rang.

"Well hello, Terrence. It's your mother."

A shiver ran up his spine and the car took an involuntary swerve on the little country road. Sweat beaded into his palm as he squeezed the phone tight in his hand and tried to calm his voice replying, "Good morning, Mother. What a pleasant surprise. I was just thinking about you."

He had been thinking about two hundred cold, dedicated, and determined American patriots risking their lives on a suicidal volunteer mission to bring liberty to an infant country. His mother could not have been further from his mind. Wendy felt his tension, and the baby inside of her felt her mother's anxiety too.

"What is your schedule, dear?" demanded his mother in a sweet voice. She pronounced the word with the 'sh' sound instead of the hard 'sc' sound as though she were telling him to shush or shut up. This British affectation had always bothered Terrence.

"I have an appointment this morning at Children's Hospital, and then we were expecting to enjoy lunch with you and Father," replied Terrence.

"Quite right Terrence, I had almost forgotten that you were bringing along a little friend. I'll have to call the club and tell them we will be four now."

"We're having lunch at the club, Mother?" Terrence said into the tiny phone without taking his eyes off the road. *Little friend*, he thought. She could be so condescending.

"Of course, Terrence, that will be best. I have gardeners and the rug cleaners coming today, and Beatrice has the day off to attend her niece's graduation. I couldn't say no, she practically raised the child. Her sister is absolutely good for nothing, and sometimes I think your father and I support the whole family, but be that as it may, lunch at one at the club. Okay, dear?"

"Yes, Mother, we'll be there," Terrence was ready to flip the phone closed.

"Your friend has something appropriate to wear I'm sure, dear?"

“We do, Mother,” he said wondering whether that was a question or a command.

“Very good, Terrence,” said his mother and disconnected before he could say good-bye.

He put the phone on the console directly in front of the stick shift and grasped the steering wheel with both hands. He stared ahead purposely, seeing nothing that registered consciously. *Good bye to you too*, he thought.

“Terry? Are you okay, Terry?” asked Wendy looking at his set jaw.

“I’m fine,” he replied.

“Yeah, right, and I’m the Miss June centerfold.”

“Oh please don’t joke like that, Wendy. That is not the kind of comment that will go over well at this little family reunion.”

“Hey, first things first, don’t you have an interview to get through in an hour?” said Wendy.

“I do. I’m sorry, you’re right. It was only a phone call, and I’m not going to let it ruin my day. I have to keep priorities straight, don’t I?”

“You bet you do, mister,” Wendy said. “Do you think it would be okay if I explored the hospital a little bit? I’d like to see the babies.”

“Of course, that sounds like a good idea. Hey, look, it’s our old friend I-95. Now how the heck do I get up there?”

“So how did Goat get his name?” Wendy asked after they had managed to navigate back onto the highway.

“Oh, it’s a funny story; it happened that day actually. After we snuck back onto campus Johnny, Gordo and I headed to bed. We told the proctor we were sick and he sent us to the nurse but we just headed back to our dorms and crashed. Campbell, that's Goat, Campbell Ferris Van Pelt. He had to go to French class first period or he would have flunked the course. Old Mrs. Leveque told him that if he missed any more class she would fail him. We all felt pretty rotten, we had polished off three bottles of Boone's Farm Apple wine that we bought in Pennington on the way to New Hope, but Goat couldn't miss that class. Mrs. L. was a goofy old lady, and she had set up a cheese tasting party for everybody to experience the joys of French cheese, did it every year I guess. I wish I had been there; it's become one of the legendary stories of Lawrenceville. I guess Goat did okay with the Gouda and the camembert and the brie or whatever else the old doll had for them to taste, but when it got to the goat cheese . . . well you can figure out the rest. All the other guys in class had heard about our night out and they could tell that Goat was hurting, so they started rubbing it in. I guess the goat cheese was runny and milky and lumpy and smelly and when Goat tried to eat it he blew everything all over the room. Pinky said the whole building smelled like sour apples and cheese. Poor Mrs. Leveque. So that's how he got the name Goat, end of story."

"You can tell me how Pinky got his name later," said Wendy laughing.

Terrence knew Philadelphia, and despite the profusion and confusion of construction everywhere he managed to get them across another river and onto the Schuylkill Expressway and into a concrete bunker of a garage attached to the Children's Hospital of Philadelphia. They found an information center and Terrence headed off to his meeting while Wendy wandered around the huge central atrium. She wanted to see the babies but discovered it wasn't that easy unless you were family, so she settled into a comfortable couch and watched the passing traffic. By the time Terrence found her she was totally distraught. She hadn't moved a muscle and still held the unopened magazine and the candy bar that she had bought at the gift shop.

"Oh Terry," she whimpered. "It's so sad. There has just been a steady stream of little sick kids and scared mothers and distraught fathers walking past here for the last hour. I can't imagine how anybody could work in such a sad place."

"I thought you were going to go upstairs to look at all the healthy little babies and the happy, grateful families and be in a wonderful mood when I saw you," Terrence consoled her.

"Me too, I mean I was, but then this steady stream of little sick toddlers and wailing adolescents started rolling by in wheelchairs, and there were devastated looking parents with their precious children in their arms, and I just froze here. I couldn't move. I feel so helpless, Terry."

"It's a wonderful place, Wendy, and sick children are precisely why people work here. This hospital is over one hundred and fifty years old and they have been treating kids here for longer than any other facility in the world." He pulled her close to comfort her and they held each other in the center of the big hospital for a long time. "Maybe I'll work here and help some of these sick little kids," suggested Terrence as he held Wendy tight.

I don't think so.

"I don't think so, Terry," said Wendy.

CHAPTER 14

"Whoa de whoa whoa, if it ain't Mr. Terrence Frazier drivin' up in a fancy damn spote car?"

"Hiya, Jonathan, I'm Dr. Frazier now if you don't mind and this is my girlfriend Wendy, and we are here to lunch with my parents. Are they here?" Terrence said to the wiry little black man in the white shirt standing at the valet sign outside of the main entrance to the Chester Valley Country Club.

"Well, 'scuse me, Doctor. Yassir, yo daddy's here and, yassir, he brung yo momma, da wicked witch a Paoli, wit him," said Jonathan. "Now, may I park this sweet little ride for you 'cause you know I gonna take it right downtown and show it off to all my po friends?"

"That's all right, Jonathan," Terrence laughed. "I'll leave this beautiful young girl here with you and park the car myself, if you don't mind."

"Hell, Terry boy, dat's better yet," Jonathan said as he helped Wendy out of the Porsche with a big toothy smile.

Wendy had been very nervous about what to wear and had changed clothes twice in the tight confines of the car on the way over. Terrence kept insisting she looked great, and now as she stood by the door watching Jonathan charm arriving members she felt better about the stylish skirt and blouse she had finally decided on, but she was anxious to sit down somewhere and hide her sandals under a table. She fingered the necklace that she had found in the envelope that her father had slipped into her purse the morning they left Rhode Island. It had been her mother's; a thin gold chain with a jade St. Christopher medal hanging from it. It gave her strength.

She had cried when she opened the envelope and found the necklace and the check for $5,000 from her daddy. They were tears of joy, and she was beginning to feel as though this crazy life of hers was somehow getting back on the track that it was supposed to follow. For the last seven or eight years she'd imagined that she was running alongside her life watching it unfold without her. She had been a witness, an observer, and she felt like she hadn't been able to outrun her sorrow, but now she was starting to recover some sense of control. The constant restlessness, the constant seeking, the constant fear that had been creating so much emotional turbulence were slowly being replaced with a sense of purpose and intuition, and she had no doubt that the baby inside of her was responsible for this positive change.

She noticed that Jonathan had abandoned his southern 'step and fetch it' accent and was greeting people with perfect diction and an aristocratic manner. Terrence was striding toward them across the flawlessly manicured lawn alongside the practice putting green when Jonathan got a break in the traffic and slid up beside her.

"Miss Wendy, I have known that young man since he was a baby boy, and I would like to tell you that he is one of the finest gentlemen I have ever met. His father is a gem and his mother treats me like crap, but the men in that family are first rate, and I don't know how you two hooked up, but darlin' you need to hold on tight to that boy because you have snagged yourself a real diamond. Now, don't you dare tell anybody I said that because I can tell you and I are going to be fast friends."

He walked away as quickly as he had approached, and Wendy was momentarily staggered by his comment. Jonathan had made her feel good, really good. She immediately lost any remaining anxiety and regained her composure and her confidence as she watched Terrence skip down the slate steps toward her, and she knew everything was going to be just fine.

He's an angel, Mommy.

"I figured that, sweetheart," said Wendy.

"What's that?" Terrence asked as he approached.

"Jonathan is an angel," said Wendy.

"Ah, he's the best. I guess I've known Jonathan my entire life. Mother treats him like crap. She treats everybody like crap, but Dad takes care of the staff here, and Jonathan has always kept an eye on me and Sarah. We love him, and he teases us shamelessly."

"Is your sister going to be here?" asked Wendy.

"I wish. But no, she won't be here. My plan is to visit her down at the beach house this afternoon and spend the night there. Is that cool with you?" They were walking through the carpeted foyer lined with old photographs and smelling of wood and leather.

"Absolutely, you never told me you had a beach house, Terry."

"It's not ours, Wendy. We've been renting the same place down in Avalon for the last two weeks in June for as long as I can remember," said Terrence.

"That sounds terrific."

* * *

"Excuse me, young lady what did you call my son?" Wendy mimicked Terrence's mother perfectly. They hadn't stopped laughing since they hit the Lancaster Pike, and now they were back across the river in New Jersey, heading down the Atlantic City Expressway to the shore.

"Please stop," said Terrence. "That was too funny. The look on her face when you told her that you'd started calling me Doctor but that I had insisted that you call me Terry was just too much."

"Terry? Terry? Dear Lord who would want to see a doctor named Terry?" Wendy mimicked again.

She dropped the affectation and slipped back to her normal voice, "You know she never once called me by my name. After you introduced us it was 'young lady' and 'dear girl' for the rest of the meal."

"I know. I'm sorry, what can I say?" Terrence said.

"When you told her to just eat her salad I thought she was going to stab you with her fork. And what was with the 'my people' routine? She must have asked me a dozen times where my people were from and what my people did and who my people knew. I felt like I was from an Indian tribe or something," Wendy continued.

"Well you certainly shut her up when you explained that Bristol was only sixteen miles up Narragansett Bay from Newport as the yacht sailed," Terrence remarked.

"Thank you, Terry. I was sort of on my game, as they say, wasn't I? I learned some very effective coping skills growing up taking care of Daddy, and one thing I do pretty well is read people. That's what makes me a good waitress. I knew your mother would react favorably to my references to Newport and Bristol's proximity to Wood's Hole, Nantucket, and the Vinyawd. I was on the verge of telling her that Daddy and I occasionally sail down the Bay to lunch with the Vanderbilt's, but I thought that might be stretching it," she laughed.

"You were wonderful, Wendy. You handled the whole thing very well. I'm proud of you. You were like Daniel in the lion's den, baby."

"Well your father is terrific. He kissed me and squeezed my hand on the way out and made me feel very welcomed. Your mom has some issues my friend. Are you sure your cool Uncle Jake, the hippie, is really her little brother?"

"Jake is a lot younger than mother. He was raised in a different time by totally different people. I mean they were the same people, my grandparents that is, but they seemed to have mellowed considerably by the time Jake came along. I think mother probably wore them out.

"She's a textbook borderline personality; she bosses people around, acts condescending and superior to others, and can't understand why they are offended. She takes no responsibility for her actions, never apologizes or feels any remorse. She's a social arsonist. She ignites fires and walks away from them expecting somebody else to put them out and clean up the mess. No regrets, that's for the little people."

"Wow, you've got her pegged," said Wendy.

"My therapist cleared it up for me when I was thirteen."

"You see a therapist Terry?"

"Saw. I saw a therapist. And don't call me Terry or I'll get an inferiority complex," Terrence joked. "My dad sent me to Mary after I had an adolescent nervous breakdown in our backyard. I could never understand why my mother was so mean to me. I kept thinking that everything was my fault, that I was a terrible kid, that I couldn't do anything right or ever make her happy. I don't know why my father stays with her to this day, but thank God he knew that I needed professional help. I saw Mary once a week for two years, and it was the best thing I ever did. Sarah still sees her I think."

"What was all that about Sarah? I don't know if you heard . . . you and your dad were talking about Stokes something, but your mother totally trashed your sister after you mentioned that we were going to visit her."

"I heard. I've heard it before, thank you. Dad and I were talking about the Joseph Stokes Jr. Research Institute at Children's. He has a couple friends on the board. It's an amazing place, world renowned. They've made some very important breakthroughs in children's disease diagnostics over the last fifty years. It would be an honor to work with those people, but Dad kind of gave me a wink and a nod. He agrees with you, I guess. Without coming right out and saying anything, I think he knows that it would be in my best interest to not take up residence in Mother's neighborhood. Can you imagine a steady diet of luncheons like that?"

"No," Wendy said forcefully. "But what's her problem with Sarah?"

"Sarah is a very dutiful daughter. She has always done exactly what was expected of her, but on one particular issue she definitely marches to her own drummer."

Wendy said nothing. She waited patiently for Terrence to continue.

"She's gay," he said.

* * *

All angels do not incarnate back to the world in human form. They exist in the wind and the solar dust. They watch from above like the winter owl or the golden eagle or the snow whitened gale blown from the mountaintop. They are gleaming crystals buried in mountain caves and the hungry, licking flames of prairie campfires. They are the breeze whispering through the treetops and the silent pause before one dove answers another. Sometimes though, they are people too.

"Is it just my imagination or does the wind always begin to blow when a cloud covers the sun?" Wendy asked no one in particular.

The four of them were lying on the beach in the afternoon quiet. The sound of the surf had replaced the happy squealing and laughter of the children that had left with their mothers moments ago. The serenity was enhanced by the cry of a gull and the heat warming their bodies from the soft sand below them. Nobody answered her. The cloud passed, the wind stopped, and the sun beat down on them again. Wendy felt her body melt into her towel and smelled her flesh cooking. It felt good.

"Wow, this feels great," said Terrence. "Has the weather been like this all week?"

"It's not your imagination, Wendy," said Sarah's friend, Kate. "I always notice the wind too, but you're the first person I've ever heard mention it. That's so strange, don't you think?"

"It's been beautiful, Terry," said Sarah. "Unfortunately, Mom and Dad are coming down tomorrow, so I'm predicting rain."

"That'll happen," laughed Kate. "I'd love to see your Dad, but I'm leaving. It's so not worth the hassle."

"Being down here during the week and going back home for the weekend is really the perfect way to do it anyway," said Sarah diplomatically.

She and Kate were both beautiful girls. Wendy was two years younger than them, but the three of them all looked terrific in bathing suits. Wendy was a little embarrassed about how pale she was compared to Terrence's sister and Kate, but she tanned quickly despite her light complexion and would have loved to stay for a week or more. The smell of the ocean had hit them when they drove across the causeway over the flats, and Wendy reflected once again on how well their week had unfolded, and thought longingly about how much she'd love to stay put for a couple of days.

"Mom and Dad will be at the Yacht Club the whole time anyway. They never go to the beach. The good doctor will golf every morning while Mother does her little bike ride thing and terrorizes the locals. You hardly even have to see them at all if you don't want to. We spent two weeks a summer down here every year, and we never spent any time with our parents," Terrence explained.

"Do you really call him Terry, Wendy?" teased Kate. The entire conversation was being held without anybody moving an inch or opening their eyes.

"Hey I didn't know it was a federal offense. The man told me to call him Terry." Wendy realized she sounded a little bit defensive. "I mean, is that okay?"

Sarah propped up on her elbow and said, "Of course it's okay, Wendy. Kate's just teasing. Everybody has always called him Terry except Mother or except when Mother's around. It's pretty much a family joke."

"I call him Terry in front of her just to tick her off," said Kate.

Terrence groaned, "You have the knack, Kate."

"Should we cook tonight or go out?" asked Kate.

"Are you two still doing your vegan thing?" Terrence asked.

"Yes," said Sarah. "We're still doing our vegan thing." She paused, "Well, mostly."

“Then we’re going out,” Terrence said. “I feel like some good fish. Maybe we should go up to the docks and buy something from today’s catch to cook at home.”

“Let’s just go out,” said Kate. That turned out to be a good decision because they all laid on the beach for two more hours.

* * *

“I’d love to stay a couple more days if it’s going to be as sunny and beautiful as it was today,” Wendy said between bites of grouper. They were seated outside at Sylvester’s on Twenty-First Street between Pennsylvania Harbor and Princeton Harbor. “I think I can deal with your mother; she’s not so bad I’m sure.”

“You’re sure?” said Kate.

“Well, it’s just so pretty here, I hate to leave.”

“It is nice, Wendy, but there’s a whole lot of coastline, and we could come back next month when the ocean is warmer. We could stay at a bed and breakfast in Cape May if you want.” Terrence pushed away from the table to head back inside to the salad bar and the shrimp buffet.

“So how’d you hook up with the handsome young Frazier dude?” Kate whispered conspiratorially after Terrence was safely out of earshot.

“Oh, Kate, please,” said Sarah.

“I wanna know,” Kate whined.

"I went to the Emergency Room in Burlington back in April and swept him off his feet," Wendy replied.

"Ha, if I had known it was that easy I wouldn't have gone for the sister," laughed Kate.

Sarah threw a napkin across the table at Kate, and they all laughed together.

"I really like him," Wendy said. "He's sweet. I've had bad luck with guys, and he is so much different from the losers I've always ended up with. Terry is a giver. There are givers and there are takers in this world, and he's the first real giver I've ever been involved with."

"Sounds serious," said Sarah.

"I hope so; it is for me, that's for sure."

They continued munching contentedly on the smorgasbord before them until Kate spoke again.

"Take Terry up on the Cape May proposal, girl child. My girlfriend here isn't real astute about these things, but despite your killer body, Wendy, you're starting to show. I'm sure it was no problem fully dressed at the club today, but believe me; Mommy Dearest will notice your baby pouch if she sees you in that sexy bikini."

Sarah stopped chewing and stared at Kate in shock.

"Please breathe, Sarah," said Wendy. "Kate's right, I'm about eleven weeks along now."

Sarah spit a mouth full of seafood salad into her hand and took a long gulp of iced tea without taking her eyes off of Wendy.

"Really?"

“What are you girls talking about?” said Terrence as he approached the table. “Do you think they might cut me off from the ‘all you can eat’ shrimp thing?” His plate was stacked high with plump shrimp. It was his third plate in as many trips since they’d sat down.

“We’re talking about you and how fat you’re getting,” answered his sister.

“Really?” said Terrence looking down at his stomach. “Are you serious?”

“No, Mr. Manorexic, she is not serious,” said Kate.

This is fun.

“This is fun,” said Wendy. “I’m really enjoying being with you guys.”

“No kidding,” said Sarah. “We like you Wendy. Big brother did good.”

“Well,” said Terrence.

“What?”

“ . . . did well.”

“Whatever,” Sarah said.

“Hey, you’re the Bryn Mawr grad.”

“You’re still a nerd, Terry,” said Kate. “We like your girlfriend, but you’re still a nerd.”

“I love you too, Kate.”

Love grows when it is shared.

“Ouch! This is great. I have to say, I’m enjoying the punch and counter-punch routine going on here because I can tell that it’s really true—you all really do love each other,” observed Wendy.

CHAPTER 15

I'm afraid of water too, Mommy. I was once one of four grooms with General Robert E. Lee. The General brought me along to help with the horses when I was twelve years old, and toward the end of the war, I was the only one left alive. I wish he had just left me on the farm. I was scared and lonely for four long years, and in '64 we were crossing the Rappahannock after another terrifying battle, and I almost drowned. I always held onto Traveler's bridle or his girth when we were crossing a river, but this time I slipped on the rocks and I lost my grip. The whole Company just kept riding and marching over me. Maybe they thought I was dead, but Traveler came back for me alone and I grabbed his trailing reins and he pulled me to the other side. That was it. I was done with that war, and I looked up into the General's face and I could see that he was done with that war too.

Water is the lifeblood of our world, but after that day I never again went in it over my ankles.

The drive back to Vermont was going to take about eight hours, Terrence figured. It was pretty straight forward; up the Garden State Parkway to the New York Thruway past Albany and Saratoga and over

Route 4 to Route 7 and into Burlington. Traffic was light and the road and the day were both clear and Terrence and Wendy and the baby were all in good spirits. It had been a productive and positive trip, and Terrence had a couple months to decide where he would do his residency. That was the hard part. It was also the least of his worries on this beautiful summer morning with a girl that loved him beside him and a car he loved to drive beneath him.

"The ocean scares me," said Wendy,

"I'm not surprised," Terrence agreed. "It demands respect, and you had one of the most frightening experiences with it that I could ever imagine. I don't know how those guys can brave the North Atlantic to fish the great banks, or those fishermen in Alaska—that's scary. What about the poor souls with Columbus? They were sure they were going to just drop off the face of the earth. Those ships were tiny, man."

"Yeah, the ocean scares me," she said again. "Who is Traveler?"

"Traveler? Do you mean the horse?"

"Um, yeah," said Wendy. "I think so."

"Traveler was Robert E. Lee's stallion. He was a big, white, handsome, strong guy that inspired the troops of the Confederacy. Union soldiers wouldn't shoot at him; bad luck I guess. They say he had a knot in his tail and he pulled the entire Army with it. He was a legend, bigger than life, and he retired with Lee and supposedly lived a pretty long life in peacetime. Why? Where did that come from?"

"I think I know who put the knot in his tail," Wendy giggled to herself.

He let it go. "I'm sorry we didn't have the time to go down to Washington. The cherry blossoms are probably gone by now but I had ulterior motives too," Terrence shared. "There is so much I want to show you, Wendy, and I guess it's presumptuous of me to assume that you haven't visited some of the places that I would like you to see, but you know you really don't talk too much about your past or your childhood."

"I know."

Terrence waited for her to continue, but she didn't. "My Uncle John used to have a beautiful estate down in Owings Mills, Maryland. He was my granddad's oldest brother, and he made his fortune in Pan Am and some clandestine CIA stuff I think. Anyway, he had this unbelievable mansion and barns and out buildings on about six hundred acres off of Reisterstown Road, and he used to entertain the Eisenhower's and other big shots from the Presidential cabinet back in the fifties I guess. He raised thoroughbreds and hosted pheasant shoots and we used to love to visit him when we were little. He had four or five wives and no kids, which was pretty weird. It's always been a family mystery where all his dough went.

Everything we gather is something we can lose.

"I really wanted to show the old place to you. It would have been right on the way to D.C. . . . but, hey, another time, right?

"It's funny, but I have this real desire to share so much of my happiness from when I was a little kid. I would love to take you to Brandywine and Winterthur. That was the old DuPont estate in northwest Delaware that is the coolest museum and garden and grounds you have ever seen. It would have been pretty much right on the way too. The DuPont's have made a lot of their property public, and you can cruise for miles on lovely little dirt roads through the prettiest land you ever wanted to see. There's a chapel I want to show you someday and a little fairy cottage at Winterthur that you would die for. It all makes you realize where the Wyeth's got their inspiration. Of course D.C. is cool too, and someday I'll take you to Bermuda and Sanibel and Pebble Beach and Aspen.

"My dad and I flew into Denver when I was about ten or so. It was still Stapleton Airport at that time. We drove west in a rented four-wheel-drive truck, and when we got to the top of Lookout Mountain and I saw the entire Front Range of the Rocky Mountains unfold before me I thought I would faint. It was also about seven or eight thousand feet above sea level. I had never been that high before so, I guess, there was a medical explanation for the dizziness. You just have to see the Rockies, Wendy, and I'm going to take you there. Dad drove us over Loveland Pass, and I swore that someday I would move out west. I love big sky and big mountains and wide open spaces, and I know you will too. Someday, Wendy, someday, we'll go to Paris and New Zealand. We'll see the Alps and Thailand and Antigua and the Hawaiian Islands. It's such a big world."

The purpose of life is to discover beauty and to describe truth.

They got gas at a rest area on the Northway, and Wendy bought a couple of sandwiches and some apples. North of Saratoga they found a quiet place to pull over without any of the regular services or distractions> It was wooded and landscaped like a park and had nice picnic tables away from the road.

A couple roared into the parking lot in a big Lincoln with Quebec plates and the man jumped out of the driver's seat and slammed the door, screaming, "Shut up, shut up, I can't take it anymore." He marched toward the tree line, unbuckling his pants, apparently to relieve himself. The passenger door flew open and an angry woman emerged. She slammed her door and walked around the car to the driver's side and got in and started the engine.

Terrence and Wendy had just taken bites out of their sandwiches when this scene started to unfold, and now they were stopped mid-chew as the woman jammed the car into reverse and skidded out of the parking slot. She put the big car in drive and yelled out the window, "The next time you want to go to Atlantic City why don't you just send the mayor a god damn check." She pulled back out onto the Northway and was gone.

The creative energy of the love force between a man and a woman can make visible the invisible beauty of God.

"They didn't get the memo, peanut," Wendy laughed to herself.

Terrence didn't ask. He was getting used to Wendy's mysterious comments. The man was shaking his head and walking back toward the parking lot.

"I'm sorry we were a part of that," Terrence said to the poor guy. "But can we offer you a ride?"

The man looked at the little Porsche and shook his head. "She'll be back," he said. He sat down on the curb in front of where his car had been, and Wendy and Terrence quickly finished their sandwiches, wished him luck, and got in the car and left.

It really wasn't funny, they both insisted, but they replayed the scene over and over and laughed until they passed the Visitor's Center outside of Rutland. Before they knew it, they were on the outskirts of Burlington and the long drive had passed in a flash. They enjoyed each other's company and time flew by when they were together and no chore seemed too difficult and no journey seemed mundane. They were both happy to be approaching their little apartment, but they were also flushed with the adventure of the last week and they felt as though they had shared a very special time together, and that's what love was all about.

* * *

June passed into July, and August was upon them as they resumed their daily routines and Wendy's baby grew. Yoga was a wonderful addition to her life, and she started taking a weekly Qi Chong class as well. The yoga had become a daily practice, though, and she never missed it. It was an affirmation of life for her. She had always felt that she had been seeking something, but couldn't quite figure out what it was. She realized now that she had been in a permanent state of continual disturbance and frustration and the meditative aspect of yoga released her from a lot of that tension.

Terrence was pestered routinely by the staff at Fletcher Allen. Nobody wanted him to leave, but they all knew how successfully his interviews had gone, and nobody really expected him to stay.

The gang at the Sirloin Saloon delighted in Wendy's ever expanding belly and mothered and nurtured her. The busboys wouldn't let her carry anything to or from her tables and her tips practically doubled. Life was good, but change was in the air.

* * *

Wendy stepped off the scale, and Grace made a note on her clipboard as she returned the triple beam to zero.

"You're right on schedule, kiddo, I'm not surprised to tell you. You've gained exactly ten pounds which is just right, and coincidentally our little baby is now about ten ounces. She's probably close to ten inches long too from her head to her toes. Now we start measuring her full body. Up until five months we measure from the top of her head to her rump, but she's straightening out now and will start losing that wrinkled look as she continues to put on weight. She's like a chubby little banana right now, but you'll start gaining faster from here on in, maybe a pound a week, but don't worry, Wendy, you look great. You're a young mother, and you're strong and staying in great shape so you're carrying her high. Our little one has fully developed eyebrows and eyelids now too, which were about the last developmental things we needed to grow. From here on she's just going to eat and wiggle and hum. Are you getting any heartburn or indigestion?"

"No," said Wendy pulling on her jeans under the gown. "I'm getting some leg cramps at night, though, but I figure that's probably from too much exercise."

"No such thing. You keep up your walking and yoga. You don't know how happy I am to see a pregnant woman staying as active as you. Leg cramps are normal. Are you getting enough iron? I know you're not crazy about meat, but try to eat some red meat anyway. Soy products are best, raisins, prunes, cereal with iron, shellfish, that sort of thing is good too. And don't forget nuts. How are you sleeping?" asked Dr. Mitchell.

"Like a log," said Wendy. "Oh, I toss and turn a little, but I fall right off. Terry says I'm starting to snore too which is embarrassing. What's that all about?"

"Perfectly normal, tell him it's the baby."

Excuse me?

"I think you've offended her."

Grace laughed and said, "You are a breath of fresh air. You wouldn't believe how many women I see that are scared to death of the gift inside them. They think it's some sort of alien taking over their bodies. Talk to her, Wendy, rub her and sing songs to her and love her."

"I do, Grace."

"I know. Be sure to let her get to know Terry's voice too."

"I do, Grace."

"I know. You're really doing wonderfully Wendy. I'm very happy for all three of you. Now beat it, and I'll see you in class."

We love you, Dr. Mitchell.

Wendy took Grace's hands in hers and looked intently into her eyes and said, "We love you, Grace."

* * *

"Come down to the marina on Monday," said Heidi. "Me and the gray-haired gentleman have settled in to life on a boat. I'm loving it. It's a little cramped, but I want you to see it, Wendy."

"The gray-haired gentleman and I," corrected Wendy. "Maybe we will, let me run it by Terry."

The following week Terrence and Wendy were trying to get comfortable on a handsome boat, under a magnificent sky, on a beautiful lake, on a gorgeous summer day. They weren't having any luck.

"It's a head, Heidi, and I know these complicated nautical terms because I was raised around boats and, yes, I do have to pee, but, no, I'm not going to pee on your boat and then have to pump it into the sanitary bilge when I can walk up the dock to the marina and pee there. But thanks anyway."

"Okay, Wendy," said Heidi. "Don't get worked up. I just thought you would think it would be fun. I love it. It's such a cute little toilet. I must admit, though, when I have to do anything besides tinkle, I go ashore too."

The men were sitting on deck taking in the warm sun and drinking beer. Terrence was mostly holding his beer. Heidi's middle-aged Romeo was drinking plenty of beer.

"Time to cast off," said Romeo. "Let's go for a little spin around the lake and see if we can spot Champ. She's all gassed up and ready to go. I swear those sails are gonna dry rot we use them so much," he said sarcastically. "They're just too much hassle." He laughed a little too loudly.

We're not casting off with anybody, Mommy, especially not him.

"I'm going up to the marina, does anybody need anything?"

"Hurry up, Wendy, we're about ready for a little sail," Heidi said.

"Not me," Wendy said forcefully. "Terry, can I talk to you?"

"We can talk in the car, Wendy. I have to get going. You guys enjoy your cruise and thank you very much for the tour and the beer; it's been a real nice afternoon. Great boat, I need to get one of these someday, but today I'm on call and can't be stuck out on Lake Champlain. Looks like a nice sunset in an hour or so, but I'm afraid we'll have to take a rain check. Watch out for Champ"

Back in the car Wendy said, "You're my hero. You sized that up didn't you?"

"A responsible doctor does not go boating with an inebriated captain." Terrence said and then paused before continuing. "Let's go to Montreal for dinner this weekend."

"Wow that sounds like fun. Montreal seems like Europe or something to me. How far away is it anyway?"

"It's an easy two-hour drive, and I want to take you to the hippest restaurant you've ever been to. It's called Queue de Cheval. It's right downtown and you will absolutely love it.

"Anything goes. It's a Sting concert one night, boxing the next, and a full-blown circus or a million dollar car show or a wine tasting event: something different night after night. There's a cigar bar and a huge ballroom and private dining rooms and the best food in North America. I've been there twice, and it's like Vegas. It never seems to slow down or close. The owner is a hoot. He sings and dances and entertains famous celebrities and some not so famous people that you just know could buy and sell the city of Montreal. It's such a cosmopolitan town; like Paris and Amsterdam and Rio all rolled into one."

Wendy's eyes were lit up. "Just say the word, Terry, it sounds great."

"Let's go this weekend; Saturday night. We'll break in the new American Express card."

Saturday was August nineteenth. It was a lovely day and they hopped in the Porsche at five and headed north to Montreal. Terrence knew the city, and they crossed the St. Lawrence on the Point Victoria Bridge and pulled up to the valet parking sign in front of the restaurant. Exactly ninety minutes later Terrence asked Wendy to marry him.

The ring glittered. The little diamond seemed to weep with joy as Wendy stared at it all the way home. She had been speechless at the table and could only cry, and now she couldn't take her eyes off of it. It was never coming off her finger; ever, ever, ever. The sun was setting in the west, and the pastoral landscape zipped by around them, but Wendy didn't see any of it. She never looked up the whole way back to Vermont except to sneak quick glances at the man that was driving the car. She intended to be sitting next to him for the rest of her life, and she was immensely happy. She fingered her mother's St. Christopher and rubbed the baby in her tummy, but she did not take her eyes off the ring on her finger. It smiled back at her. This ring had found a home.

"You know you scared me for a minute back there. You went completely white and I thought you were going to faint or throw up," Terrence spoke for the first time since the valet had delivered the car.

"I still can't talk," said Wendy without looking up from the hand in her lap. "You floored me, Terry. That was totally unexpected. Are you sure you want to marry me. You don't have to, you know?"

Terrence laughed and said, "I had been planning that little surprise for quite awhile Miss Applegate. I want to marry you more than anything else in the world. By the way, you still haven't answered me."

"I'm not going to either. I want you to ask me that question every day for the rest of my life; preferably every morning when we wake up and you don't have a half a bottle of Chateau de Whatever in you."

Terrence laughed some more and agreed that that was a deal he could keep and Wendy continued to stare at her ring and finger her jade necklace as her baby spoke to her.

Many years ago, I was a Princess in the valley of the Hindu Kush deep in the protective Karakoram Range of the Pamir Mountains. My father was the royal host of our Shakas tribe when the Yuezhi Mongols from the north attacked our land. They killed all of the men and stole my sister and me away to the ancient city of Jalalkot. I thought Father was dead, but then I saw two snow leopards playing in the sun on a cliff far above the mountain pass we were crossing and I had hope. A jade stone and a diamond were the only possessions I had managed to hide from the Kushan savages, and when I saw a falcon dive out of the air at the leopards I somehow knew that Father was alive. They had taken him to Kabul and held him for ransom. When it was paid he was released and he found us and brought us home. For that entire year of captivity I held onto my diamond and my stone of jade, and they gave me hope. Finally the Holy Mother returned me to my family. I was never without my jade or my diamond again.

"That's a wonderful story, Annabelle. I'll hold onto my jade and my diamond forever too. They are my hope and my faith and some day they will be my legacy. Some day they will be yours," said Wendy.

"Annabelle?" said Terrence. "You're talking to your mother now, Wendy?"

"No silly. Annabelle is our baby's name too, and by the way . . . yes, I'll marry you, sweet man."

CHAPTER 16

Joe and Rebecca were married in a tasteful, quiet ceremony on the beach early in the morning on the first Saturday in September. Rebecca had called Wendy the Monday before and asked her and Terrence to join them in Wellfleet out on the Cape. Wendy was thrilled to be Rebecca's maid of honor, and the weather cooperated with a beautiful day hinting at the first whisper of autumn. Tommy Gunn was the best man, and his wife and brother were there with a few other friends from town. Rebecca's mother and father were honored guests and everybody enjoyed themselves immensely. It was a Unitarian service which as Joe said was no service at all. He and Wendy had been members of the Presbyterian Church back home but Rebecca's family did not care for organized religion so they had asked a Unitarian minister that they both knew from the program to perform the civil duties. Joe joked that Christians prayed to a cross but Unitarians prayed to a question mark.

The bride's mother was a very spiritual lady, though, and she gave a wonderful, moving toast at the reception afterward that had everybody in tears. There was a higher power operating in this woman's life, and she thanked the Lord deeply for her daughter's happiness. She spoke of the soft silence of devotion and the joys and rewards of motherhood and the gifts of patience, tolerance, and forgiveness. She told Joe and Rebecca that they had a choice to be ruled by love or to be ruled by fear, and she expressed her gratitude that they had both made the decision to follow the path of love.

It was a moving and simple ceremony and by mid afternoon the luncheon on the porch of the Holden Inn Lodge was over and the guests were departing. Joe and Rebecca had a double suite in the cottage of the Inn and offered the other bedroom to Terrence and Wendy, but it was still early, and they had already decided to drive back to Vermont. Rebecca's parents were planning to stay, and they had planned dinner with the newlyweds. Everybody hugged and kissed and promised to stay in touch as they made their departures. Wendy held her father tightly and cried, of course.

"I guess it's no secret that Becca and I have both been pregnant for about the same time," Wendy said to her father.

"No, sweetie," Joe laughed as he held her close. "It's not a secret and I'm delighted. Rebecca thinks that you both got pregnant about the same time, as a matter of fact. Wendy, your old man couldn't be happier. I think it's terrific and I respect your independence and your courage and I judge no man or woman, especially living in this glass house of mine. Terry is a great guy. You'll be wonderful together darling. Today is proof to me that there is always hope and that joy is around the next bend. I know your mother is looking down on us right now, and I know that she is relieved that we have both found the love we lost when she left us. She'll always be my wife and she'll always be your mommy and she'll always be with us both. I'm so happy you were here today."

Shared joy is a double joy. Shared sorrow is half a sorrow.

"Oh, Daddy, I'm so happy I could be a part of this too. I love you so much. Thank you for loving my mother so much and thank you for being my daddy."

Terrence drove out past Great Pond back to the beach. He pulled over just before Wellfleet by the Sea and got out without a word. Wendy followed him over the dunes to a deserted stretch of beach and they kicked off their shoes and sat down and gazed out at the Atlantic and watched the perfect waves curl into the sand.

"I'm so content, Terry. I was very proud to wear your engagement ring today, but I couldn't help thinking that even though I'm anxious to get married before you change your mind, I really don't think I want to be pregnant at my wedding. Is that a problem?"

"Of course not, and I was thinking the same thing coincidentally. It doesn't bother me one bit that we haven't even discussed a date. Let's just let it happen. It's worked well so far. I'm content too Wendy and I am not going to change my mind. Today was lovely."

"It's hard for me to be happy, I think. I'm really happy for my daddy. I love him so much, Terry, and things have worked out better than I could ever have imagined. What's wrong with me?"

"What do you mean? Nothing's wrong with you. Your life is good, Wendy."

"But it seems as though there has always been a part of me that could never be completely satisfied. There is a part of me that I don't think I will ever know. Could that be normal?"

Terrence looked hard at the ocean. He looked at Wendy as though he was seeing something in her for the first time. "Yeah, Wendy, yeah, that's normal. There is a place of mystery within you that has been there forever, perhaps before this lifetime, if that doesn't sound too weird. I don't know where this is coming from, but I know there is a part of you that was here before you were here, if that's not too bizarre. I'm a doctor and I believe in science but I also know that the mystery within you has beauty and it has meaning. I don't know what it means, but I know that just knowing that and accepting it and appreciating it is enough."

Mother sends divine messengers to help the people of this world, but they can only recognize and acknowledge the presence of these angels if their hearts are open.

Their hands found each other and they hugged and sat there in a state of rapture, loving each other and loving themselves for feeling loved like neither one of them had ever felt before.

"The ocean is so beautiful, Terry. Why does it scare me so? Is it the mystery, the power, the unpredictability?"

"Maybe it's just your bad experience, Wendy, and maybe you've had bad experiences with it before and they are buried deep in your subconscious."

The seas will rise up in anger along the length of this coast and the non-believing warrior tribes, those living without harmony and those existing in fear and those thriving on ego will attack the great cities of this land.

"Maybe I have an intuition that the sea will bring danger and pain."

"Maybe."

"Terry, why do you want to stay here on the East Coast? Why did you only look at hospitals in the northeast? You spoke about Colorado and California the other day; do you have any interest in living somewhere else?"

"I never really thought about it, Wendy. I guess I have this elitist attitude about the east but now that you mention it, I would like to maybe expand our horizons," said Terrence.

Follow the sun, Mommy.

"Come on, let's go home."

* * *

"Hey, talk about coincidence," Terrence shouted out of the bedroom. "I'm checking my e-mails and I got one here from Johnny S. He's my old roommate from Lawrenceville. He works in Winter Park, Colorado, now."

They had made it back to Winooski from Cape Cod in record time with Terrence pushing the Porsche the way the car liked to be driven. Wendy was in the kitchen making a salad and she had all the windows in the apartment open and the fresh air was blowing in from off the lake.

"Cool," said Wendy. "What news does Johnny S. bring?"

"You would love this guy, Wendy. He was the antithesis of the Lawrenceville snob. John Sgarlatti from Staten Island; he came to school on a baseball scholarship and he hated the place. Well I think he liked the school, but he was a rebel and was always banging heads with the administration. Did not take too fondly to the dress code or the preppy culture or the old money gang, but the kid could pitch and now, ironically enough, he's the head of our class reunion committee. What a hoot. Says he loves Colorado. He's on ski patrol up there, and he wants me to come and visit him. We were great roomies, we always got along well. I helped him with the books and he was the dean of sports, parties, and girls."

"Is he still the dean of girls?" Wendy asked.

"I'll ask him," laughed Terrence.

The dean of girls was happily married and had two little girls of his own. He worked construction in the summer and was on his way up to Estes Park to repair cabins and bridges for the park service. Life was good, he was happy, and he was anxious to see his old roommate, but it didn't look like he would get back east until the Lawrenceville reunion which was still a year and a half away.

Terrence brought him up to date with his life, and the two of them renewed their old friendship through the miracle of the internet and they continued trading barbs and old stories.

Johnny had sparked a nerve, and on September twenty-third, Terrence took Wendy out to dinner to celebrate her twentieth birthday and informed her that he and Dr. Howe had been in touch with a couple of hospitals out west and that he was planning a quick trip to Denver and Phoenix to interview with four hospital administrators; two in each city. He had sent resumes to Salt Lake, Monterey, and the little health center in Sedona as well, but he thought he'd get an initial feel of the opportunities in Denver and Phoenix first before committing to a longer trip.

Wendy was delighted. Adventure was in the air, and her baby did a little dance when Terrence broke the news.

She decided to break routine and enjoy some birthday cake and asked Terrence if he knew who else celebrated their birthday on the twenty third. She responded to his shrug with an emphatic, "The Boss!"

"Whose boss?" Terrence asked.

"The Boss," said Wendy. "Bruce!"

"Bruce who?"

"Are you for real, Doctor Frazier? Bruce Springsteen, The Boss." And they celebrated Wendy and The Boss's birthday by dancing to the E Street Band until the baby got tired and they all went to bed.

Terrence was up early Sunday morning for his flight to Denver. He would arrive in Colorado that afternoon and visit St. Joseph's Hospital downtown and the Boulder Medical Center on Monday before flying over to Arizona. If all went well he would be back in Vermont late Wednesday night.

Wendy had finished her book about the protective octopus and was starting another about a little wooly mammoth that did not yet have a name. He was a baby mastodon and he had fallen asleep in the noonday sun with half of his body in the shade of a fig tree and the back half of his little round elephantine torso exposed to the hot sun. He awoke to find his lower half badly sunburned and all of his beautiful wooly mammoth hair singed off his prodigious rear end. Needless to say the other animals were teasing him mercilessly and Wendy was having fun drawing the little guy and developing the story.

She missed Terrence after only a couple of hours, knowing that he would be gone for a couple of days, but she realized that she did not feel alone or lonely. Feelings were meant to be felt and she looked at herself as if from above and thought that, yes, she was alone, but she had her baby and her man would be back and she had nothing to fear. Her present circumstances simply were what they were, and it was no cause for anxiety or panic. *How liberating,* she thought and concentrated on weaving that theme into her new wooly mammoth story. Life was full of daily discovery and new insights, and she felt complete and refreshed and enthusiastic about everything.

When the phone rang she assumed that it was Terrence so she was surprised to hear his mother's voice.

"Is Terrence there, dear?"

"Uh, no, Mrs. Frazier, he's not here right now. Can I take a message or have him call you?" She wasn't sure if Terrence had told his mother about his trip out west or not, but she sure wasn't going to say anything.

"Is he working at this hour?"

"I'm not sure," said Wendy. *He could be working,* she thought. *I'm not lying.*

"You're not sure? Dear girl, you should be more aware of these things I should think. Nevertheless, please have him call. I wanted to tell him that his dear old friend Stuyvesant Templar is getting married this weekend up in the Hamptons. Doctor Frazier and I will be going, of course. The reception is at the Maidstone. I suspect Terrence received an invitation; perhaps he didn't mention it to you, though. Please tell him to ring us up. Thank you, dear." And with that she disconnected.

Wendy held the phone in her hand, looking at it and listening to the dial tone and burst out laughing. "Up your butt and around the corner," she said aloud in her most proper British accent.

Twenty minutes later the phone rang again, and Wendy looked at it warily. *Has the old snob forgotten something,* she wondered? She answered more cautiously this time and was relieved to hear Terrence's voice.

"I'm so glad it's you, Terry. How is Denver?"

"All is good, sweet darling. What's going on with my girls?"

"I just got off the phone with your mother. Your old friend Irvington Templar is getting married, and she wanted to know if you were going," reported Wendy.

"Irvington? You mean Stuyvesant."

"I guess," Wendy said. "I wasn't really paying attention. The wedding is in South Hampton or East Hampton or West Hampton or North

Hampton," she laughed. "Some darn Hampton, and the reception is at the maid's house I think."

"Have you been drinking?"

"No, but I might have taken a double dose of hormone pills this morning because I knew you were going to be out of town and I felt like getting crazy."

Terrence laughed too. He loved Wendy when she was in one of her goofy moods. He didn't like being away from her, and this conversation made him feel good. He missed her and he told her so.

"His name is Stuyvesant Templar the Fourth. He doesn't like me and I don't like him and it would be a cold day in hell before he invited me to his wedding and colder yet before I ever went. Mother likes that crowd, but Stuyvie number four is a pompous windbag and it tears her up that I'm more comfortable with guys like Johnny the Scar from Staten Island than I am with dorks like Stuyvie. So what else is going on?"

"Wow, I might have to take a couple more hormone pills to get over that rant," Wendy giggled. "Anyway, your mom thought that you were probably invited but I think she assumed that you RSVP'ed that you wouldn't attend because you didn't want to hurt my feelings."

"Yeah, right, other than that . . . ?"

"All good here," said Wendy.

"Great, I'm going up to Idaho Springs to have dinner with Johnny and his family and I'll be back in my motel room by eight or nine if you want to call. Wait, I guess that would be ten or eleven Vermont time, forget it, unless you're up." He gave her the number and they kissed into their phones and hug up.

He loves you, Mommy.

"I know," Wendy said to her baby.

CHAPTER 17

Joe Applegate had decided to sell the house. He needed a change and he was tired of Rhode Island winters and he wanted to make a fresh start with his new wife. But he was nervous about Wendy. How should he break this news to his daughter, he wondered? She had grown up in this house. It held memories of her mother and her childhood, but it also had some pretty harsh recent history, and he did not know how Wendy would take it.

"You know how I feel about stuff like this, Joe," Rebecca said to him. "Honesty is always the best policy. Wendy is twenty years old and almost seven months pregnant and engaged to a man that loves her. I think she can deal with this, Joe. As a matter of fact, I think she'll be relieved and the money will be a blessing and a great start for her and Terry. Pick up the phone and just tell her." That's what the baby inside of Rebecca told her to say, and it worked.

Joe walked into the kitchen and called Wendy.

"Hi, sweetie, it's your daddy."

"Daddy, what a pleasant surprise, how are you and my new step-mother getting along?" Wendy said mischievously.

"We're great," Joe snickered. He paused and thought that there was no beating around the bush. "I've been thinking about going back to work, Wendy. I got an offer from a resort in Tucson, and I'm considering selling the house and relocating to Arizona."

"Daddy, that's wonderful. When are you going?"

That was easy, thought Joe. "You know," he paused again, "I don't know why I get myself so twisted up in knots worrying about stuff, Wendy. I was scared that you would freak out at this news."

"That's crazy, Daddy. I'm delighted. I'm really happy for you. I want you to take Becca and my baby sister away from the East Coast. I've been worried about you living so close to the water. Terry is in Phoenix today looking at a hospital coincidentally."

"You're kidding," said Joe. "Really, he's in Arizona? I thought you two were looking around here at hospitals. What's the sudden interest in the West?"

"Three hundred days of sunshine a year, clean air, beautiful mountains, a better climate; how about you?" asked Wendy.

"Same thing, I guess," said Joe. "I've always wanted to be in the resort racket and I want to play more golf, and Rebecca wants to get away from the cold and I want a fresh start. Wow, this is neat, little girl. Anyway, I put the house on the market just to get some feelers, and we got an incredible offer right away. The guy is being transferred to Providence. He works for Mobil, ExxonMobil, I guess, out of Virginia and he needs to move quickly and everything is sort of falling into place at the same time. I didn't commit because I wanted to talk to you first, but they can move right in with some of our furniture and we don't have to close until the beginning of next year. Larry, you remember Mr. Diehl, he's my financial advisor, he said to wait until the first of January to do it for tax reasons and that seems to be okay with the buyer. They're real nice people, Wendy. The neighbors-Nit that is-will be happy to have a young family move in, and we can feel good about good people living in our home. I'm psyched. I'm psyched that you're so okay with this. Rebecca said you'd be cool, I was just worried as usual, but there's a lot of stuff that I want you and Terry to have, but there's no rush, and I thought . . ."

"Daddy, Daddy, you're running off again. Slow down," Wendy admonished. "It's all good; this is going to work out fine. I'm glad that you're taking back your life and I do want some of mommy's things, so we'll figure it all out. Wait until I tell Terry. I think he'll be pleased too. Tell me about the job."

"Well, there are actually two places that are interested in hiring me. What do you mean you want us to get away from the water?"

"Nothing, it's just an intuition I guess. I think something bad is going to happen. Like terrorists, maybe, I don't know. But tell me about these resorts," said Wendy.

"Terrorists? What do you know about terrorists?"

"Forget it, Daddy, what about the jobs?"

"Well, I sent resumes to a bunch of places. I like Canyon Ranch and the Lodge at Ventana Canyon and Lowes Ventana Canyon Resort the most, I think, and the Lodge and Lowes both want me to come out for an interview."

"What will you do?" Wendy wanted to know.

"I don't know. I didn't ask. I just sent my resume—heck I've only really ever had one job. I included a nice generic cover letter and said that I wanted to work with nice people in a nice place. I followed up with a few phone calls and somehow ended up talking to the right people. I figure people on vacation are generally in a good mood and those are the type of folks I want to spend my day with. That's pretty much what I said in my phone interviews and the folks I spoke with all seemed anxious to talk with me some more. So that's what I'm going out there to do." Joe was warming to the subject. "I think I would like the desert. It's only really hot in August, but it's dry, of course, and everybody lives in air conditioning anyway. Your mother and I drove through that whole area back in the early eighties and we loved it. We always said we were going to take you to a dude ranch when you got big enough, but . . . but that . . . well, you know." He seemed to have lost his train of thought.

"Yeah I know, Daddy. It sounds fabulous." She wanted to change the subject from her mother. It was still difficult for both of them. "I'll talk to Terry tonight. He should be arriving tonight, but I'm sure it will be late. Maybe tomorrow would be better," she thought out loud. "But we can rent a U-Haul and come down and pick up some furniture next weekend maybe. Well, maybe not, that might be too soon. Let us talk about it, and I'll get back to you. You keep doing what you're doing and thinking like you're thinking, Daddy. Somebody is giving you good advice, I think."

"You're right, and I think somebody is giving her good advice too. I love you, baby."

"I love you too, Daddy. I'm so happy we're talking like this again. Good night."

"Good night, Wendy."

This is good news, she thought to herself and questioned why she suddenly felt so anxious. She should be happy for her father. She was happy for him. Maybe she was just nervous about Terry. Maybe she was nervous about the uncertainty of their future. *Why was she feeling agitated*? she wondered. Wendy had always been a very independent person; well, certainly she had had to be after her mother had died. She'd always found it hard to trust others. She had been disappointed by unmet expectations too often. She wasn't sure she could depend on others, so she had determined to be self sufficient and not open herself to that vulnerability.

Now she had Terry, and she wanted to let him run her life. She was tired of doing it all by herself, and she had to admit that up until meeting Terry things hadn't really been working out so well. But she hated the thought of becoming dependent upon him. She felt as though she was becoming dependent upon the baby inside of her as well and that too made her uncomfortable. She decided that what she really wanted was to make a commitment to turn her life over to God, but she hesitated. Letting go was so hard. The little one inside of her told her that the balance between the loneliness of independence and the desperation of depending solely on the whims of another was a state of interdependence. This previously unconsidered joy of sharing herself and her life with another human being in a reality of equal cooperation and love had never before occurred to her and she was frightened.

Be still and know that I am with you.

"Okay, I'll try," she said aloud to an empty room.

Mother gave you the gift of life and living it to the best of your ability is your gift back to Her.

* * *

Terrence got home on the last flight into Burlington. They had been delayed landing in Newark and he almost hadn't made the connection and now, as he stepped into the deserted terminal, he could see that there were no cabs and no transportation available into town, so he walked the three miles and got to the apartment about one in the morning. The walk felt good after being cramped in an airplane seat all day, and he made himself a cup of tea and flipped on the television and flopped down in his chair knowing that he was going to sleep in late the next morning.

That's where Wendy found him when worry woke her up in the middle of the night. She pulled his shirt over his head and grabbed his arm pulling him out of the easy chair and guided him into the bedroom. They both slept late, and Wendy told Terrence about her conversation with her father the previous day as they were eating breakfast.

Terrence didn't respond. He had a far-away look in his eyes and Wendy assumed that he was exhausted from his long and quick trip across the country. A smile slowly grew across his handsome face, and he reached out to Wendy as she turned from the sink and pulled her close to him. He buried his face in her chest and mumbled and growled to the baby inside of her. Wendy laughed and tried to pull away but he wouldn't let her.

"Here's the plan," he said. "Next week is the end of the month and our lease is up. I'd like to give Mr. Shapiro more notice but we've been good tenants and he'll understand. This is a college town.

"We'll rent a U-Haul and pack up all of our stuff and drive down to Bristol and load up everything that you want out of your parent's house and then you drive the Porsche and I drive the truck behind you to Colorado. I want to take the job at the Boulder Medical Center and we'll rent a place and put everything in storage until we find a house we want to buy. The baby is due sometime toward the end of December, so we'll have plenty of time to find something we love and get it ready for our little one. Boulder is a great town, you'll adore it and the Medical Center has two locations and I can work hours in both. The money's not quite as good as Massachusetts General but I already know that's where I want to be. It's pre-ordained, Wendy. It's meant to be. It's perfect."

"Whoa, this is kind of fast," said Wendy.

Follow the sun, Mommy.

"No it isn't, Wendy, the timing is perfect. We make a clean break here and a fresh start out west. It's even a full moon. Please, Wendy, let's do this. I thought about it all day yesterday, and this is what I want.

This is what I want for us. Please trust me on this, Wendy. This is our shot. The coincidence is so strong. Everything's right for this move. Life is about taking action Wendy—seizing the day. Please want this as much as I do, Wendy, please. I know this is right for us and I know that it's all happening pretty fast and I know that change is frightening, but we have to follow our hearts, darling. I know that you want this as much as I do. Follow our intuitions, right? Isn't that what you've been telling me? It's scary, I know, but if we let anxiety affect our motivation, Wendy, it will sap our will. Our strength and our effectiveness and our courage are decreased by fear. We need to be brave together. We give each other power. Wendy, we need to do this." Terrence was staring intensely into Wendy's eyes.

Please, Mommy. The future belongs to those who believe in the vision of their dreams. Let's follow the sun.

"Yeah, okay, let's do it," she said and started to laugh and twirl around the little kitchen. "Yes, you're right, Terry, it is meant to be. Yes, yes, yes, let's do this," she yelled to the ceiling. "Let's be brave, let's be strong, let's be spontaneous, let's be together and be happy forever and ever, Terry. I trust you. I believe in you. I'll follow you anywhere."

"I'm driving the truck," he laughed. "I'll follow you, or you can follow me. I don't care. Let's just be together."

"You bet we will, handsome. You follow me." She pulled him off the kitchen stool and spun him around and around and said, "Follow me, Terry Frazier, and when I get tired I'll follow you and we'll follow each other to Colorado or Timbuktu or the end of the world. I love you. I love you. I love you. Should we pack?"

"Heck no," said Terrence. "We should celebrate." So they went down to Church Street and got milkshakes and walked to the lake and sat in the park holding hands and talking for hours about nothing and everything and looking into each other's eyes. The sun settled brilliantly over the Adirondack Range on the western side of the lake and the first star of the night sparkled dimly in the northern sky.

"I'm going to miss Lake Champlain," said Wendy.

"I think we're both going to miss Vermont a little."

"We've had a good time here."

"Good friends too."

"Yeah, tomorrow I'll quit the Saloon; they were expecting it pretty soon anyway. Heidi's going to freak."

"Tomorrow I'll talk to Doctor Howe and solidify things with the folks in Boulder and talk to the landlord and get a truck and give my notice at Fletcher."

"Josephine is going to be devastated," said Wendy.

"We'll have to cancel the phone and the cable. I guess we can forward the mail to the Health Center until we get an address. I'll check on a storage place around Boulder. I'm sure somebody can point us in the right direction for a monthly rental. Good thing we didn't get that puppy, huh?" Terrence reflected.

"That puppy is coming Terry."

"I know, Wendy, but first things first."

"Right, first things first," she agreed. "Job, house, yoga class, baby, wedding, puppy; ought to take about six months I figure," said Wendy.

"Yoga class is a priority?"

"It certainly is. Darn I'm going to miss Grace. Who's going to deliver Annabelle?"

"I think we might be able to find someone, Wendy," Terrence teased.

"I know," she agreed. "I'm thinking yellow lab."

"You just keep thinking, sweetheart. Come on; let's go home, we've got a big day tomorrow."

CHAPTER 18

The Boulder Medical Center has two locations; one on Arapahoe Avenue in Boulder and the other in Louisville right down Route 36. Terrence could not believe his luck when the Administration Director told him about the house that was available for free. It was located about equidistant to both locations. One of the senior handicap therapists was going to Switzerland for three months of training and seminars and workshops beginning the following week, and she was looking for someone to move into her house and take care of her cats until she got back at the end of the year. The sprawling three bedroom ranch was on a big piece of property between Marshall and Eldorado Springs off of Eldorado Springs Drive. It had a barn and a jacuzzi and a view up the canyon toward Eldorado Springs with the famous Flatirons in the background. It sounded too good to be true.

"Unbelievable," Terrence said to Wendy. "I spent about forty minutes with the guy and he's going to recommend us to live in her house. I mean he does know Doctor Howe and he did go to school with my dad, but even he said that he didn't remember Dad too well. Dad didn't remember him at all. The most surprising thing is that he didn't meet the best part of me: you."

"You're so sweet, Terry. You also totally underestimate yourself. I knew you were a special person the minute I met you."

"Wendy, you thought I was impersonating a doctor, if you remember correctly. We did not exactly get off on the right foot," said Terrence.

"But I knew you were special."

Mr. Shapiro was sad to lose them, but he was happy for the young couple too, and he returned the full month and a half deposit that Cameron and Wendy had put down and which Wendy had promptly forgotten about. One of Terrence's classmates jumped at the chance to move in, and Mr. Shapiro didn't even have to paint the place. Wendy and Terrence did not plan on taking a lot of the stuff in the apartment with them, and the new tenant was delighted to have it. They didn't even clean out the refrigerator. Wendy still hadn't decided what to do about all of her plants.

She went to see Grace Mitchell the next day. When she called, she was told to come right down to the clinic; she didn't need an appointment. Word was getting around town and Grace had heard about the impending move at the evening yoga class and told her secretary to make room for Wendy whenever she wanted to come in. It was going to be a tearful office visit and both women were determined to be stoic and professional. Wendy walked into Grace's office and they both burst into tears and ran into each other's arms.

Oh well, so much for keeping my cool, thought Wendy.

"It's going to be okay, honey," Grace assured Wendy. "My old med school roommate is at the Women's Care Center in Boulder. I'm pretty sure they're affiliated with the Medical Center. It's in the Foothills Medical Office, I think, but I'll check and make sure. Her name is Emily Nicholson. I'm going to send Emmy your complete file and talk to her as soon as she and I get a chance. She's a wonderful obstetrician—almost as good as me," she laughed.

"You'll love her, Wendy, and I know the feeling will be mutual. I'm going to miss you so much, girl. I told my husband to break out the frequent flier miles because we're going to Colorado for the birth of Annabelle and for your wedding. Jim's little sister lives in Avon right down the road from Vail so we do an annual March ski trip anyway. And of course I have a goofy old aunt who lives up near Boulder, so we drop in on her too. She's toothless and senile, but harmless. Jim and his sister and nephews go skiing and I drive back down out of the mountains to spend the day with my crazy old aunt, so you see, you can't get rid of me, Wendy. You've been my favorite patient ever. I'm serious, I mean that, Wendy. We'll always be friends for life. I love you."

Wendy couldn't speak. This woman had become such an important part of her life. There was some sort of transference with her mother going on, but mostly she felt as though Grace was the caring, protective big sister that she had never had. This was going to be very hard. She tried to speak and choked up. She couldn't get anything out but sobs and blubbering, so she turned to the door and waved her arm over her head and started to walk away. Grace caught her from behind and spun her around and they held each other tight.

"I'll tell Clara to reschedule my next couple of appointments. Come on, let's go get some lunch."

Wendy choked out a laugh and swallowed hard and said, "Grace, it's nine forty-five. I'm going to take a walk. I have a lot to do. I'll be back."

We'll be back.

"We'll be back," said Wendy.

"Okay," said Grace. "I'll be here. I'm going to call Emmy. She's a lucky baby doctor, and I plan on telling her that. I love you, Wendy."

That didn't go so well, thought Wendy; *not quite how I planned it anyway.*

Life rarely goes the way we plan, Mommy. We follow a road between the dawn and the dark of day, and we simply do the best we can. You're doing wonderfully.

"Thank you, sweet pea," Wendy said aloud to the surprise of the man holding the door for her on the way out of Grace's office.

* * *

Joel Silver left a message on their machine that he would like Wendy to do one last party at the Sirloin Saloon if she thought she could manage to spare a couple hours Sunday afternoon. It was a wedding reception, Joel had lied to her, and he was going to need all the help he could get. He said he had her final paycheck which was unexpected, and that he could assure her a big bonus and tip for working this gig. No need to call back, Joel's message said. He was sure she could help them. Thanks a lot, etc. etc. yada, yada.

Wendy discovered that Heidi was working the wedding reception too, and that she couldn't pick Wendy up because her car was in the shop and she was having Romeo run her over to Shelburne. Terrence would be happy to drive her, he'd said.

He knew something was up when they arrived at the restaurant that Sunday. The parking lot was already full and he recognized some cars from the hospital so he thought he should probably walk Wendy in.

"That's okay," Wendy said, pulling herself out of the Porsche. Her little belly was starting to make mobility an issue. "You don't have to walk me in; I'm a big girl, Terry." She slammed the door, and he yelled at her.

"Hey, not so hard," he smiled and started to pull out of the lot when Josephine's husband, Ramon, stepped from behind the hedges and flagged him down.

"Smart doctor like you, I woulda thought coulda figure dis out," he said as Terrence rolled down the window. "Park the car, Terry, we goin to a party, my man."

Terrence and Ramon walked through the door into a raucous scene. Music was playing, balloons and flowers decorated the entire restaurant, and sixty people or more were all trying to hug Wendy or waiting in line for their turn to hug her. Wendy, of course, was bawling.

The 'going away' party was in full swing with the entire staff from the Saloon, friends from yoga and around town, and most of the people from the hospital that weren't actually working that day. Favors had been called in and schedules had been rearranged and none of the regular Sunday crew were actually on duty at the hospital. Terrence took a quick inventory of the faces in the room and hoped that a major disaster did not occur in or around Burlington for the next couple of hours.

There was an open bar and tables full of food. People drank and danced and toasts were made and tears were shed and everybody promised to visit the brave couple in Colorado. The last of the revelers staggered out as the evening sun was setting over the painted Adirondacks. Joel slipped an envelope into Terrence's hand and told him to give it to Wendy when they got home. Wendy had cried and laughed all day, and she and her baby were exhausted. Before she fell asleep she told Terrence that besides the night of his proposal this had been the best night of her life.

"I have never had so many friends, Terry," she mumbled into her pillow. "I don't want to leave. I love these people."

Terrence teased her, "Baby, we absolutely have to leave now," and he went into the kitchen to turn out the lights. The red light was blinking on the answering machine and Terrence listened to nice messages from his father and his future father-in-law and went back into the bedroom to join Wendy. He felt full. His life was great. He was current with everything and everybody and he had absolutely no worries or regrets. He was so optimistic about their future his entire body tingled.

He gazed at his sleeping fiancée. Her eyelids fluttered and she yawned the innocent yawn of a sleepy child as Terrence slipped back out of the bed onto his knees and thanked God for the blessings in his life.

* * *

They spent the first night in Bristol with Joe and Rebecca. Wendy had gone on Mapquest and navigated the way from Burlington to Boulder with stops in Bristol, western Pennsylvania, central Missouri, eastern Kansas, and finally into Boulder. They had tentative reservations at Holiday Inns each night and were planning to stay in contact with their cell phones. That got old half way through the second day, though. There just wasn't too much to talk about. They took turns leading as they had discussed, but Wendy was mostly content to follow the cowboy painted on the back of Terrence's U-Haul truck and lose herself in her own thoughts. Driving the Porsche was fun and easy, but the truck was a different story. Terrence was on full alert, concentrating on the road, the traffic, and the route. The open road wasn't too difficult, but piloting the big rig through Pittsburgh, Columbus, Indianapolis, and St. Louis was a challenge. Kansas City still lay ahead as they approached their fifth day on the road. The nights in hotel rooms were fun for both of them; room service dinners and television, but Wendy was starting to worry about her plants in the back of the truck and she was glad that they didn't have a pet to deal with.

The U-Haul was full. Joe had insisted that Wendy take practically all of the furniture that he and Rebecca and the new family wouldn't absolutely need, but Terrence and Wendy could see a big yard sale in the near future. She had the things that she really wanted and paying to store stuff that they weren't going to use was silly. There were a lot of her mother's things that she was anxious to show baby Annabelle when she got older. They were a reminder and told the story and the life of her mother and that was a story that Wendy looked forward to keeping alive and passing along to the next generation of gentle people in her life.

How much farther, Mommy?

"Are you joking, Annabelle? Of course you're joking," said Wendy to the baby inside of her. "Please tell me you're joking. You may be a baby in my womb, but you are an angel with thousands of years of life experiences and even though you may never have driven across America in a Porsche, you've probably scaled the Alps with Hannibal or something, so please tell me you're joking."

I'm joking.

"Good, Annabelle. Do we need to eat? I'm hungry. I think I'll call Daddy, oops, I mean Terry. Wow, that was a slip . . . or was it? No, it wasn't," she decided. "He's going to be your daddy no matter what color, brand, make, or model you end up being. He is my future husband and I'm your mommy, and we'll cherish you together so that's that. Terry will take care of both of us, little girl."

Wendy was enjoying these long thoughtful hours motoring across America. She had time to think, and the broad, wide open plains of this beautiful and bountiful country put her at peace and promoted leisurely and deep meditation. The expansive landscape somehow expanded her soul.

Silence is the language of the spirit and solitude is the nurse of the soul.

"Hi, girls," Terrence said into his cell phone. Wendy had her speaker feature on automatic and his voice cackled into the sports car. "Let's eat." Terrence was a man of few words when he was hungry. "We're coming up on Kansas City, and then it's a long push into Colorado. I'm about tired of all these CD-'s. I've listened to everything three or four times."

"I'm worried about the plants, Terry. Do you think it's too hot for them in the truck?" asked Wendy.

"Yes, I do, but I don't know what we can do about it. We'll be in Boulder in about ten hours I figure, unless you want to spend another night on the road, which is fine with me. The plants are in the back and we can let them out for a night if you want. Let's eat."

"Oaky doaky," said Wendy. "I haven't listened to anything since we left Vermont. This little buggy only has an AM radio, in case you forgot. But I don't mind. I've spent four days talking to my baby and dreaming. I love this country. It's so pretty and so big. Hey, there's a Stuckey's. Pull in."

"I'm there," said Terrence.

They parked at the end of the lot with plenty of room in front of the truck so Terrence wouldn't have to back it up, and then they found a table in the restaurant across from a big Nascar display advertising tires, batteries, and motor oil.

"Why would you order spaghetti in a Stuckey's?" Wendy wanted to know.

"Because I like spaghetti," said Terrence. "I'm all for making another day of this journey if it's all right with you. The plants will be okay, I'm sure. We'll set them free in a parking lot for a night. How are you holding up?"

"Good, really, I feel great, but I get the feeling that driving that truck is a lot more demanding than driving a Porsche, so let's do five or six more hours today and arrive fresh tomorrow. We could find a motel in Hays or somewhere," Wendy supposed.

We aren't in a hurry, Mommy and I feel fine. I think this is fun.

"We aren't in a hurry, Terry, and we think this is fun."

"Done," Terrence agreed as he shook his head to the plural reference. "My butt will not argue with any reasonable logic. I like sleeping with you in hotel rooms; both of you."

* * *

They enjoyed another night in another Holiday Inn and pulled into Boulder shortly before noon on the sixth day of their trek from Vermont to Colorado. Terrence locked the U-Haul and they left it in a commuter lot along Route 36 and took the Porsche to the hospital on Arapahoe Avenue. Dr. Benedict was happy to see Terrence again and delighted to meet Wendy. He gave them the keys to Dr. Ashgar's house in Eldorado Springs and offered directions.

"I'll email Madeline that you've arrived. That's Doctor Ashgar; she's lived in that house her whole life. Her father was a physics professor at C.U. when she was a little girl, and she inherited the place when they retired and moved back to India. She's about ten hours earlier in Switzerland I think, but she'll be happy to hear that somebody will be taking care of her precious cats. You'll get along fine with both of them, I'm sure. I've been handling the daily feeding duties but they're an affectionate pair and they'll welcome somebody spending the nights with them until Madeline gets home." Benedict was obviously relieved to be freed from the cat obligation.

They picked up the truck and drove through Marshall and found the house with little trouble. Wendy was stunned.

"Are you kidding me?" she said as she took in the scope of the house and the property. "We get this place for free? This is beautiful, Terry. We could never afford a place like this. Wow, what a great way to start our life in Boulder."

"I'm going to dig out the plants so we can give them a little drink and then we can relax and spend the next three months unpacking." He said this with a sense of relief and then reconsidered. "Actually, I should turn in the truck, so let's scope the place out and decide what we want with us, what we should sell, and what we should store. Tomorrow, I mean. No rush. Is that Jacuzzi working?"

The Jacuzzi was working fine and so was the fireplace. They found fresh sheets in the hall closet and remade the master bed and ate some Campbell's soup they had discovered in the pantry and collapsed into bed.

"Do we need to feed the cats?" Wendy wondered.

"Maybe," said Terrence.

"Will they let us know if they're hungry?"

"Maybe," Terrence said again.

"When do you have to go to work, Terry?"

"I'm not sure, but I'm going to go see Dr. Benedict tomorrow and ask."

"What was your nickname at prep school?"

Terrence rolled over onto his side and looked at Wendy and said, "Where did that come from?"

"You never told me what Pinky stood for either," Wendy pointed out.

"You never asked," said Terrence.

"I'm asking."

"Go to sleep."

CHAPTER 19

Everything started falling into place right off the bat. The cats were sweet, and they made friends with Wendy the very first day, and with Terrence within a week. The new cat sitters separated the furniture in the truck and had a moving-in yard sale the first weekend after they had arrived. It was a great way to meet the neighbors and get rid of the excess baggage that Joe had insisted they load in the U-Haul. Terrence took the stuff they wanted to store down to a place in Arvada and signed a three month storage lease on a twenty foot unit.

Wendy made an appointment to see Dr. Nicholson and Terrence told her about the yoga classes at the hospitals. She was also starting to get along very well with the cats. They were twin girls, Madison and Lexington. Lexie had a little white spot on her chest but other than that they were both solid black and hard to tell apart. Maddie was the affectionate one and was a little chubbier than her sister. Lexie was more adventuresome and spent more time outside. Dr. Ashgar had named them after the famous New York City avenues because her parents had taken her back east to visit her grandparents in Manhattan every summer when she was young and she still had a fondness for the city.

Her parents and their parents were all Sikhs, and both sets of grandparents still lived in the same rent controlled apartments in Alphabet City that they had first moved into after emigrating from India. Madeline had grown to love her trips to the Big Apple and visits to the Empire State Building, Coney Island, the Statue of Liberty, F.A.O. Schwartz, and Central Park. Her maternal grandmother took her to children's plays and her paternal grandfather took her fishing along the Hudson River piers on the west side of town. All of her grandparents were appalled by her love for Nathan's hot dogs.

Wendy e-mailed Madeline in Zurich to thank her for her generosity and assure her that her kitties were being loved and cared for. To Wendy's surprise and delight this set off an almost daily stream of electronic mail from Dr. Ashgar who was happy to begin a correspondence with the keeper of her precious cats, and who seemed homesick for Colorado. She filled Wendy's computer with descriptions of Switzerland and Lake Geneva and the Alps, and Wendy mailed back daily news of local events, the neighbors, Terrence's job, and hospital gossip.

Terrence loved his new job. He was splitting time between the two hospital locations and working long and demanding hours. As low man on the totem pole he was pulling all of the weekend shifts and spending a lot of nights at one of the two facilities. He had a cot set up in the doctor's lounge for slow nights, but he didn't get the opportunity to use it much. Consequently when he did have sixteen or twenty hours at home he spent a good bit of the time catching up on his sleep. He was also 'on call' practically twenty-four hours a day, every day of the week, but he knew the score. These were the dues he had to pay to move along in his career, and he was happy to do it.

Wendy had no resentment for the long shifts. She knew that this was Terrence's calling, and she was willing to do everything she could to help him. On days when she needed the car, she simply drove him to the hospital, and he usually got a ride home. This is how Wendy met many of Terrence's co-workers and friends and how she got a lot of the news that she forwarded along to Madeline in Zurich. Nobody ever just dropped Terrence off. His associates always came in for a cup of coffee or an iced tea and spent time chatting with Wendy. Terrence and Wendy were the popular new young couple and they were making friends and adapting to life in Boulder quickly.

Wendy would never forget the day she first met Emily Nicholson. She'd arrived early for her scheduled appointment and a very pleasant young receptionist handed her a clipboard with a questionnaire and release forms to be signed. Wendy saw Grace's picture hanging in a frame on the wall as soon as she sat down and was temporarily stunned by the image. *What is Grace's picture doing here,* she thought?

After completing the necessary paperwork, Wendy returned it to the desk and couldn't contain herself.

"I'm sorry, excuse me, but I just have to ask. Why do you have a picture of Grace Mitchell hanging here in your waiting room?"

The pretty girl looked at Wendy and smiled. She took off her glasses in a slow, dramatic manner and said, "That's right, I'd almost forgotten. You were Dr. Mitchell's patient in Burlington, weren't you?"

"Yes, I was," Wendy smiled back. "And Grace and I had become . . ."

"Hello, Wendy," said Dr. Nicholson as she entered the room from an inconspicuous door behind Wendy. "I'm Emily Nicholson," she said offering her hand warmly.

"Grace!"

"No Wendy, I'm Emily. My sister and my family call me Emmy, though, and I would be happy if you did too," she said.

Wendy was speechless. She finally managed to sputter a couple of 'buts', "But, but, but . . ."

Emily Nicholson laughed and said, "Please sit down, Wendy, we don't want to have little Annabelle right here in the waiting room. I didn't mean to shock you. Apparently my sister did not inform you that she has a twin. An identical twin sister who, by the way, just happens to be an obstetrician as well, please sit down."

Wendy sat.

"I think we should get you a glass of water and let this sink in a moment," Emily said over her shoulder to the receptionist who was already bringing a paper cup of cool water around the desk to hand to Wendy. "Let me finish up with Mrs. Turtleheart and I'll be right with you."

Emily walked back through the door and the receptionist sat down beside her and put her hand on her knee.

"I'm Caroline, Wendy. I haven't ever met Doctor Mitchell, but I've seen pictures, and I'm not surprised you're shocked. They sure look like the same woman to me. I can't tell them apart in the photos of them standing side by side. Twins actually kind of creep me out. It's like they have a separate dimension than the rest of us . . ." She looked at the ceiling for a minute and shrugged. " . . . or something. I don't know what, but it's weird. I'm glad the other one is all the way back in Vermont. I've never even been out of Colorado."

"Thank you, Caroline. That was a little shock. I guess it really showed. I mean, I had no idea." She laughed at herself. "Wait 'til I get my hands on Grace, boy she really set me up. She said she had a senile old aunt that lived around here. These two have probably been pulling stunts like this all their lives."

"Yeah," said Caroline. "Twins, you just can't trust 'em."

"Have you worked for Dr. Nicholson long?" asked Wendy.

"Not too long. I met her at the Planned Parenthood clinic last year when I took a friend from school in to get an abortion."

"An abortion? Boy that seems like a strange place for a baby doctor to work," said Wendy.

"Yeah, right? That's what I thought too, but Dr. Nicholson volunteers there as a counselor. She tells girls about their options. She wants them to have the whole story, you know? A lot of these girls are from good families, and they don't want a baby to mess up their lives, but Dr. Nicholson tells them about adoption and depression and regret and tries to make them see all the angles."

"Did your friend go through with it?" asked Wendy.

"Yup, nobody was gonna change her mind, but I sure listened. If I got pregnant, which isn't going to happen, I couldn't kill it. I'd go the adoption route. Working here has been an eye opener for me. There are so many people who would love to have a healthy baby from one of these college girls." Caroline jumped up to answer the phone and greeted a patient warmly and confirmed her appointment and then came back around the desk and sat with Wendy again.

"Do you go to the college, Caroline?"

"No, I mean not yet. Someday maybe, but I could never afford C.U., maybe Front Range though, or Metro or Red Rocks; one of the Community Colleges, you know, but all in time. I like what I'm doing. I make enough to ski and have fun. I still live at home with my folks, and I just want to find a boyfriend and climb and ski and bike and enjoy the mountains for now," Caroline told Wendy. "Actually, if I had the money, I'd want to go to Regis. I know a really cool guy from high school that's there now."

She continued with a laugh, "This isn't the greatest place to meet guys, but I get Fridays off when Dr. Nicholson is at the clinic, and I get afternoons off a lot when she makes rounds and I get weekends off, so I have plenty of time to ski. Working with Emmy is really great, even if she is a twin. Twins creep me out."

"Yeah, you said that," Wendy told her. "Where do you ski?"

"Well I have a pass at A Basin which is the bomb, but I run up to Eldora when I get an afternoon off, and the guys all know me so they let me on for free. I mostly stick to the Front Range areas, Eldora, the

Basin, Berthoud, and Loveland. I try to avoid the tourists," Caroline said. "Arapahoe Basin on the weekends is the greatest, especially in the spring; lots of hot dudes up at the Beach, that's what we call the parking lot, with reggae blaring and weed and wine and partying 'til they chase us out. I love it."

"Wow," said Wendy. "That really sounds like fun. Sometimes I wonder if I got pregnant a little too early, like maybe there's a lot of life out there I'm missing."

Once the rain has fallen only God can put it back. Trust your instincts, Mommy. Don't question your heart.

"But then again, I'm very happy about the choices I've made recently. I think having this baby is the best thing that's ever happened to me."

Caroline looked closely at her. "I envy you, Wendy. I'm happy for you, you seem really together. I think it's going to be real nice getting to know you more."

It's nice to be admired, but it's more admirable to be nice.

"Thanks, Caroline; you've made me feel very welcome. I think it's going to be really nice getting to know you too."

"Can I get in on this budding friendship?" asked Emily Nicholson as she entered the waiting room. "Caroline and I have become pretty good friends, and from what my sister has told me, I'm thinking you and I are going to hit it off pretty well too, Wendy."

"Dr. Nicholson, I'm so sorry about my reaction before. I had no idea that Grace had a twin sister. She told me about your senile old aunt, but nothing about you," Wendy explained.

"Relax, Wendy." Emily laughed as she took Wendy's elbow and steered her through a door into the examination rooms. "There is no senile old aunt and I really should apologize for my sister's juvenile prank. We've been doing stuff like that our whole lives. It's time for both of us to grow up, but it seems we can't. Please come into my office. We'll take a look at you and the little one in a minute. I want to call Grace and scold her in front of you."

So that's what she did. Emily put the phone on speaker and hit the speed dial for Grace's private line and the three of them yelled and laughed like teenagers. Wendy felt like the third sister and the warm feeling of camaraderie made her feel good and connected. The baby was happy to hear Grace's voice, and she kicked and rolled about and it was the most fun Wendy had ever had in a doctor's office.

After Grace reluctantly disconnected, Emily told Wendy about the two of them going to Hopkins on scholarships and rooming together just like home and both of them falling for medical students and how much she loved Grace's husband, Jim, and how her marriage fell apart in Ohio when her husband started fooling around with the nurses at the Cleveland Clinic. After an hour, Wendy felt as though she knew Emily as well as she had known Grace. She told her how frightened she was to leave Grace and how close she had grown to her sister, and Emily assured her that they would have a strong relationship too and that together they would bring little Annabelle into a world of love and compassion.

In the examination room, Emily confirmed the report that her sister had sent her.

"Just like Grace said, mother and daughter progressing perfectly," she said as she pulled her smock over her head. "Grace has talked to you about diet and exercise and the warning signs to look out for so I'm not sure I have anything to add. I'm anxious to meet Terry though, Grace says that he's a catch, but that'll wait. I know the poor guy must be busy and probably a little sleep deprived as well. Have you found a yoga class?"

"It's funny, Doctor Nicholson . . ."

"Emmy, please, Wendy. All of my friends call me Emmy."

"Okay, it's funny, Emmy, but yoga was at the top of my priority list when we decided to make the move, but I still haven't gotten around to finding a class. I'm a little hesitant, I guess, because I want it to be just like the one back in Burlington. I had such great friends there and it was a daily routine and Terry told me about classes at the hospital, but I don't know . . ."

You are paralyzed by perfection.

"That's it; I'm paralyzed by perfection."

"Okay," said Emily with a funny look on her face. "Um, well, what are you doing tonight?"

"Going to a yoga class with you?"

"Yes."

* * *

Wendy was walking in the back of the property with Lexie when the storm exploded over the mountain behind her. The crash of thunder and the sudden and complete darkness was shocking to a girl that had never experienced the dynamic temperament of the Rocky Mountains. The cat was gone as suddenly as the peace and sunshine and tranquility of the day. The house was about one hundred yards away but the rain and hail came down so quickly and so hard that the building disappeared before Wendy's eyes. She wanted to just curl up on the ground where she stood and surrender to the overpowering elements. She was instantly soaked, but the scorching lightning bolt that pierced the wall of water behind her catapulted her toward the safety of the house somewhere in front of her. She skidded onto the slate patio in the back of the house and yanked hard at the sliding glass door and threw herself on the floor behind the leather couch.

Was this the end of the world, she wondered? Had a terrorist explosion leveled Boulder perhaps? The thunder came in quick, loud booms rocking the roof and tearing at the walls. She thought the windows would explode in. The percussion was a bass drum, and she imagined invaders banging on heaven's door. The hail was the size of peas and nuts and rapped a staccato on the porch and the patio. They were little missiles sent from the clouds; riders on the howling wind of the storm. Just as she was starting to adjust to the repetitive din of the thunder, the lightning took over, bathing the landscape in the eerie whites and grays of a photographic negative exposing the world for brief flashes and then plunging everything into instant and total blackness before the brain could register objects familiar or strange.

It was over as quickly as it had begun. She peered warily around the end of the couch to the yard outside and saw the sun burst across the field and roll up the Flatirons in the near distance. She breathed deeply, and the air tasted fresh and cleaner than it had a moment before. She felt as though the sudden outburst had washed the atmosphere and brought a weird and wonderful peace to her little world. There was a coppery taste on the tip of her tongue.

"Well, little girl," she said to her baby. "Welcome to Colorado."

Laugh in the sunshine, Mommy, and sing in the rain. Mother will protect us and show us her glory.

"I don't think that exactly qualifies as a little summer drizzle, peanut. We could have been killed out there. We certainly saw the glory though."

Mother will watch over us.

"I hope so."

Let's go to yoga.

CHAPTER 20

"Hi, my name is Willow," the girl said. "You might want to be in the maternity class."

Wendy had arrived at the studio about thirty minutes before Emily told her to meet her there so that she could check things out. She hated being late anywhere for anything and always liked to make a good first impression. Her mother had taught her that. She didn't mean to arrive quite this early, but since she didn't know where the place was, she took the precaution of giving herself plenty of time.

Wendy was trying to be current in all of her endeavors these days. She had grown to realize how much serenity she experienced by not having any regrets about not being up to date with everything in her life. Procrastination had never been a serious problem for her, but sometimes she didn't say things she later wished she had said, or she delayed doing something for no apparent reason. It had become increasingly important to her to stay on top of things in order to avoid the disappointing feeling of an opportunity lost. She was probably making too much of it, but it was essential to her to live in the present. Her baby was teaching her that.

"I guess I'm really early," she said to the thin girl named Willow. "I wanted to give myself plenty of time. I'm meeting my doctor here tonight, and I'm pretty sure that I want to be in the regular yoga class. I mean for now anyway."

Willow was the instructor, and her name could not have been more appropriate. Wendy wondered if they had willow trees around here and then she wondered if it was a nickname or if her parents had named her Willow. If they did, how did they know that their daughter would grow up to look like a willow tree?

"Oh, no, that's okay. The regular class is cool if that's what you want. We're pretty laid back here. Everybody's really on their own level anyway, and I don't judge or criticize. I help with poses when people need help or ask for it, but we don't really do the beginner, intermediate, expert stuff, you know. I mean no qualifications or anything. Do what you're comfortable with, that's where it's at. My name is Willow," Willow said again.

"Yeah, I got that, Willow. That's a pretty name," Wendy said as she slipped the sack holding her mat and sweatshirt over her shoulder so that she could shake hands with Willow. "I'm Wendy."

"Hey, Wendy," said Willow shaking hands. "We have about a half hour or so. Would you like some water or fruit juice or something?"

"That's okay, no thanks. I take it there's a special class for pregnant women then?"

"Yup, but it's only one night a week and tonight's not the night. We have two classes in the morning and one class, this one, every night but Sunday, and then the maternity class an hour earlier on Tuesdays," explained Willow. "I lead them all."

"Wow, that's quite a schedule," said Wendy.

"It's not so bad, and I can always find someone to pinch hit for me if I need to. This evening class is all regulars. I could put on the music and go take a nap if I wanted to. Who are you waiting for?" asked Willow. "Oops, I'm sorry I don't mean to be nosy."

"Not at all," Wendy replied. "We just moved here and Doctor Nicholson suggested I come to this class."

"Oh cool, Emmy, yeah. She's a regular. We have a great group. You'll like it."

The class started filtering into the studio, chatting in groups of two and three, and Emmy arrived and pulled Wendy over to a spot on the floor near her. The class began without any kind of signal or announcement and just like Willow said, these ladies all knew exactly what they were there for and what they were doing. Willow gave quiet instructions barely audible over the soft music, and the class moved from one position to the next without comment. Wendy felt very much at home and drifted into that meditative state that she loved so much. The hour was over before she knew it.

Emmy and Willow praised her technique and introduced her around the room, and Wendy felt as though she would fit in nicely with these folks. There was a shared calmness and an inner peace and a common sense of restraint and confidence that came with people who knew each other well. Wendy had discovered back in Vermont that the practice of yoga was metaphorical to life in that learning requires exaggeration but living requires subtlety.

Wendy and Emmy walked out to the car lot together and Wendy told her doctor how frightened she had been by the sudden storm. Emmy described the dynamic weather patterns of the foothills and agreed that she too had been unprepared for the force and the fury and the unpredictability of Mother Nature when she first arrived in Boulder.

*   *   *

Life fell into a comfortable and predictable pattern. The baby grew in Wendy's stomach; Terrence worked brutal hours and raved about it. Wendy took care of the house and the cats and corresponded with Madeline and stayed in touch with her father and Rebecca. She went to yoga class every day and made new friends at the market and the car wash and the library where she had begun to spend time researching and polishing her latest book. She explored the area in the Porsche, getting thrills out of driving the tight little car through the mountain passes. She got to know the area around Boulder very well. She had found a private spot about a mile from the house just inside the Eldorado Canyon State Park. She would have liked to have a dog with her when she hiked to her spot, but she wasn't going to rush the future. Her puppy was somewhere in her life just ahead of her.

She met a realtor in yoga class and began driving around with her to look at homes, but she quickly got discouraged by the prices. She prayed each day and tried not to project about the future. Her life was great; there was no reason to be anxious or nervous. They would find a place before Madeline was ready to return and Annabelle was ready to be born. She knew that in her heart.

Her life was really so much better than she could possibly have imagined, and she couldn't figure out why. What had suddenly happened? What had she done to make things so good?

She had read about sacred places and she was convinced that her private meditation spot in the canyon was some kind of vortex where the air and space was very thin between this world and the next. It was there that she realized one morning that the deciding factor that had changed her life so significantly in the last year was prayer. She believed in God and she believed that God was watching over her. She had faith where previously she had had none.

Faith is the bird that sings when the dawn is still dark.

"That's it," she said to Annabelle. "It's not at all complicated is it, little one?"

* * *

Wendy couldn't believe her eyes when she read the e-mail, so she read it again, and then she read it again, and again. When Terrence got home that night she told him that he was not going to believe the e-mail she got.

"Try me," he said warily dropping onto the couch with a bottle of cold water in his hand.

"I'm telling you, Terry, you will not believe it."

"Try me, honey," he repeated.

"You are absolutely going to freak out," Wendy assured him.

Terrence just looked at her. He really wasn't in the mood, but he could see that she was overjoyed. She was bursting to tell him her news. She looked like a little kid on Christmas morning, and his fatigue melted away. He still didn't say anything, though.

"Well?" she prodded.

"Well what, Wendy?" Terrence laughed. "Just tell me what the heck is going on. You look like the cat that ate the canary."

Her face soured and Terrence could see that she didn't like that analogy, but it passed in a second, and she recovered her look of euphoric happiness at this secret that she was so anxious to reveal.

"Okay, okay, this is so cool. You are not going to believe this Terry. Guess what?"

"Guess what? What? What? What, for crying out loud, Wendy, what?" Terrence was getting a little louder now.

"Terry, calm down," Wendy admonished. "Do you want to hear my news or not."

"Yes!" he bellowed.

"Never mind," she said and walked out of the room.

"Oh my God," Terrence mumbled to himself as he sat up on the couch and put both hands on his head. "Wendy, hey come back here. I want to hear your news. I'm sorry." He stood to walk into the bedroom as she answered.

"Never mind, I said," she yelled down the hall.

Terrence slumped back onto the couch and pulled a pillow over his head.

"Well, all right," said Wendy, returning into the living room, "If you really want to know."

"I really want to know," he mumbled into the pillow.

"I got an e-mail from Madeline," Wendy began.

"You don't say."

"Yeah, and she is getting married to some French guy named Guy. They've been going to his chateau in Marseilles for the last couple of weekends. She told me about this guy before. It's Guy, but you say 'Gee', you know. Anyway, he proposed last weekend, and . . . are you listening?"

"Yes, I'm listening," said Terrence with the pillow on his head.

"So Madeline said yes," Wendy gushed triumphantly.

Terrence said that he was thrilled. Wendy said that he should be thrilled and Terrence asked her why, were they invited to the wedding or something?

"No, goofball, because she wants to sell us her house and she wants us to take care of her cats and she wants us to keep all of her furniture that we want and sell the rest and send her personal family things like photos and stuff to Zurich. That's why."

"Really?" said Terrence pulling the pillow away from his head.

"Yes, really, Terry."

"Wow."

"Yeah, wow. She wants Prakasha to come over and help us sort through her stuff and she wants us to go talk to her lawyer and she said that she would take any reasonable offer for the house and furnishings, and yes, by the way, we're invited to the wedding on the French Riviera."

"Who's Prakasha?" Terrence asked.

"Prakasha Patel. You remember Prakasha. She was here for the yard sale. She introduced herself and bought my parent's wine glasses. She is Madeline's old friend from when they were little girls. You remember," insisted Wendy.

"No, I don't. What does Prakasha do?" wondered Terrence.

"Nothing."

"Huh?"

"I don't think she does anything. I mean she has a husband and kids, but I don't know if she works," said Wendy. "We only met her once."

"You only met her once," corrected Terrence.

"Okay, I only met her once . . . here," agreed Wendy. "But what do you think, pretty amazing, huh?"

"I guess," Terrence shrugged.

"What do you mean, you guess, Terry? This is wonderful news. This is a fabulous opportunity. This is a dream come true."

"Wendy, a reasonable offer on this house with this land in this beautiful spot could be a million bucks; maybe more. We can't afford this place, sweetie. I'm sorry, but not yet anyway. Maybe in a couple of years we can find a place like this, but now? Sorry, kid, no way." Terrence was sorry too, but this just wasn't going to happen.

Only those who have known darkness can truly appreciate the light, Mommy.

"You're right, sweetie," said Wendy to her baby. "Terry, we can too buy this house. I don't know how, but we can and we will. I want us to live here and we will figure out a way to make this happen. It's just too much of a coincidence. We will buy this beautiful place and it will be our home and we will have our baby here and that's all there is to it."

"Sure," said Terrence. "Okay, whatever you say, sweetheart. I'm going to take a shower and go to bed."

"You're going to eat first, Terry Frazier. I made a nice salad with chicken. Then you can take a shower and then you can go to bed."

"Yes, ma'am," Terrence said.

They were silent at dinner. Terrence really did look exhausted. Wendy wanted to snap him out of his funk.

"What was Pinky's real name?"

"Woodrow Knox Pinkerton," Terrence replied with a smile.

"I was guessing something like that," said Wendy. "Now the sixty-four thousand dollar question—What was Terrence Abercrombie Frazier's nickname?"

He walked his plate over to the sink, and washed it off, put it in the dishwasher, and turned and smiled at her. "Over my dead body," he said and hugged her tight. "Thank you for that delicious dinner. I'm going to be in the shower and then I'll be in the bedroom. If the hospital calls, please wake me up. If you figure out how to buy this place, definitely wake me up. I would love to live here too, Wendy." He let the rest of it go unsaid and headed down the hall.

Wendy gazed through the kitchen door from her place at the table and she could see the big beautiful mirror over the fireplace in the living room.

"I hope she lets us keep this mirror," she yelled down the hall.

CHAPTER 21

"Your husband is a publisher?"

"Yes, Wendy," said Prakasha in her formal tone. "He works closely with the University. There are quite a few students and professors trying to get their work into print, and it is fertile ground for a small independent publishing company."

They were sitting in the living room drinking tea on a cool November morning. Prakasha had a list of personal things that Madeline had asked her to pack up and ship to Zurich. She and Wendy had located all of the books and photographs and trinkets and mementos that were important to their friend, and they had boxed a lot of it and tagged the rest with little green sticky dots. To Wendy's surprise, UPS offered a packing and shipping service and they had contacted the company and were waiting for the people to arrive as they sat on Madeline's couch sipping their tea and chatting.

After Wendy had sheepishly told Prakasha about her efforts at writing children's books, Prakasha had insisted on looking at them, and now they were both laughing out loud at the misadventures of Maury, the sunburned baby mammoth.

"I am taking these home with me and I will not take no for an answer," insisted Prakasha. "This is precious stuff. You are very talented, Wendy. I make no promises, but don't be surprised if my husband likes them too. He spends all day reading very dry material written by very pretentious people. These books are refreshing, my young friend. I know what sells and . . . well, we shall see."

The doorbell rang, and the three men in brown uniforms made quick work of Madeline's list. They packed all of the boxes into their brown truck and were pulling out of the circular driveway within the hour. Prakasha told Wendy to take her time deciding what she would like to keep and to not worry about hurting anyone's feelings. Madeline was very much in love, she assured her, and would pay no attention anyway. They would take a list of items to the lawyer and decide on a fair price for the whole kit and caboodle and sell the rest.

Wendy was not going to let herself get frustrated. She kept telling herself that they would figure out a way to buy this house. She felt connected to it now. It was their destiny, she was sure. She willed her mind to think positive thoughts and reviewed options of renting, delaying payment, extending payments, leasing part of the property, or subdividing the land. Her mind was working overtime, yet still nothing seemed feasible. Reasonable was the word Madeline had used. She e-mailed her delight back to her landlady in Switzerland but tried hard not to sound desperate or unsure or defeated. Like a mantra, she kept repeating that this house would be her home. Finally, she knew she had to get to her yoga class and clear her mind.

The way of progress is neither swift nor easy, Mommy. Turn it over to Mother.

"Okay, baby. Dear Lord, it's all yours."

When she got home later that evening, she told Terrence that they had to pray for their home. So he did.

"Are you sure you should still be going to yoga, Wendy? You're pretty far along," said Terrence with a worried tone. He had been working too hard he decided, and had not noticed how big Wendy was.

"I'm fine, doctor," she said raising her hand for Terrence to help her off her knees. "Emmy, the obstetrician, remember? says I'm doing just fine, thank you, and that I'll know when the time to quit walking and exercising comes. And frankly I don't think it'll come until you're driving me to the hospital. I want to paint the baby's room sky blue. Annabelle isn't going to be a little delicate flower in a pink baby room. I want her to feel a part of the mountains and the sky right off the bat."

"Wendy, that's probably fine, but I think we should talk to the attorney about it. I'm sure Madeline will let us stay here until he finds a buyer, but we shouldn't start painting rooms without his permission, or Madeline's permission."

"Terry, this is going to be our house," Wendy said defiantly. "I promise."

* * *

Rebecca called and told Wendy all about their great adventure. They were relocating to Tucson. The movers were packing up the house, and

Joe had gone up to Providence to rent an RV that they were going to drive across the country. Sammy was coming with them of course.

"Oh, Becca, I would love to see Sammy," Wendy said into the cell phone as she wandered through the house taking mental inventory of the furniture. "Are you planning on driving through Colorado? We would love to spend some time with you, anywhere. A rest area on the interstate would be fine for me. I miss you both so much."

Wendy brought Rebecca up to date on what was happening in their lives, and the two expectant mothers compared notes on the status of almost eight months of pregnancy. Then Rebecca dropped the bombshell.

"I should really let your father tell you this, he's so excited about it, but I'm excited too and I just can't hang up without making your day, Wendy. You are going to be so blown away. I mean we know how much you want to stay in Dr. Ashgar's house and we know how frustrating it's been searching for a place and I guess it's really been all up to you because Terry's working so hard and everything, and it must be driving you crazy and you're probably driving him crazy too but . . ."

"Rebecca."

"I know, I know, I'm getting to the point, don't interrupt me. I should not be telling you this little sister. Joe will probably kill me. He's been so anxious to tell you, but you know how men are, he wants to set it all up just right and get you hooked up with Merrill Lynch or something first and that will probably take forever, that kind of stuff always does. Actually I was thinking Morgan Stanley. I hate it when . . ."

"Rebecca."

"Okay, okay, don't rush me. Your father sold the house, and he's sending you five hundred thousand dollars. There I said it. Forgive me, Joe. But he wants to make sure that he transfers it directly into an IRA at Merrill or like I said, maybe . . . Wendy? Hello? Wendy, did you hear me? Wendy?"

Wendy didn't hear her. She was on the floor in the baby's bedroom, fainted dead away. The sound of Rebecca's voice brought her slowly back to consciousness. She realized that she was on the floor and she didn't know what had happened or how she had gotten there. The phone was a couple of feet away, and her step-mother was insistently calling her name with a tone of panic in her voice. *Step-mother?* How odd it seemed to be thinking of Rebecca as her step-mother as opposed to her big sister or her father's wife or just her friend. *What happened?* She wondered. Why was she down here looking at the phone and listening to the sound of the wind competing with Rebecca's voice for her attention?

"Oh my God, please answer me, Wendy. Where are you? What's happened? Wendy, I'm calling 911. Please pick up the phone. Oh heck, that's it. I'm calling the police. Wendy? Wendy I'm calling the cops. Are you there? Oh my God. Hello? Hello?"

The windswept forest was singing to her as a steady breeze blew through the tall conifer trees on the other side of the yard. She heard waves tumbling onto a rocky shore as her brain struggled back from beneath warm, clear water. Her fingers and her toes tingled and she felt her knees sinking into deep spongy moss as she crawled across the deep carpeting toward the squawking telephone.

"Becca? I'm here," Wendy whispered gingerly picking up the phone.

"Oh my God, oh, thank God, Wendy where did you go? What happened? Did you drop the phone?"

"Yes, I dropped the phone. I think I fainted. I must have fainted, Becca."

"Wendy, you have to get to the hospital right now. Are you sure the baby is okay? Is the baby okay, Wendy?" Rebecca demanded.

"How long was I out?" asked Wendy.

"Oh my God, Wendy, you have to get to the hospital. Can you drive? Did you hurt yourself? Wendy, are you all right, sweetie?"

"Five hundred thousand dollars?" she repeated. Wendy was sure she hadn't heard right. "Is that what you said, Becca? Did you say five hundred thousand, like a half a million dollars, Becca?"

"Yes. Yes, your father sold the house for six hundred forty thousand and we're using some of it to close and move, and your dad's sending you the rest. Please don't faint again. Wendy, I think you should go to the hospital right now. Call Terry, Wendy. I think you were out for like two or three minutes. Oh my God, Wendy, did you absolutely fall, like collapse somewhere? Did you bang your head? Did you land on the baby?"

"Five hundred thousand dollars Rebecca, are you sure? Is that what Daddy told you or do you know that beyond a shadow of a doubt?" Wendy needed confirmation.

"I know that, Wendy. Yes, it's five hundred thousand, oh, please don't faint again. Hello? Hello? Wendy, are you there? Oh Christ, oh no, she did it again. That's it, I'm calling an ambulance. Oh dear, Wendy, I never should have said anything. Damn, why didn't I let Joe do this? Hello? Wendy?"

"I'm here, Becca. Sorry, I'm just trying to process this. When's Daddy getting home?"

"It's the truth, Wendy, I promise. Don't faint. I'm hanging up so you can call Terry. I feel terrible. I shouldn't have ever told you this. It's not my place. Okay, I'm hanging up. Call Terry, okay? Wendy, Wendy?"

"I'm calling him right now," Wendy assured her.

"You're okay, right?"

"Becca, I have never been better in my life. I love you. I love you. I love you. Tell Daddy I love him too, and tell him to call me right away. It's really five hundred thousand dollars, Becca? You're sure? Becca?"

"I'm sure. Are you sure you're okay?"

"I'm sure. I'm real sure. Oh my God, am I ever okay."

The phone rang again as soon as Wendy and Rebecca had disconnected. Wendy assumed it was Rebecca again. Maybe she had made a mistake. It couldn't really be that much money. Maybe it was just a joke. She would kill her if it was a joke. She snapped open the cell phone.

"Rebecca, honest to God, if that was a joke I'll kill you. I swear I'll rip your heart out."

"Wendy? Hello, Wendy, it's Prakasha, is that you?"

"Oh, hi, Prakasha," said Wendy. "Sorry about that, I think a friend might be playing a joke on me."

"Oh, well I don't mean to interrupt. I just thought you'd like to know that my husband loved your books. He took the liberty of passing them along to a colleague who specializes in children's literature and he liked them too. He just called me to ask you to give him a call at his office. Apparently, they are prepared to offer you quite a bit of money to publish them."

Silence.

"Hello? Hello, Wendy, are you there?"

Wendy was back on the floor.

* * *

Terrence gazed into her left eye with his little flashlight and then he looked into the other eye. Wendy was lying on the couch in the living room with a cold, wet washcloth on her forehead, and she was thinking that she hadn't been real crazy about this couch when they had first arrived back in October, but that it really was a nice couch and she thought that maybe they should keep it. It was better than the couch they had brought with them from Rhode Island, and that couch would really go much better in the guest room. Maybe she could get slipcovers made for both of them and keep them both here in the living room. She could sort of offset them so that one part of the living room would be for television and the other could be more for entertaining.

She really had plenty of furniture for the guest room and she didn't want to junk it up just because they had the pieces. She preferred to simplify as opposed to putting too much stuff in her new home. Feng Shui was the way to go, she thought.

"Your eyes are bopping around in your head like they're watching a ping pong match," said Terrence. "But I don't think that has anything to do with the fainting. Why do I get the feeling that you're not too worried about dropping to the floor twice within a couple of minutes? This is nothing to play with, Wendy." He held her wrist, feeling her pulse, and searched her face for something only very serious young doctors search for. "You have never fainted before in your life and now you've done it twice in the span of like no time and you don't seem to think it's much of a big deal."

"It isn't a big deal, Terry. I feel fine. Now quit playing Marcus Welby and let me up," Wendy insisted.

"Wendy, you are eight months pregnant, please take it easy," said Terrence helping her to her feet. "Do you feel dizzy?"

"No, I told you that before. I thought I was seeing double for a second, but that was because I had two identical black cats licking my face when I came to. I'm fine now."

"I don't mean to sound dramatic," said Terrence sounding very dramatic, "but I think we're lucky those two black cats were here."

"Oh, please, I would have come to regardless, but, yes, you're right, it's nice to be loved. Now let's call Daddy and let's make an appointment with Merrill Lynch and with Madeline's attorney and let's get this ball rolling."

"Man, you are all business, woman. I want to savor the moment. What about the book deal? I mean that's wild. You should be so proud. I'm totally blown away by that, Wendy," Terrence said.

"Yeah," she paused for a moment. "That's pretty cool, but it can wait. Let's buy our house, Terry. Oh, I'm so excited." Wendy ran down the hall to the bedroom.

"Hey, no running anyway." Terrence was trying to be in charge of this situation. He regarded it as a medical issue, after all, but Wendy was done being a patient. She had called Terrence to rush home because of their financial windfall and the coincidental happy consequences. What was a little faint or two?

The next couple of days passed in a blur, arrangements were made, money was wired, a contract was signed, a mortgage and terms were drawn up, and Terrence never missed an hour of work and Wendy made it to every yoga class.

In the paint department of Home Depot they got into a silly argument and Terrence pointed out that they were both exhausted. Joe and Rebecca were arriving with Sammy and the RV in two days and Johnny and his family had been invited down for a barbeque to round out the reunion. Wendy and Terrence needed some time to recharge their batteries.

They told the lady at Home Depot that they'd be back in a week and they got in the Porsche and drove home and took off their clothes and crawled into bed in the middle of the day and slept for eighteen hours. Wendy got up to pee a lot, but Terrence never moved and when they finally left the bedroom, Terrence made scrambled eggs and they watched the sun set over the Flatirons from their stools around the counter in the kitchen of their own house.

"I prayed for this, Terry," Wendy said. "I think somewhere deep down inside of me I've been praying for this my whole life. We are so blessed. I am so happy to be with you here, Terry. I told you this was going to happen, didn't I?"

Mommy, there is a graceful way of being right and there are many disgraceful ways of being wrong.

"You're right, baby. Terry, we must never forget our spiritual connection to this earth and this universe and to our Holy Mother. I love you, Terry."

"I love you too, Wendy."

CHAPTER 22

Hey! Queer Bait," Johnny Sgarlatti bellowed as he stepped out of the four-door Jeep after parking it behind the massive RV that was taking up most of the driveway. His wife got out of the passenger side and leaned into the back seat to unbuckle the baby from her car seat as the five year old in pigtails and blue jeans launched herself out the window into her daddy's arms. John put the little girl down and then ran across the grass and grabbed Terrence in a big bear hug and lifted him off his feet and kissed him on both cheeks before setting him back down on the ground.

"Don't call me that, Scar," Terrence hissed when his old roommate had plopped him back down on the lawn.

Wendy and Joe and Rebecca were standing in the yard waiting to be introduced to John and his family and were slightly taken back by the affectionate reunion. John's wife and daughter and baby seemed unfazed by their daddy's behavior and were walking up to the small gathering with big smiles on their faces. They were a beautiful little family and John was not at all chagrined by Terrence's reproach. He jogged back to his wife and scooped the baby out of her arms and grabbed his daughter by the hand.

"Hi, everybody, I'm John and this is my wife, Marie, my daughter Cheyenne, and my baby, Dakota."

"What did you call him?" said Wendy.

"Hi, Marie," said Rebecca. "I'm Becca and this is Wendy, Terry's fiancée, and Wendy's father, Joe."

"Hello, everybody," Joe said stepping up to shake John's hand. He shook Marie's hand next and then he leaned down and took Cheyenne's hand and shook it vigorously and said, "What a pretty name, Cheyenne." He kept shaking the little cherub's hand until she giggled and blushed.

John walked over to Wendy and embraced her warmly and kissed her on the cheek surprising her. He said, "I am so happy to meet you, Wendy. You are marrying the guy that was my best friend in school. I'm so happy for you both, aren't we, Marie?" he said over his shoulder to his wife who nodded and shook her head laughing.

Wendy pulled back and looked at John squarely in the face and said, "What did you call him?"

"Never mind," Terrence said.

Marie took Wendy's hand and said, "Just ignore him Wendy. He doesn't know when to shut up."

"He called him 'Queer Bait'," Joe laughed.

"This one doesn't know when to shut up either," said Rebecca referring to Joe.

"Was that your prep school nickname that you wouldn't ever tell me?" Wendy said accusingly.

"I'm not surprised," said Joe still laughing.

"What's wrong with 'Queer Bait'?" John asked.

Terrence was bright red. "Can we just let this go? How about we start over? Let's pretend you're just pulling up and you get out of your car, Scar, and you say, 'Hello Terry, old buddy'. Can we do that?"

"Queer Bait?" said Wendy again.

"That's his name," John said again. "Everybody at school called him Queer Bait 'cause he was so darn cute. He was the only one of us that never had a pimple."

"Nobody called me that but you, Scar."

"That's 'cause you went postal on everybody else, but you couldn't kick my butt," John laughed.

"Okay, Johnny, leave Terry alone," said Marie. "We're guests here, you moron. Honestly, you just can't take the boy out of Staten Island."

"Queer Bait?" Wendy looked like she had eaten something rotten.

"Come on, everybody, let's go inside. I made a pitcher of Bloody Marys and the girls might want to play with the cats," Terrence said. He bent down and took Cheyenne's hand and said, "Do you like kitties, Cheyenne? Wendy's daddy brought Wendy's kitty to visit the kitties that live here and they're all in the house playing." That wasn't exactly true. Sammy didn't like Madison or Lexington one bit and they were all keeping their distance.

"Bloody Marys," asked Johnny? "Got any beer?"

"Oh, be quiet," said Marie. "I'd love a Bloody Mary, Terry."

They all filed into the house and immediately went in separate directions. Wendy began giving Marie the tour of the house that she had given Joe and Rebecca when they had arrived the night before. Terrence and Johnny and Joe walked right through the living room and out onto the back patio through the sliding glass doors and looked across the yard to the canyon and the mountains. The view still humbled Terrence. It was really breathtaking. He saw it every day and had not yet gotten used to it. Joe and Johnny were impressed and made complimentary noises about the yard and the view beyond.

"Heck, you could get horses, Bait," Johnny said. "Is the barn in good shape?"

Joe nodded that it was, and Terrence said, "It's in great shape; clean too. I don't think we're quite ready for horses, though, I'll leave that up to Wendy, but they would be very happy horses living here, I think."

Rebecca was in the kitchen fixing an apple juice for Cheyenne and pouring drinks. Terrence had made the drinks without booze, but the vodka bottle was on the counter for anyone who wanted to fortify their spicy tomato juice. Everybody wandered around the house for twenty or thirty minutes before finally settling in the living room with refreshments and a bowl of nuts and a bowl of popcorn. Johnny drank a Coke out of a can and tossed peanuts in the air and caught them in his mouth. The baby quieted back down and fell asleep with a pacifier in her mouth, and Cheyenne sat on the floor stroking Madison. The conversation flowed easily and Terrence got up to start the grill before sitting back down between Rebecca and Marie who were talking about babies. Wendy was once again recounting her fainting incident for Johnny and Joe.

Joe told everybody about his new job and the house in Tucson that they had found on line. Their trip from Bristol to Boulder had been easy and they enjoyed travelling in the comfort of the big recreational vehicle.

"How long did it take ya, Joe?"asked Johnny.

"He is so concerned about time," said Marie. "Every trip back East is a race with this guy. I would love to get a big RV like you guys have and just take it easy and see the country."

Rebecca said that was pretty much what they had done. They scoped out RV parks along the way and stopped and set up camp and got to know other RV people.

"Ours is small compared to some of the rigs you see in the parks," Rebecca remarked. "Some of those people spend a week or two in those places too. They aren't all old and retired either. Those RV parks rock. They have water parks and bingo halls and crazy events like dances and bonfires. It's a whole other culture. There are a lot of Canadians we noticed."

Johnny was getting ready to kick off the ski season at Winter Park, and Cheyenne was full of chatter about the nursery school she had been going to three days a week since September.

Rebecca and Wendy were talking about how grateful they were to be enjoying problem-free pregnancies and Marie envied them because both of Marie's babies had been tough the last couple of months before birth.

"Did you both get pregnant the same night?" Marie joked.

"Don't laugh," said Wendy.

"We think we might have," Rebecca explained with a wink.

"Wow," said Marie. "That's wild. Do you have names yet?"

"Of course," answered Rebecca. "Wendy's carrying Annabelle, and I'm carrying Maria. I hope you don't mind Marie."

"Heck no, that's great. I've been called Maria all my life. It's a beautiful name. I love Biblical names."

Terrence threw burgers and hot dogs and a few chicken breasts on the grill and told Johnny that the old Weber was the best part of the deal they had struck with Madeline and her attorney.

Everybody remarked about how lucky Terrence and Wendy were to end up with this wonderful house and how fortunate they were to have pulled off this negotiation with their former landlady. They had nothing but gratitude for Madeline, and Terrence offered a toast to her.

Wendy made a nice salad and some macaroni and cheese, which was a hit with the little girls, and dinner, was noisy and busy and fun.

The older girls were in the kitchen cleaning up when Rebecca asked Wendy if Annabelle was still talking to her.

"You bet," said Wendy. "More than ever, actually. It's more of a two-way conversation these days, not like she's just giving me advice."

"Yeah," agreed Rebecca. "Me too, it's like Maria is talking about more mundane and routine stuff."

"Well, I don't know about that," Wendy thought aloud. "Annabelle is getting a little heavier. I don't mean just physically," she giggled. "Sometimes she gets pretty deep, and I'm not sure I really understand what she's trying to tell me right away. Sometimes it takes awhile to sink in, you know?"

Marie was leaning back against the counter with her hands behind her on the counter top and a cautious look on her face.

"Your babies talk to you?" she asked quietly.

"Yes."

"Yup."

"Okay," Marie said expectantly. "Anything else you want to tell me?"

Dakota started to cry in the other room as if on cue, and all three women looked toward the living room and laughed.

"I guess my baby talks to me too, but she waited until she was born."

The smaller the bird, the sweeter the song, Mommy.

"Ah, that's sweet, Annabelle," Wendy said back to her baby.

"What did she say?" asked Rebecca.

"She said, 'the smaller the bird, the sweeter the song,'" Wendy answered.

"Ah, that is sweet," Rebecca said.

"You two are nuts," said Marie. "I better go get Dakota and see if Johnny is ready to go home. We should leave you weirdoes alone," she teased.

Johnny wanted to drive up the canyon and home through Nederland, Central City, and Blackhawk, but Marie nixed that and they ended up headed for the highway and the easier route back to Idaho Springs on Interstate 70.

Joe and Rebecca were planning on getting an early start in the morning, and the four of them sipped tea in the kitchen from oversized ceramic mugs that Rebecca had made and brought along to give to Wendy. They talked softly and laughed together and got sleepy and sad that they were parting after too short a visit. Wendy held Sammy and softly stroked her as her oldest friend purred contentedly.

"I can't thank you enough for your generosity, Joe," Terrence began. "No way could we have afforded this place without your help. We put a pretty good chunk down to keep the mortgage payments reasonable, but I'm happy to say we've got all of the rest conservatively invested for your granddaughter and, oh by the way, I do promise to make an honest woman out of your little girl."

Joe chuckled into his tea mug and Rebecca asked about marriage.

"When are you two going to formalize this relationship?"

"August nineteenth next year," Wendy answered quickly.

"We are?"

"Yes, Terry. Sorry I hadn't filled you in yet. That's a Friday. Annabelle will be eight months old and so will her Aunt Maria. She'll be at the wedding along with her daddy and mine and, of course, you, Becca. I'm still working on my list, but I'm hoping we can give Grace and your parents plenty of time to plan to be here.

"I thought about getting married at a regular church. I think we should look for a Presbyterian Church, Terry, but the best one I've found is Broomfield Presbyterian, and I don't want to drive all the way down there every Sunday. Church of the Apostles here in Boulder is probably the one we should join. It's really pretty, and I like the pastor. I looked at Trinity in town and it's really cool. Boulder Valley would be a good place for a wedding too; it has beautiful views, and Peace Lutheran and the Mennonite Church are both really cute, but the more I think about it, the more I think we should get married outside somewhere in a natural setting. I was talking to Caroline about where to get married and she suggested Estes Park, so we're going to check that out, but anyway I've pretty much settled on the nineteenth of August."

Terrence looked a little shocked. "That was a mouthful. I'm glad you've got this all figured out sweetheart."

"What is the significance of August nineteenth, if you don't mind me asking?" asked Rebecca.

"The girls will be a good age, the weather will be nice, we'll be settled in better, and I'll be able to fit into a pretty wedding dress," replied Wendy. "It's also the anniversary of the night Terry proposed to me in Montreal."

Rebecca liked that. She clasped her hands together on her chest as if to pray, tilted her head to the side, and made a little whimpering noise.

"Okay," said Terrence, clearly out of the loop on this not-so-minor decision regarding his life. "Anything you say, sweetheart." He just shook his head. "What does the baby think?"

"She agrees with me," Wendy confirmed.

"Of course."

"We'll be here, Wendy," Rebecca assured her. "Right, Joe?"

"Yeah, right," Joe responded. "Anything you say, sweetheart," he mimicked Terrence. "I'm going to bed."

* * *

The surprise baby shower was held at the yoga studio the night after Thanksgiving. Wendy had no idea. Willow and Caroline and Emmy and Prakasha put it all together and invited all the students that Wendy had been practicing with as well as a lot of the staff from the Medical Center that had become friends with the popular new couple. Annabelle's gifts were practical since Emmy and Prakasha knew exactly what the baby and her young mother still needed, but they were also ridiculous, excessive, unnecessary, vulgar, and downright funny. Wendy was overwhelmed. She cried and she laughed and she hugged everybody over and over again and, for a moment, Terrence thought she was going to faint when she suddenly went white and looked like she had that night back in Canada three months ago. Emmy called a halt to the festivities in the interest of the baby's and the mommy's health and all the girls finished off the carrot cake and headed into the night.

"Wendy Applegate, you sure have a knack for making friends," said Terrence on the way home.

"I just can't believe it, Terry. My life has changed so much since I met you, since I got pregnant, since this angel inside of me started calling the shots. I don't really know what I've done or how I've changed or why I am suddenly so surrounded by love and positive intention. When I get into my meditative yoga state I feel as though my mind is taking me on a trip that has no destiny. I think that I'm in full flight from reality but then I realize that it's just the opposite; I've never been more present in my own life or more intuitively aware of the wonderful and mysterious destiny that I am certain is ahead for us. Then I realize that it's not a happy future I'm so sure of, it's a happy present that I'm living and I'm fully in it. It's weird. I guess I can't really explain it."

Mommy, you have learned to give more than you ever expect to get. You care.

"Oh, thank you, baby," Wendy said, and Terrence just drove without comment.

CHAPTER 23

Both babies were born on Christmas Day.

The full moon bathed the snowy backyard in a brilliance and glow that seemed unearthly. Wendy thought that heaven must have light like that as she sat in the white wicker rocking chair looking out the window of the baby's room at midnight. The room was prepared and waiting patiently for the new addition to their lives, and Wendy couldn't sleep because she was worried; Annabelle had been strangely quiet for two days now. The crib, the little changing table, the bassinette, the dresser with bunnies painted on it, the jungle animals on the wallpaper border around the top of the room all waited for Annabelle to arrive. Wendy felt as though the room was holding its breath. She had slipped out of bed, trying not to disturb Terrence and had wandered around the house holding her belly and talking gently to her baby. The full moon was perched like a snowy owl over the Flatirons and Wendy told herself not to be anxious; everything was all right, everything was fine, this was all going along according to God's plan. She felt her mother looking down upon her and she felt safe and loved.

And then her water broke.

"Terry!"

* * *

"Okay, Terry, I think I'm being pretty calm about this whole thing, you know," Wendy said as they sat in the Porsche at a red light two blocks from the hospital.

"Yes, um, yes, Wendy you're doing really good." Terrence was not doing nearly as well. He was a nervous wreck. *Some doctor,* thought Wendy.

"Well, Terry, I'm doing really well," she corrected.

"What? Oh, yeah," he said. "You are." He stopped and then continued, "Doing really well, I mean."

"The thing is, Terry, it's like one in the morning on Christmas Eve you see, and there isn't another freakin' car within ten miles of here."

"Yeah, I noticed that. It's pretty quiet, isn't it?" Terrence agreed with Wendy.

"So, not that I'm really nervous or anything, but my water broke and my contractions are about every twenty minutes or so . . ."

"Yeah," Terrence agreed, "about every twenty minutes or so."

"Right, so do you mind telling me why we've been sitting at this stupid light for like . . . well, I dunno, Terry, what do you think, maybe twenty minutes, since about my last contraction and you know I'm thinking, heck I could pretty much get out and walk from here for all the good you're doing?" Her voice was starting to get considerably louder, “I mean I could practically spit on the stupid hospital from this distance and yet here we sit.”

“The light is red, Wendy.”

“I know the god damn light is red, Terry,” Wendy screamed at the top of her lungs. Terrence winced and the little car shook. “Go through the god damn light Terry or I’ll push you out and drive this flipping car myself, you shit for brains excuse for a doctor.”

It’s okay, Mommy, I’m all right. We still have an hour or two. Please don’t swear.

“Oh, Annabelle, thank God you’re okay. I’ve been so scared the last two days. Where have you been?”

Right here, Mommy. Don’t yell at Daddy. God moves the way God wants to move.

“Well I wish She’d tell him to move this little buggy from here to that Emergency Room door over there,” Wendy said impatiently. And then she screamed again as another contraction twisted her gut, “Right freakin’ now, Terry!”

He threw the car into first gear, but it was third, and he popped the clutch and the Porsche stalled and Wendy moaned like a wounded rhino and Terrence’s hand shook as he turned the key and grinded the motor and finally got it into the right gear and they shot into the intersection, right into the path of an oncoming bread truck. The truck’s brakes squealed and the horn blared and the driver yelled out his open door at them as he swerved to avoid the Porsche.

“Whaddaya drunk?”

"He thinks I've been drinking," Terrence said, clearly offended.

"I'm starting to wonder myself," Wendy hissed through clenched teeth. "At least you'd have an excuse for being such a moron."

They pulled up to the Emergency Room entrance and an orderly and a nurse and Dr. Nicholson rushed through the double doors as they opened with a swish. The orderly was pushing a wheelchair and he and the nurse quickly transferred Wendy from the car to the chair and Emmy asked, "Where have you two been?"

"Stargazing," spit Wendy glaring at Terrence who was trying to get the bag that she had packed a month ago out of the back seat.

They rushed Wendy into the hospital and Terrence started running with the bag trying to catch up to them, but the security guard grabbed him by the arm.

"Dude," he motioned to the car. "What about the ride?"

Terrence spun around and looked at the Porsche as if seeing it for the first time. The engine was running and both doors were open and it was blocking everything. Terrence ran back to it and then turned around and ran back to the guard and handed him the bag and then ran back to the car again and jumped in and stalled it. He got it going and leaped forward toward the parking lot. When he ran back, he found the bag on the pavement where the security guard had left it and he snatched it up and ran inside.

He had been working in this building at least four days a week for the past three months. His time had been split between the two Medical Center locations, but he was mostly here and most of the time he was in the Emergency Room. Yet as he walked into the waiting area he saw it all as though he had never seen it before. He hesitated just inside the door, unsure of which way to go. The girl behind the wide desk pointed to the left and said, "They're in one-oh-four, Doctor Frazier. Hey, your buttons are wrong."

Terrence ran down the hall to Examination Room 104 and burst in to find Wendy and Emmy comfortably organized.

"Your buttons are buttoned wrong, Terry," Emmy said as she stepped away from Wendy, pulling her stethoscope from around her neck. "Can I see you out in the hall for a minute?"

Terrence had a panicked look on his face. He started fumbling with the buttons on his shirt.

Out in the hall Emmy turned to Terrence and gently held him by his shirt collar. "Doctor, you are scaring my patient. Do you think you're okay?"

"Yeah, I'm fine, I mean I'm, well, okay, I mean. I'm okay, don't worry."

"All right, Terry, we're going to have this baby pretty soon, so gown up and put on a mask and try to lose the deer in the headlights look. Wendy is totally cool, but this is her first time and it's scary enough without you adding to her anxiety, so pull yourself together or you're going to be sitting in the waiting room like all the other daddies. Got it?"

"Yeah, I got it," Terrence said, but he wasn't sure and neither was Emmy.

"She's got an IV drip going, and I just administered an epidural. Do you need something?" Emmy was totally in control of the situation.

"No," said Terrence. "I'm fine. I got it. I'll be okay."

Wendy was doing her breathing exercises with the nurse when they returned to the examination room. Dr. Nicholson wanted her upstairs so the orderly arrived again to get the patient onto a gurney and into the elevator and up to Delivery.

They all crowded in the elevator and Wendy said, "Just like yoga, right, Emmy?"

"That's right, honey, long deep inhale but kind of pop the breaths out in little machine gun spurts. You two did Lamaze right?"

"Yup, no problem," Wendy responded.

The nurse was Caribbean. Her nametag said Gwenevere, but everyone called her Gwennie. "This is fun, huh, Terry?" she said. "I've never been on a delivery with you and you bein' the chauffer, the attending, and the daddy. Wow, you multi-taskin' tonight."

Wendy was starting to feel a little woozy, and she asked Gwennie, "Do you know Josephine?"

"No dearie, I don't know Josephine, who's she?"

"You talk just like her," said Wendy.

"Josephine is a nurse back in Burlington. She's an old friend and she's from the Virgin Islands," Terrence explained. Emmy was glad to see that Terrence was starting to pull himself together.

"Nope," said Gwennie, "don't know no Josephine."

They were in the delivery room now and Emmy had Wendy in the stirrups and she said, "Big dilation, Annabelle's in a hurry."

Ten minutes later there was a loud piercing cry and Gwennie was taking the baby to the wash table. "She is so beautiful, Wendy girl. You done good, sweetheart. This is about the prettiest little thing I seen in awhile."

Wendy's hair was soaked under the cap on her head, and her back and throat and everything else was sore. But she had a huge smile on her face and stared at Gwennie's back as she washed out Annabelle's mouth and ears and nose, hoping to catch a glimpse of her baby.

"Is she black?" asked Wendy in a sleepy voice.

"Is she what?" said Gwennie glancing over her shoulder. Terrence stopped folding the sheet in his hand and Emmy looked up at Gwennie with a questioning look on her face.

"Black? I think you got too much juice in that drip Dr. Emmy. This baby is pink as sunrise. Why you ask that, Wendy girl?"

"Is she Chinese?"

"Chinese?" Gwennie laughed bringing Annabelle over to put her in Wendy's arms. "Next you gonna ask me is she a puppy or a turtle, I guess. Here, darlin', look for yourself. This is a beautiful pink, American girl wid a little bit a red hair. Not much maybe, but it's red."

Wendy took the little bundle and pulled back the soft terrycloth blanket to look for the first time into her daughter's face. Gwennie was right. This baby wasn't African or Asian at all. This baby was all Wendy, and Wendy burst into tears and said a silent thank you prayer to God. She didn't understand it, but right then and there she decided that she didn't need to understand it and she reassured herself that Mother works in mysterious ways.

Terrence's cell phone vibrated and he stepped into the hall to answer it. He returned a moment later with a big grin on his face and told Wendy that her father had called and Rebecca had just delivered a healthy seven-and-a-half pound baby girl. Annabelle and Maria had been born within ten minutes of one another.

* * *

Two months later, Annabelle's hair had begun to grow in with beautiful soft, reddish—blonde, bouncy curls. Her bellybutton was almost healed, and she was growing like the chubby little puppy that Gwennie had suggested she might be. She rarely cried, and she smiled a lot. Her blue eyes were the color of Terrence's, and she was the picture of contentment, nursing with her eyes closed and sleeping in her little bassinette. Wendy spent most of her nights in Annabelle's room, asleep on the rocker. Terrence woke up practically every night in an empty bed and went into the baby's room and brought Wendy back to their bedroom. It was a routine they were all comfortable with.

Wendy was back at yoga on a regular schedule and Patel Publishing had picked up all three of her books as a series. They launched a modest advertising campaign and had gone to a second printing to meet the growing demand from nursery schools, elementary schools and children's libraries across the country. Patel was looking for a company to translate the series into Spanish with the hope that they would be successful enough to publish in French, German and Italian. The royalty checks were in the mailbox once a month like clockwork, and Wendy had received a bonus and an advance against her next book which was the story of an owl that lived high in the Flatirons. She found that she was having difficulty finding the time to write; the artwork though, was all over the house.

Caroline had persuaded Wendy to go skiing with her, and they took Terrence along to babysit Annabelle while Wendy tried to follow Caroline's instructions. They laughed and screamed and fell all over the beginner's slope, and Wendy clung to Caroline, and pulled her down in the snow when she lost her balance, and they had a blast. Wendy loved the mountains, and the deep blue sky, and the bright sunshine, and the lodge, and the cute outfits, and the healthy, outdoorsy people. She enjoyed the drive up to Eldora through the canyon and the sudden weather changes and the conversation and hot chocolate and laughter and camaraderie and the soreness throughout her whole body. She fell asleep on the short drive home in the backseat of Caroline's little Subaru beside Annabelle sleeping soundly in her baby seat.

The next day she arrived home from yoga class and Terrence and a young guy she didn't recognize were standing in the driveway beside a brand new, maroon Land Rover LR2.

"Do you like it?" said Terrence with a broad smile on his face as Wendy stepped out of the Porsche leaving Annabelle asleep in her car seat.

Wendy didn't say a word, but got in behind the wheel and adjusted the seat and fiddled with the mirrors and started the engine and turned on the radio and the lights and the wipers and finally said, "Oh, Terry, I love it."

"It's yours, Mrs. Frazier," said the young salesman. He turned to Terrence. "If you want to give me a lift back to the dealership Doctor Frazier, we can finish up the paperwork and your wife can slide the baby right into the back and enjoy that new car smell while you're gone. I'd love a ride in that old Porsche. I've seen you two around town in it. She's a classic, never seen a color like that, I have to say."

Wendy nodded, absorbed in the dashboard of her new car and Terrence and the young salesman discussed insurance and financing as Terrence carefully picked up the baby and strapped her seat into the back of the LR2.

When he got home, Wendy was in Annabelle's room nursing and he said, "Do you really like it?"

"I love it, but what I really loved was being called Mrs. Frazier," she said with a dreamy smile on her face. Wendy always looked so calm and relaxed and at peace with the world when her baby was nursing. "It'll be perfect for our ski trips. Emmy's coming with us to Winter Park on Friday. I called Marie and she said she has a great sitter for Annabelle so we can all ski together. I'm so excited, Terry. I really like skiing. Do you think it's bad of me to leave our baby with a stranger?"

"Don't worry," said Terrence. "If Marie has someone she trusts I'm sure Annabelle will be okay. By the way, my boss has a condo in Vail he said we could use anytime."

"I'm so happy we moved, Terry. Sometimes I worry that my life is so perfect, I'm afraid something bad might happen. I need Annabelle to talk to me. I miss that."

"Let me try to help," said Terrence. "I'm thinking that Annabelle would probably be reading your mood right now and would tell you to leap blindly into change. Embrace the spontaneity and trust your good intuitions. Live without fear and take a chance on happiness. What do you think?"

"Very good," Wendy cheered up. "That's exactly what she would tell me, but it's different coming from you. I miss her little voice in my head."

"I know you do, but you have her little voice right there in your arms right now."

"You're right." The baby gurgled and Wendy pulled her away from her breast, wiped her mouth with a diaper, and gently draped her across her chest and started patting her back gently. She changed the subject abruptly. "So how much did you finance my new buggy for? What are the payments going to be?"

"Wendy, do you look at the checks you get from Patel Publishing?" Terrence asked with a patient tone.

"I looked at the first couple. They were pretty big," said Wendy.

"They're getting bigger," said Terrence. "I bought the Rover outright. We got a great deal. Wendy, you're rich."

"Rich?"

"Yeah, Wendy, I've been depositing the checks into our Merrill Lynch investment account, and we're getting a nice return of five or six percent on a pretty substantial and growing principal. Wendy, we aren't really rich by some people's estimation, but we have a lot of money."

"That's nice, Terry. I've made reservations for our wedding at the Black Canyon Inn up in Estes Park in August, and I'm trying to figure out how many rooms I should ask them to hold."

"Wendy, rent out the whole darn place. Don't worry, we'll fill it up."

So she did.

CHAPTER 24

Zeke and I were settled in the tall, cool grass of the Grove listening to Gabriel off in the distance laying down some smooth blues riffs. We were on our backs with a warm breeze rippling the deep green grass around us, watching white clouds against an ink blue sky when Mother approached. Zeke gave me a shot in the arm and jumped to his feet to greet Her, but I didn't know She was there until She spoke. Zeke was much more tuned in to those vibes than I was.

"Hello boys," said God. "How are you two today?"

"We're fine," said Zeke and I scrambled to my feet and told Her that we were fine too.

"Fine," God repeated. "Augustus, do you have a moment?"

"Certainly, Mother," I said. "What can I do for You?" That was stupid. I mean, what did God need me to do that She couldn't do Herself? "I'm sorry, I mean, how can I help You?" Stupid again.

Zeke snickered and said "Nice, Gus," under his breath.

"It's all right, Augustus," God said, shooting Zeke a look. "I do need your help, please excuse us, Ezekiel."

"Sure. You're excused." For an angel, Zeke was a bit of a smart ass.

God was rarely impolite, but She looked at Zeke and said, "Leave us now." He left.

"There, that's better now isn't it, Augustus?"

"Yes, Ma'am, much better," I agreed, not having any idea why this was better.

"I'll get right to the point, August. You don't mind if I call you August do you?"

"No, Ma'am," I said. *God can call me anything She wants,* I thought to myself without thinking.

"Quite right, of course I can, nevertheless I do believe I raised you all with manners and I try to practice what I preach. Some angels, Ezekiel for instance, need a refresher from time to time I'm afraid," said God.

"Yes, Ma'am."

"August, you were a wonderful and glorious knight in the service of St. John in defense of the fortress of St. Elmo at Malta a short while ago." God's conception of time was a little abbreviated. "That was an unfortunate affair, but you were certainly resolute in your guardianship of the Word and the Way and I would like to call upon you once again to return to the world, and to be a witness for love and tolerance."

"Certainly, Mother," I said recalling that I had been impaled through the heart on the beach trying to evacuate the women and children. It didn't seem very glorious to me.

"But it was glorious, August, and your death alongside Alexander in India, and your demise at Bastogne, and your work in Bangladesh, and atop those pitiful ramparts of Hadrian's Wall, I could go on. There have been countless other battles that you have fought in My name, and a hundred other deaths that you have suffered, and a hundred more to come; all glorious, August, all heroic and dedicated to your beliefs. You have been an inspiration, my precious angel, and I do not want you to minimize or forget it.

"August, we are once again challenged by infidels. Lucifer, bless his soul, never seems to rest. My concern, Augustus, is the proliferation of atomic and nuclear weaponry which has unfortunately found its way into irresponsible hands. I should like to utilize this energy for the good of mankind, but I will not force it. That time will come, I assure you. Destruction of the civilized world again, however, would be an inopportune set back. I need your talents and your devoted service yet again, my boy.

"I am not willing to sacrifice the progress that mankind has made since the recent reawakening age of the sixth decade of this century past. Great progress and mindfulness, and care and concern for the planet and for one man for another are seeds that are just beginning to sprout. I will not have radical fundamentalists with misplaced fidelity tearing those seeds from the ground. I call upon you, my faithful servant, to serve for the future, and for the welfare of the people of Abraham."

"Certainly, Mother."

"You will be the second child of a wonderful young couple in the village of Boulder, in the province of Colorado on the continent of North America. I believe you have been there before, Augustus."

"Yes, Mother, I was a horse gentler with the Iroquois Nation."

"Quite right. You will be the son of a healer and his wife, a spiritual guide. Opportunities will arise for you to serve Augustus. Your intuition and your heart will lead you as always, my dear boy."

"Certainly, Mother."

* * *

Wendy didn't recognize the address when the e-mail popped up on her computer screen. It was a Blackberry message from someone named Barefoot Bart sent from Cabo San Lucas in Mexico. She scrolled through the text and realized that it was Willow. Willow had met this person, Barefoot Bart, at a concert at Red Rocks two nights ago and now she was on a Mexican beach with him and she said that she was going to marry him. She was asking Wendy to cover her yoga classes for a couple of days until she got back. *Holy cow*, Wendy thought, *how exciting*, and then she realized that she was flattered that Willow was asking her to stand in for her and under the circumstances she hardly felt that she could refuse. So she didn't.

The elopement was the talk of the class. Willow had been very busy on Barefoot Bart's Blackberry, and most of her class was aware that Wendy was temporarily in charge. Wendy was a little nervous at first, but then everybody settled down and they had a great hour together. After two weeks, Wendy was thoroughly enjoying her new duties and only vaguely concerned about the whereabouts of Willow. She had changed the music, hoping nobody would mind and was pleasantly surprised that it was greeted with enthusiasm. Annabelle was the star of the nursery, and the lady that ran the studio asked Wendy to consider joining the staff on a full time basis. Except for the approaching nuptials, Wendy had nothing on her calendar or in her life that would prevent her from working regularly at the yoga studio. It was another coincidental opportunity to have a place for Annabelle to interact with other babies, for Wendy to assume more responsibility and discipline in her life, and to exercise and practice her craft for free.

When Willow returned they would work out a schedule that was beneficial to both of them. The studio was also considering expanding classes and hours during the summer, so it was all working out well.

Spring skiing was in full swing, and Wendy and Annabelle were joining Caroline and Emmy and sometimes Terrence for glorious sun-drenched days at A Basin and Loveland Pass. Caroline had joined Wendy and Annabelle for a ride to Estes Park to go over the wedding plans, accommodations, and menus at the Black Canyon Ranch. Invitations were printed and sent to seventy-eight people. Although she had not yet received any RSVP's, everybody on the invitation list that ran into the bride-to-be around Boulder confirmed their attendance. Rebecca called, Grace called, Sarah and Kate called, and even Josephine called to say that they wouldn't miss it for the world.

Wendy put Annabelle down one night and sat in her favorite wicker rocker looking out over the Flatirons and felt the inspiration to complete her book. She went to Terrence's briefcase and found his little tape recorder and returned to the baby's room and softly dictated the story of Oliver the wise old owl who lived in the Front Range high above El Dorado

Canyon. She hadn't been consciously aware of writing the book while she doodled and drew fun pictures over the last two months, but the drawings told the tale and Wendy simply wrote the words to correspond with her sketches. She went to the kitchen and boiled water for tea and resumed her spot listening to the sweet, regular breathing of her baby and reflected with a sense of awe upon how well her life was turning out.

Willow returned from Mexico and her visit to Sedona, Arizona where she had met her new mother and father-in-law. She was delighted to find out that the studio had permanent plans for Wendy, and the class of regulars chattered like careless parakeets, bright and busy and noisy. Everybody was happy for Willow and looking forward to a wedding weekend in Estes Park.

Spring melted into summer and, before they knew it, the festivities were around the corner. Joe and Rebecca arrived with baby Maria in an RV that Joe had bought shortly after they turned the rental in at the agency in Phoenix last fall. They loved this mode of travel and had visited the Grand Canyon, Vegas, and Zion and Arches National Parks since the baby had been born in December. They spent a night at Mesa Verde National Park on their way to Boulder.

Terrence's parents were being weird. They had received no word or confirmation from them.

"Your father hasn't been feeling well at all, dear. I'm worried about him handling that thin air at his age," said Terrence's mother on the telephone three nights before the wedding.

That was baloney and Terrence knew it. Harold Frazier was as strong as an ox. Terrence's mother was the one with the problem. She wasn't running this show and it pissed her off, but Terrence wasn't going to let it impact his marriage. He decided not to tell Wendy anything until she asked. He knew she would ask, and then he would call his folks and ask them point blank if they planned to attend their son's wedding or not. He had a sudden revelation that Annabelle would have said:

Honesty is ineffective as a weapon.

It pleased him to think that his sweet little daughter had been such a positive guiding influence on both of them, but on Wendy in particular, for nine wonderful months. He knew now that she was heaven-sent and he got down on his knees in the kitchen in the middle of the day and thanked God for their blessings. That is where Rebecca found him as she walked in to reheat Maria's oatmeal.

"Excuse me Doctor Groom," she said. "I didn't mean to interrupt, but I must say that I find it very reassuring that my daughter's uncle prays. Is everything okay?"

"Of course, Becca," said Terrence. Annabelle would have said:

It is what it is.

"As my little angel would say, 'It is what it is'."

"Indeed," Rebecca agreed. "Sounds like advice from Maria too." She crossed the kitchen and took Terrence in her arms and whispered, "We are so lucky, Terry. We are so blessed."

"Sarah just called," Wendy said walking into the kitchen. Annabelle was crawling along behind her at full speed doing a pretty good job of keeping up with her mother.

"Mama, mama," she repeated contentedly looking down at the wood floor and concentrating on her crawling.

"She and Kate and Grace and Jim just got back from a four mile hike up to Timberline Falls, and they are totally psyched." She scooped the baby up in her arms and said, "Jim's on his way down to Denver to pick up Josephine and Ramon. Sarah says they all love the place and they want to stay an extra week, which is great I think. What about your parents, Terry? I asked Sarah if they were there yet and got the silent evasion."

"Mom's playing games, Wendy, but it doesn't matter. The show will go on with them or without them."

Wendy frowned with a look of confusion on her face. She was holding Annabelle and Rebecca had gone into the bedroom and picked up Maria from her nap and now the two little girls were looking at each other from the safety of their mother's arms with childlike curiosity.

The mothers settled their babies gently side by side on the small sofa in the kitchen and the tiny girls seemed to snuggle up closer to one another. The moment dragged on and time seemed to slow perceptibly for the three adults as the little ones stared at each other more intently.

"These two have very serious looks on their little faces," said Terrence.

Wendy and Rebecca saw it too. The light seemed to brighten as if the sun outside were turned up a couple of notches. The air died and the silence roared with anticipation as Annabelle reached purposely for Maria. Wendy felt a chill and Rebecca tried to alter the mood.

"Maria, you are sitting beside your niece, Annabelle." She tried to make it sound funny. "Annabelle, say hello to your Aunt Maria." The little eight-month-old girls reached slowly for each other with their index fingers.

"Hanna," gurgled Maria.

"Hia," cooed Annabelle.

Their fingers touched and there was an instant explosion of thunder and a spear of lightning pierced the earth in the yard outside of the sliding glass doors just beyond the patio. All three parents jerked in fear, but the two little girls did not move. They were transfixed on one another. Their index fingers held their tiny hands tightly together. They smiled at each other warmly and adjusted their grips to hold hands firmly. Rebecca and Wendy were afraid to move. A snowy owl glided from the mountaintop above them and soared over the house screeching, and Terrence, Wendy, and Rebecca felt a wave of love that brought tears to their eyes.

"She just called Maria, Hia," said Rebecca.

"And she called Annabelle, Hanna," said Wendy through her tears.

The three grown-ups hugged each other as the little angels squeezed comfortably closer together. The adults slowly glided to their knees and thanked Mother for the adorable blessings holding each other on the couch before them, and that's where they were when Harold Frazier walked into the room.

Dr. Frazier silently lowered himself to the kitchen floor and reached for Wendy. He held his daughter-in-law tightly and reached out to his granddaughter and a single tear ran down his cheek.

* * *

They whole gang crowded into the Land Rover and the Porsche for the trip to Estes Park. Joe was happy to leave the RV in the driveway behind Dr. Frazier's rental car. Nobody asked Terrence's father about his wife and he didn't offer any explanation either. Once they arrived at the resort, everybody got checked in and went to their rooms.

The rooms were lovely. The rest of the crowd was arriving and checking in and Terrence went downstairs to make sure everything was in order for the rehearsal dinner which was to begin in a couple of hours. When he got back, Wendy was just emerging from the bathroom staring at something in her hand.

"What is it, baby?" Terrence asked quietly so as not to disturb the sleeping eight-month-old.

"It's blue," said Wendy not taking her eyes off of the little gadget.

"What's blue?" asked Terrence.

"I did it twice, Terry. It's blue."

"Wendy, what are you talking about?"

"It's a pregnancy indicator. Five bucks remember? I'm pregnant, Terry," she said raising her eyes to meet his.

When Terrence came to, his father was leaning over him and Terrence's head hurt. His eyes took a second to adjust and he focused on his dad's face and saw little red bells in his hair. He blinked and they looked like tiny rust colored Christmas tree bulbs. They faded away when his father smiled warmly.

"Pretty good bump on the noggin, young man," said the elder Dr. Frazier. "What's the story? Getting cold feet?"

He looked around the room. He was dazed. He was confused. He felt as though he was swimming through wet air. "Wendy?"

"Yes, daddy?" she giggled holding the little five dollar contraption behind her back.

Be gentle with him, Mommy. It's been a big day.

Wendy looked suddenly surprised. She glanced at the crib and saw that Annabelle was sleeping soundly. She looked down at her flat belly and said in a barely perceptible whisper, "Are you kidding me?"

No mommy, no kidding. Mother calls me Augustus.

"Uh oh, here we go again."

THE END